Pity the Rebellious

A Legion Archer

Book #2

J. Clifton Slater

A *Legion Archer* series and the associated books are the creation of J. Clifton Slater. Any use of *Pity the Rebellious* in part or in whole requires express written consent. This is a work of fiction. Any resemblance to persons living or dead is purely coincidental. All rights reserved.

I'd like to thank Hollis Jones for guiding and correcting my wandering mind as I authored this book. She has kept me on the path, adjusted the structure, identified rough spots, and called my attention to overly long descriptions. Because of her, *Pity the Rebellious* exists.

And, I'd like to extend my sincerest 'thank you' to you. My readers are the reason I can spend my days doing research and writing stories. Rendering a hand salute to you for being there for me. Ready, two!

If you have comments, contact me:

GalacticCouncilRealm@gmail.com

To follow my progress on the next book, read blogs on ancient topics, or to sign up for my monthly Author Report, go to my website:

www.JCliftonSlater.com

Act 1

Although Carthaginian General Hannibal Barca humiliated Publius Scipio at the Ticinus River and soundly beat Tiberius Longus on the banks of the Trebia, the citizens of Rome didn't fear for their city. The Legions of Consul Gaius Flaminius patrolled southwest of the Apennine Mountains, and the Legions of Consul Servilius Geminus held the eastern end of the Po River Valley. Their positions blockaded Barca and prevented his army from penetrating southward into the Republic.

Then, a messenger ship arrived from Iberia with grand news. Proconsul Gnaeus Scipio, brother of Publius Scipio, had brought a Punic General named Hanno to battle along the Ebro River. The populous, however, missed the importance of the victory. Not until Senators pointed out that General Gnaeus Scipio's success meant Rome controlled the land north of the Ebro river between the Balearic Sea and the Pyrenees mountains. This stretched Hannibal's supply lines and required his reinforcements to take a longer route over the mountains from Iberia. In short, while the battle of Cissa didn't stop the Carthaginian army from attacking the Republic, it reduced Hannibal's options.

The citizens of Rome celebrated the battle for three days. On the fourth, a squadron of cavalry and mounted couriers arrived from Rimini with news of the battle at Lake Trasimene. In response to the loss of twenty-five thousand Legionaries and allied troops, the people took to the streets in mourning and the Senate went into an emergency session.

Welcome to 217 B.C.

Chapter 1 – Cool Mountain Water

Bird songs reverberated through the calm forest. Leaves crunched underfoot, and a soft afternoon breeze rocked the high branches. On the trail below, sixty-two men hiked wearily eastward.

"File Leader Kasia, are we not men long out of the agōgē?" Lieutenant Gergely inquired.

"We are, sir," Jace confirmed. "Each graduated as a full master archer."

"And I haven't seen a Carthaginian mercenary since yesterday," Acis Gergely added. "Have you?"

The Cretan officer hobbled on a carved branch. Using the crutch, he gritted his teeth, focused his mind, and kept up with the line of archers.

"I have not, sir," Jace admitted. Then he studied the men behind the Lieutenant. Their shoulders slumped, and their empty waterskins lay flat on their hips. "Perhaps we should find a place to rest."

"An excellent idea," Gergely agreed.

Jace tapped an archer names Eachann and another young archer on their shoulders.

"Find us a defensible position with a source of water," he instructed.

Mountainous with steep terrain, the Island of Crete, and the archer school, produced bowmen with endurance far beyond most soldiers. In the tradition of Cretan archers, the two sprinted away from the group without a hint of exhaustion. The same couldn't be said for the older or the injured bowmen.

After fighting their way off the banks of Lake Trasimene the archers, along with a group of Legionaries, scrambled up a slope to escape the killing field. Following a dispute, the archers and Legionaries took separate trails. While the Romans marched along a track between hills, the Cretans struggled up a goat path to higher ground. Moving just below the ridge lines, the archers spent a fitful night in the open. In the morning, they continued eastward with no sign of the Legionaries. No one cared or complained about the absence of the snobbish heavy infantrymen and their hostile Centurions. They had parted ways and were all the better for it, according to many of the bowmen.

"What do you suppose happened to Tribune Scipio and his Legionaries?" Jace asked.

"I imagine he and his men have joined a Republic patrol. They're probably mounted and riding to Rimini," Gergely replied. "We'll get there later and report to Captain Zoltar. He'll be surprised and angry."

The rest of the Company of Cretan Archers, under the command of Pedar Zoltar, should have landed at the seaside town of Rimini. If not, then the units of bowmen would arrive from Crete within the month.

"The angry I get. We lost archers," Jace commented. "Why the surprise?"

"Because some did survive," Gergely told him.

One of the two scouts appeared between the trees. He ran to Jace and slid to a stop.

"Just ahead, down the slope, and across a valley is a small mountain pond," he reported. "On the other side of the water, the grade is steep and thick with trees. It's defendable from there."

"Where's your partner?" Jace questioned.

"He headed up the valley to be sure the area is safe."

"Good looking out for us," Jace complimented the archer. "Take us to the mountain oasis."

As the scout and File Leader Kasia marched ahead, Lieutenant Gergely limped forward and said a silent prayer to the Goddess Algea. His plea was for a reprieve from the agony of his injuries.

When they forded the Tiber River and started across the valley, Jace sent a scout to the south. He didn't want to be caught in the open if any Carthaginian soldiers happened by.

To Acis Gergely's displeasure, the Goddess of Pain must have been occupied elsewhere. Her gift continued to torment him all the way down the trail, across the river and the valley floor, around the pond, and up into the trees. Only then did he lay down and allow the injury to become a dull ache.

***

For two days, the Goddess Algea had been busy. From the deep cuts that didn't kill but mutilated, to the bones shattered on sharp steel, men cried out from her blessings. Only those souls in the arms of the Goddess Nenia avoided the agony by dying.

"I will not give you the satisfaction of crying out," Appius Pulcher growled.

The Legionaries shoving the Tribune onto the back of the horse didn't understand his hesitation. They had pulled the injured staff officer up the hill from the lake and carried him on a shield for over a day. If he wanted to scream, they would understand.

"Appius, we can rig a real stretcher," Cornelius Scipio offered.

"Stick a stretcher up your cūlus," Pulcher cursed. "I'm an officer of the Republic and I will ride this horse."

"Despite the pain?"

"Yes, despite the pain," he groaned while shifting and trying to get a comfortable seat. "We need to report our loss of the Legions to Consul Geminus."

"Or he'll march into Hannibal's army," Cornelius added.

"Tribunes, we should be moving," a cavalryman suggested.

Around them, two thousand Legion cavalrymen filled the valley. Farther north and in the distance, Cornelius could make out the lead elements of another two thousand mounted Legionaries. Ranging far in advance of the Legions from Rimini, the two groups probed, searching for the Legions of Gaius Flaminius. Unfortunately, they would only find a few thousand survivors.

"We should get…" Cornelius stopped and stared to the south.

A lone Cretan Archer stood in the center of the valley. At five hundred feet, it was difficult to make out details, but the case with the war bow jutting over his shoulder helped Cornelius identify the bowman.

"I see the rats from Crete are lost," a combat officer remarked.

"Those rats are the reason we got out of the ambush. Without their arrows, you'd be dead."

"Sorry, Tribune Scipio," the Centurion apologized. "I know how much affection you have for the foreigners."

Cornelius started to protest the framing of his association with the Cretan Archers. But the bowman in the valley began jumping up and down and pointing at him.

"What's that, their war dance?" the Centurion laughed. Then he sneered. "Undiscipline rubble."

At first Cornelius waved back, thinking to return the greeting. Then the sounds of nervous horses and angry voices from the cavalrymen drew his eyes to the north. The neat line of Legion horsemen in the distance had been replaced by dust, panic, and Punic mercenaries pouring down from the surrounding hills.

"Hannibal Barca at his finest," Cornelius declared, "trap, pressure, and follow through."

"I won't chastise you for that," Appius Pulcher said. "The Punic has proven his talent too often to deny his leadership abilities."

Neither staff officer noticed the look of disgust on the Centurion's face at the compliment to Hannibal's tactics.

The Legion cavalry around Cornelius and Appius created ranks and began riding to the aid of their fellow cavalrymen. As they rode towards the fighting, Appius inquired, "Do we get involved or go the other way?"

"We should fight," the Centurion declared.

Cornelius twisted around and focused on the archer. With one arm pointing back, the Cretan jerked his head to the south.

"We go south," Cornelius instructed. "Our information is too important to risk in a melee."

"You think we should follow the stickman?" the Centurion challenged. "And desert the Legions?"

Appius Pulcher took a deep breath, fought down nausea from the pain, and commanded, "We are going with Tribune Scipio. But anyone who wants can go join the battle. And may the God Mars bless you with courage."

In a Legion combat line, the Legionaries and their Centurions were kings of the battlefield. But in the press of horseflesh and slashing steel, their inability to create a barrier, left the infantrymen as raw meat to be ground under the hoofs of the mounts.

"No offense to the God of War, Tribune Pulcher, but we'll accompany you," the combat officer informed him.

The Cretan archer's arm movements grew frantic. Then he spun and jogged away. To the north, more Carthaginian riders and light infantrymen joined the battle. In moments, the Legion horsemen vanished behind a wall of Punic riders.

"We're heading south," Cornelius informed the group. Taking the reins of Pulcher's horse, he kicked his mount and the two staff officers trotted down the valley.

Behind the Tribunes, the mounted Centurion and his twelve Legionaries on foot raced to keep up. Their cavalry escort guided their horses around and charged towards their squadrons and the fighting.

Jace Kasia stood with one foot on the valley floor and the other on the first hill of a ridge.

"Keep it moving," he urged the archers. "Fill our defensive positions from the top down before you send water parties to the pond."

"How long are we staying, File Leader Kasia?" an older archer asked.

It was an unnecessary question. Cretan Archers could march or run for days without rest. What the inquiry did was reiterate Jace's position as an NCO of archers. During the relief of escaping death, men would cheer even the slightest bit of heroism. In that frenzy, they had acknowledged Jace as a File Leader. Since then, despite Lieutenant Gergely using Kasia as a proxy for command, a few archers were backsliding on their support of the young file leader.

"We'll stay until we our bellies are full of water," Jace answered. "And the wounds of our injured are washed, salted, sewed, and dressed. Or until the Lieutenant says to move out."

"Fair enough," the archer responded. He grabbed a tree trunk but stopped before pulling himself up onto the steep grade. "Perhaps a few moments for a nap?"

"There may be Punic soldiers and riders in the area," Jace cautioned. "But if you can sleep with one eye open, be my guest."

Behind the older bowmen, the next archer in line pushed him.

"Come on, one eye," the archer teased, "move up or get out of my way."

"You couldn't beat my record during the archer's test," the mature archer boasted, "and you can't beat me now."

The two climbed with renewed energy as they raced up the ridgeline.

"Keep it moving," Jace advised the next two archers. "Fill our defensive positions from the top down before you send water parties to the pond."

Above File Leader Kasia, fifty-five of the survivors had been swallowed up by the forest. The last six approached his location.

"Three of you find a place with a clear shot down into the draw," Jace told them. "You last three give them your waterskins."

"Why am I giving him my skin?" one questioned.

"Because he's going to fill it," Jace told him.

"Why am I collecting water for him?" one of the first three demanded.

"You can swap out if you want," Jace informed the six. "But I need three archers to cut branches and join me in erasing any sign of our passage."

"Oh, come on, Kasia that's agōgē protocol," one declared. "No one in the field really does it."

"Sixty-three wet footprints emerge from that river," Jace described. "Leave them and you might as well post a sign that says, this way to a small number of stupid Cretan Archers. They are sleeping on the hill and have left an invitation for you to come up and slaughter them. But if that's what you want, it's fine with me."

Jace stepped fully onto the hill, then paused to let his meaning sink in. He didn't want to, but he thought of a thank you to his Uncle Dryas Kasia for teaching him how to use words to persuade people to do what he wanted.

"Hold up, File Leader. You're right."

After cutting three tree branches, Jace and the archers recrossed the valley. From the banks of the Tiber, they began sweeping away any signs of the Cretans' passing. At first Jace stood back looking north and south. Two of the archers grumbled under their breaths.

Between the river and where the land rose into the forest, open ground stretched four thousand feet or thirteen hundred steps. It would take a lot of sweeps back and forth with the branches to cover their tracks. At five hundred steps, Jace reached for a branch.

"I thought you were supervising?" the archer mentioned.

"Keep watch," Jace encouraged as he took the branch and began brushing the dirt. "I don't want to get trampled because an archer felt guilty."

"What me, guilty?"

"Sure, you're standing around while the rest of us work," another bowman responded.

"But I'm on guard duty," the man deflected. He pivoted his head looking north and south. "I'm making sure you don't get trampled. Just ask File Leader Kasia."

"Don't ask me," Jace shot back. "I'm too busy working."

The archers laughed because a file leader had the right to avoid menial tasks. But young Kasia didn't take advantage of the perk. Jace's gesture was appreciated.

***

The backtrail appeared undisturbed with no hint of footprints. Along the ridge, the archers reclined under the trees and sipped the cool mountain water.

An archer slid to the bottom of the slope.

"Lieutenant Gergely wants to know how long we should stay," he told Jace.

"I think one more climb to get us out of the valley before we rest for the night," Jace replied. The archer started to climb away when Jace reached out and pulled him back. "And be sure to tell the Lieutenant thanks from me."

"Thanks for what?"

"For trusting a stick of an NCO."

"You're more than that, File Leader Kasia. But I'll tell him."

The archer scrambled away and Jace sat with his back against a tree trunk. Above him a pair of birds squabbled. Since the morning of the attack, Jace had been active. Even when the rest slept, he walked the sentry posts checking on the ones assigned to guard duty. Now, with his thirst sated and the bird noises letting him know there was nothing stirring around him, File Leader Kasia drifted…

"File Leader, we have troubles," an archer blurted out.

Jace's eyes popped open.

"Well, out with it."

"There's a patrol of riders coming from the south. They're walking their mounts and looking at the ground. I sprinted back. I don't think they saw me."

"Then we should be fine," Jace consoled him. "Go up and spread…Wait. You said troubles."

"On the way here, I saw Eachann to the north," the archer reported. "He'll get here before the patrol. But the young Tribune is following him. What do you want me to do?"

"On your way up to the Lieutenant, wake everyone, and have them warm up their bows."

The archer crawled up the slope and Jace jumped to the valley floor. He glanced to the south. After confirming it was empty of riders, he sprinted to the north towards Archer Eachann and Tribune Scipio.

Chapter 2 – Sometimes, Panic is Warranted

Cornelius yanked on the reins encouraging Appius Pulcher's mount to keep up. Not far behind, and a testament to the reluctance of the horse to be led, the jogging infantrymen remained close to the mounted Centurion and Tribunes.

Afraid the Punic cavalry would notice them, Cornelius rotated his head, while thinking of contingencies. From looking back at the fighting to studying the blood dripping down the leg of the wounded Tribune, he worried about stopping if Pulcher fell. After checking on the location of their Cretan guide to be sure they didn't lose him, Cornelius

12

returned his attention to the north in the direction of the Punic cavalry.

He had just finished another check of Pulcher when the bearing of the Cretan seemed wrong. Rather than guiding them away, the archer sprinted at the small Legion detachment.

"Tribune Scipio, with all due respect, sir, move your behind," Jace instructed as he stopped in front of the horses. He took the line to Pulcher's mount, pulled the beast's head down, and whispered something in its ear. Then he addressed Cornelius. "We've a patrol coming from the south and Eachann told me you have enemies to your rear."

"How could the archer have told you anything?" the Legion Centurion disputed. "You never stopped to talk to him."

"And I'm not stopping to have a debate with you. Hold on Tribune," Jace warned Pulcher. Then to the others, he said. "Follow me."

After gently tapping the side of the horse's jaw, Jace sprinted away. Without a moment's hesitation, the horse and Appius Pulcher raced away with him.

"Forward," Cornelius ordered.

The gear of the infantrymen rattled. Big infantry shields bounced on their backs and helmets tied by leather braids knocked against their hips. But none of the equipment fell or came untied. Legionaries were taught to secure the tools of their trade from the first day of training. And although they ran hard, the horses soon outpaced the twelve infantrymen.

At the entrance to the draw, Archer Eachann divided his attention between the south and the Legionaries coming from the north. Jace slipped by him. At the pond, he released the reins, and eased Pulcher to the ground. A quick hand sign from Eachann caused Jace to stand and face the ridgeline. Another flurry of arm and hand signals brought four archers down the steep slope.

"We can't outrun a patrol," Cornelius said from the back of his horse. "Where are your Cretans?"

"We're positioned along the ridge," Jace answered while motioning at the slope with his hand. "Once we have Tribune Pulcher on the heights, we can disappear into the forest."

"Do we have time?" Cornelius inquired.

Jace made a fist and pumped it in the air. In response, Archer Eachann slashed his hand across his belly.

"The patrol has spotted your infantrymen," Jace advised. "If you hurry, we can get you, your Centurion, and the other Tribune away from here."

"We're not running," Cornelius declared. Then to the Legion officer he directed. "Centurion, as soon as our Legionaries arrive, stage them behind the trees on the left side of the draw."

"Where will you be, Tribune?" the combat officer inquired.

The look on his face displayed mistrust of the staff officer and the Cretan File Leader.

Cornelius Scipio didn't acknowledge the expression, but he did say, "I'll be watering my horse at the pond."

When the Legionaries staggered in, the Centurion sent them into the forest on the opposite side from the ridge.

"Get to the trees, gear up, and stand by," he instructed.

"Standing by, Centurion," the responses rippled through the dozen infantrymen.

The four archers snatched Pulcher off the ground and ran for a path to the ridge. In moments, Jace and Cornelius were the only ones visible in the draw.

Jace gazed across the pond. On a hump of land on the far side, the mount drank from the cool mountain water, and Cornelius Scipio sat relaxed on the horse's back.

"Don't you ever panic?" Jace called over to the Tribune.

"Only when it's warranted," Cornelius responded. "You should go."

Sprinting to the line of hidden Legionaries, Jace dove behind a tree and untied his bow case.

"The Tribune takes unnecessary risks," the Centurion observed. "And he keeps questionable company."

"You can't let it go, can you?" Jace asked.

"Let what…"

Horses coming off the valley floor interrupted the conversation.

"I will accept your surrender," Cornelius called out to the Carthaginian mercenaries.

Ten Gaelic cavalrymen urged their mounts closer to the pond. Four hoisted spears to their shoulders. Once the Tribune was targeted, a Punic officer squeezed between his riders.

"You have until the count of three to dismount and lay down your arms," Cornelius warned.

Fifteen more riders crowded into the mouth of the draw. Seeing a Legion Tribune sitting alone on a horse across the pond in a narrowing gully, caused several cavalrymen to chuckle.

"None of them understands Latin," the Punic officer told Cornelius. "Save your breath. It is you who will surrender."

More riders squeezed between the ridges to watch the arrogant Latin Tribune brought down.

"Sometimes, panic is warranted," Cornelius stated. "Centurion, advance your line. Seal the draw."

The twelve Legionaries stepped from behind tree trunks. Once free of the obstructions, they created a line, and raced to block the exit. Then, as if bricks being set, they collapsed the space between them until their shields interlocked. Their speed from hiding in the trees to forming a shield wall, almost thirty-feet-long, took the Gaelic riders by surprise.

"Standing by, sir," the Centurion roared.

Twenty-five of the horsemen turned their horses and leveled their lances. The rest remained in position to guard the Punic officer.

"Kill them," the officer ordered with a lazy wave of his arm.

Zip-Thwack

The arm froze in mid-motion and an arrow appeared in the Punic officer's throat. Gurgling his last breath, he leaned over the side of his horse before toppling to the ground.

Jace lowered his bow and waved across the draw to the Cretan Archers on the ridgeline. In response, the air filled with shafts from war bows. Shooting downward at a relatively close range, delivered death to the Gauls. Realizing the gully was an ambush, the survivors of the first volley kicked their horses, attempting to turn them. But in the confines of the narrow space, their mounts bunched up, not moving.

Across the entrance, twelve Legion shields and steel spearheads presented a solid barrier. For a moment, the horses stood, motionless, while, *Zip-Thwack, Zip-Thwack,* arrows from across the gully entered the backs of their riders.

Jace sprinted to Cornelius and asked, "Do we take prisoners?"

"Trap, pressure, and follow through," the young Tribune mouthed as if seeing Hannibal's tactics in the slaughter. But, for a moment, he almost felt remorse. Then, the vision of Gaelic light infantrymen running through the night with the heads of Legion Velites came to him. Cornelius in a commanding voice shouted. "Non capimus!"

"What's that?" Jace inquired. "My Latin is a little weak."

"It means take no prisoners, File Leader Kasia," Tribune Scipio answered.

"Advance, advance," the Centurion ordered.

The assault line of Legionaries stepped forward and bashed horses with their shields. Retreating in panic, the horses stampeded back over the fallen Gaelic riders and disrupted the ones still mounted.

One stallion shouldered through the panicked clusters, the rider screaming and leaning forward over his mount's neck. He savagely kicked the horse's flanks to overcome the beast's fear of the wall of yelling Legionaries. As the stallion approached the assault line, the steel of the rider's lance pointed directly at the Centurion.

Even targeted for death on the steel tip, the Legion combat officer didn't flinch. Expecting to be skewed at any moment, he bellowed, "Keep your lines straight, your shields tight. Advance, Advance."

If the stallion breached the shield wall, other riders would break free. With room to maneuver, they could easily swing around and destroy the Legionaries.

Zip-Thwack

The Gaelic rider stopped yelling. Part of a shaft with an arrowhead on the tip appeared in his mouth. He collapsed. Without the rider's encouragement, the stallion swerved away from the shields.

The Centurion swung his head following the path of the arrow. At its point of origin, Jace Kasia raised his bow. In response to the archer's gesture, the Centurion saluted by bouncing the hilt of his gladius off his chest armor.

***

Cretan Archers shoot birds-on-the-wing out of the sky. With that pedigree, men on bucking horses presented no problem for the bowmen. Shortly after it began, all thirty-four mounted Gauls and their Punic officer lay dead in the draw.

"Centurion, report?" Cornelius requested.

"A couple of scratches," the combat officer replied. "Can we get out of the valley, sir?"

"I thought you wanted to go fight with our cavalry?" Cornelius questioned.

"No sir, I've had enough horseflesh for one day," he added. "I believe it's best to report what we've seen to the Legion at Rimini."

"A fine idea. File Leader Kasia, show us the best route to the ridge," Cornelius said. He dismounted and confirmed for the Legionaries. "We are leaving the valley and this gully."

***

On the high part of the ridge, Cornelius bent over Appius Pulcher.

"I told you we'd get you a real stretcher."

"It's slower, but somewhat more comfortable than horseback," Appius replied. He eyed the archers selected as bearers. "Remind me about this if I ever talk bad about Cretans in the future."

"Are you ready?" Jace asked.

"We're ready," Cornelius answered. He climbed to the File Leader. "After we report to Consul Geminus, I'm returning to Rome. I want you to go with me."

"Why would a Legion staff officer want the company of a Cretan Archer?" Jace questioned. "Plus, I don't know if Captain Zoltar will allow it."

"Because twice you've saved my life and the lives of my Legionaries," Cornelius told him. "I would like you to meet my father. And, I want you to see what you're fighting for. Consider it a holiday or a diplomatic mission. In either case, you're coming with me."

"Yes, sir," Jace stated. "As they teach in the agōgē on Crete, the client is always right."

***

19

Tribune Cornelius Scipio wasn't the first to deliver the news about the disaster at Lake Trasimene and the slaughter of Legion cavalry in the Tiber River Valley. Those messengers left Rimini the same morning as Cornelius and Jace. But the hard riding couriers arrived in Rome two days before the pair.

"Take a side street, Tribune," a Centurion of the city guard instructed as they came through the east gate. "We're keeping the boulevard free around the east walls."

"Has the city been attacked?" Cornelius inquired.

"Not yet," the officer replied.

Cornelius and Jace headed off the wide roadway and entered a commercial district.

"It must be market day," Jace commented.

"Why do you say that?" Cornelius asked.

"The doors to the buildings are closed, and the streets are empty," Jace said. "In Eleutherna on market day, the streets are empty because everyone goes to the agorá to buy, to sell, or to visit."

"Buying and selling, File Leader Kasia, is every day in Rome. But the citizens don't go to a specific market. They go to another street. Look around, we're riding through the greatest market in the world," Cornelius informed his traveling companion. "Deserted walkways and empty roads mean something different."

"Like what?" Jace inquired.

"We'll ask my father when we get to his villa."

They rode down a street bordered by shops in single-story buildings. Even from horseback, they didn't have a view of the center of the Capital. Then they reached a boulevard and the landscape opened before them. Across the city, structures of travertine on Capitoline Hill glowed in the midday sun. Jace reined in his mount.

"What's the matter?" Cornelius inquired.

"That's higher than the acropolis in Phalasarna," Jace gushed while indicating a hill. "And the buildings are taller."

"Those are the temples of Jupiter, Juno, and Minerva," Cornelius explained. "Perhaps we'll visit Capitoline Hill and pay homage to the Gods while we're in the city."

"I'd like that," Jace said.

They were several paces along the boulevard when a vagabond limped into the path of their horses.

"Surely a pair of young Patricians can spare a few coins for a crippled Legionary," he begged.

"Where did you serve?" Cornelius questioned.

"In the Po River Valley with the Legions of Gaius Flaminius," the man boasted.

"It must have been hard duty up there," Cornelius sympathized. He pulled three bronze coins from a pouch and tossed them to the veteran.

"May the Goddess Clementia bless you," the beggar offered before limping out of the roadway. Then from the side he added. "And her mercy and clemency be with you for all of your days."

With the way clear, the pair nudged their mounts into motion and the archer stared at the Tribune.

"I didn't know General Flaminius had Legions that far north," Jace remarked.

"He didn't. The vagabond was lying."

"Then why give him coins?"

"Because he thought we were a couple of noblemen," Cornelius replied. "It's another reason I wanted you to accompany me. I'm curious about your family."

"Tribune Cornelius, I don't have a family," Jace informed him. "At least not in Rome as far as I know. The only thing I have is this."

Jace reached under his hooded doublet and pulled the silver chain over his head. He handed the chain and bronze medal to Cornelius.

After admiring the she-wolf on one side, he flipped the medallion over and read, "The Romiliia Household with bravery and the fierceness of wolves. I don't know the family name. But we'll ask around while we're here."

"You act as if this is going to be a short visit," Jace commented while dropping the chain over his head. "I would think you'd want time at home after fighting four battles against the Carthaginian General."

"Hannibal is the reason we're not staying long," Cornelius clarified. "I want to be there when he's defeated and crucified. However, before that, I'm studying his field tactics."

"So, you can defeat him in battle?" Jace asked.

"He'll be brought down by the Legions long before I have the opportunity," Cornelius projected. "In the meanwhile, I'll learn as much as I can from observing him. And for that, I need to be on the battlefield."

Chapter 3 – Any Assignment

The Villa Scipio occupied a high section of Palatine Hill. Nestled between a couple of grand homes, the villa covered a double lot. The entire length of the yard was being used and it worried the elder Scipio.

"Is that dangerous to our neighbors?" Publius Scipio inquired while squinting at the far corner of his garden.

"Not in the hands of a Cretan Archer," Cornelius replied.

In quick order, Jace Kasia aimed and released five arrows. The shafts shot down the length of the patio. They traveled through passages in a couple of hedge rows, zoomed across several flower beds, and flew over a section of lawn. In a heartbeat, the arrows lodged in a straw bale that rested against the far wall of the estate. The Cretan Archer sprinted towards the target.

"It's a little frightening. With enough quality bowmen on a battlefield, no one would be safe," Publius remarked as Jace raced by the seating area. Then Publius locked his eyes on his son. "Now that your friend has seen the city, it's time to send him away and pack for Iberia."

Cornelius gazed over the city, popped an olive in his mouth, and chewed. All the actions delayed his response to the instructions. Finally, he poured more watered wine, picked up the mug, and saluted his father with it.

"I'll not be going to Iberia with you, sir," he informed the elder Scipio.

"After your presence at four losing fights against the Punic General, no one wants an unlucky officer in their Legion," Publius pointed out. "Come with me and I'll make you the Senior Tribune for a Legion."

"That's very generous of you, father. But I'll decline," Cornelius said before expanding on the reason. "General Hannibal isn't using magic to win. But he is executing his tactics flawlessly. I want to learn how. If I must, I'll enlist as a Legionary."

"Cornelius, I want to tell you the truth. However, our conversation cannot go any farther than the two of us."

"Yes, sir, I understand."

"Although yesterday the Senate consolidated authority in Quintus Fabius, they fear giving anyone too much power," Publius explained. "Today the Dictator's second in command will be chosen. And I can bet, the Master of Horse will be selected to balance Fabius."

"Isn't balance good?"

"Do you think Hannibal has anyone second guessing his orders or questioning his intuition?"

"Probably not," Cornelius replied.

"Yet when we combine Legions, our Consul/Generals switch off command of the Legions daily," Publius described. "And each man can do as he pleases on his day of Generalship. In short, the Republic elects Generals then after a year of experience, we pull them out of the field. A few are elected to Proconsul positions. But even as a commander of

Legions, they spend as much time justifying their actions to the Senate as they do fighting the enemies of the Republic."

"You and Uncle Gnaeus are excellent Generals," Cornelius protested. "And he is winning battles in Iberia."

"Gnaeus is an adequate strategist and I'm a good administrator. Neither of us has designs on being a King of Rome. It's our mediocrity that frees me to join him in Iberia. Send your friend away and pack your bags. I want you out of the politics of this war."

"With all due respect, father, I would rather become an infantryman then travel to Iberia."

Zip-Thwack

Five arrows from Jace's war bow struck a second hay bale. Even with the archer on the other side of the estate, the shafts formed a tight circle in the target near the patio.

"Frightening," Publius observed before saying. "Cornelius, I can't have a son of the Scipio family standing in an assault line. Come to the Senate tomorrow. After we see who Fabius is saddled with as Master of Horse, I'll point you to a Senator who might help."

"Father, did you just make a joke about the Master of Horse?"

"I haven't the foggiest notion what you're talking about," Publius said.

Then he chuckled.

***

Jace shifted the belt on his linen tunic. Trying to get the material straightened and the leather even on the fine fabric. Seeing him fidget, Cornelius scowled.

"If you didn't insist on wearing the war hatchet, the belt would rest on your hips."

"You made me leave my bows and quiver at the house," Jace reminded him. "You can't expect me to go around unarmed."

"Most people are satisfied with a dagger," Cornelius offered.

"Most people aren't foreigners in a strange Capital," Jace informed the Tribune.

A few people in the gallery of the Senate glanced at the teen noblemen. Both had even features. From their high brows, down their prominent noses to their strong jawlines and chins, they were fine examples of Latin youths.

"Pay attention to your real clients," Cornelius advised. He directed Jace to the tiers of Senators seated around the chamber. "King Hiero of Syracuse may pay your fees, but the Senate picks the Generals of the Legions."

"The client is always right," Jace replied.

Below them the President of the Senate stood at the dais and pounded on the surface until the chamber settled.

"Senators of the Republic, I present to you Quintus Fabius, Dictator of Rome."

The side doors flew open and twenty-four Lictors marched into the Senate. Each enforcer wore a white toga. In their arms, they carried a bundle of birch branches wrapped around an axe handle and tied with red leather straps. The Lictors spread around the chamber and took up stations as if sentries at guard posts.

"See, they brought their war hatchets," Jace mentioned.

"Those are fasces, symbols of the Lictors' office," Cornelius corrected him. "Not war hatchets."

"What's the difference other than mine has a single blade and theirs are double-headed axes."

"The difference, Archer Kasia, is a Lictor can put you on trial for any offense, sentence you to death, and carry out the execution. And no one will question him."

"Not even the Archon of the city?" Jace asked.

"If you mean the chief magistrate of Rome, there are two," Cornelius lectured. "And each Consul has his own set of Lictors. Beyond being his enforcers, the Lictors symbolize the importance of the Consul's office."

"Your Dictator has twenty-four. How many does a Consul have?"

Cornelius pointed at the open doors. A tall, older man strolled in, waving at specific Senators. With dignity in the way he held his head, and in his measured pace, the man descended the tiers and approached the dais. With a flick of his wrist, Quintus Fabius dismissed the President of the Senate.

"Today, we end the senseless loss of Latin and allied lives," Fabius announced. Cheering broke out in the chamber. When the enthusiasm subsided, the Dictator continued. "Our walls will protect Rome. And our sacrifices to the Gods will lead to the end of the Punic incursion into our Republic."

Again, applause and shouts of agreement greeted his words. But a few sections of the chamber weren't as vocal or as animated at his comments.

"Some of your legislators aren't keen on the Director's words," Jace whispered.

"He wants the citizens to sacrifice their livestock and the harvest to appease the Gods," Cornelius informed him. "Some factions think there's another reason to destroy crops. They believe Dictator Fabius' plan is to starve out Hannibal's army rather than defeat him in battle."

"A win is a win," Jace commented. "What difference does the method make? Other than your people starving along with the Carthaginian soldiers."

"I was going to say honor, but you have a point."

Noises at the doorways drew their attention. A dozen more Lictors entered. Also dressed in white togas, they carried fasces in their arms. However, instead of spreading around the chamber, these enforcers remained near the entrance.

In contrast to the slow dignity of Dictator Quintus Fabius, a middle-aged man marched into the chamber. His hobnailed boots clicked on the travertine floors, and the gold inlays on his armor gleamed. He halted before saluting the Senate.

"Greeting from the Rimini Legions that now guard the approach to Rome," he exclaimed. "I, Consul Servilius Geminus, am here to report to the Senate."

Cornelius and Jace would learn later that only half the Consul's Legions protected Rome. The rest remain in the Po River Valley, fending off attacks from the Boii tribe.

"Servilius Geminus, you will dismiss your Lictors, relinquish your position as Consul of the Republic, and submit to the will of the Dictator of Rome," Quintus Fabius ordered.

A current of tension rippled through the tiers of the Senate.

"Are they going to fight?" Jace inquired.

"With the death of Gaius Flaminius and the loss of his Legions, General Servilius Geminus commands the only marching Legions in the Republic," Cornelius responded. "And he holds the only Consul seat. If he chooses, Geminus could seize power and make himself King of Rome."

"Will he?" Jace asked while resting a hand his war hatchet. "If so, who will you back?"

Cornelius ignored the question because Servilius Geminus took off his helmet and handed it to an assistant. Then four servants took his gladius, the armored skirt, and his torso armor. Left standing in a plain gray tunic, the Consul faced his enforcers.

"Lictors of the Consul, as there is no Consul, you are dismissed from duty," he directed before turning to face Fabius. "Dictator, I stand before you as a citizen of Rome, acknowledging your authority."

"Senate of Rome, I put before you a request to make citizen Servilius Geminus the Proconsul of the Navy," Fabius proposed.

A unanimous choir of voices agreed to the new position for Servilius.

"Not much of a fight," Jace commented.

"For a transition of power to go that smoothly," Cornelius told him, "there were major negotiations going on last night. Now, let's see who the Dictator picks as his Master of Horse."

"He needs the approval of the Senate for a stableman?" Jace questioned. "You Latians sure do over govern."

"You have no idea," Cornelius said, thinking of his father's comments. "But to help you understand, the Master of Horse is second in command to the Dictator. Just as the Senate elects two Consuls every year, they seek equilibrium by having two men in positions of authority."

Fabius tapped on the dais and waited. The gracious call to order and his patience reflected the nature of the Dictator.

When the chamber settled, he announced, "For my Master of Horse, who shall assume the Dictatorship should I fall, I call upon Marcus Minucius to serve beside me."

Audible gasps came from several sections.

"I take it, Master of Horse Minucius is a surprise," Jace remarked.

"That he is," Cornelius began when a Greek slipped through the gallery crowd and stepped in front of them.

"Master Scipio?" the Greek asked Jace.

"Oxi eyw, autov," Jace replied while pointing at Cornelius.

The Greek stared at the young archer for a moment then acknowledged, "Your accent is excellent, Latian."

"It should be, I was raised on Crete," Jace told him.

"I wasn't aware Rome had a colony on the Island."

"From what I've been told, it was a short, wet invasion," Jace remarked.

"You were looking for me?" Cornelius inquired.

The man faced young Scipio.

"Greetings," the Greek said while bowing. "I am Hektor Nicanor, administrative assistance to Senator Alerio Sisera. We've been told you are seeking a position in a Legion. Is that correct?"

"Yes, oh yes," Cornelius confirmed.

"The Senator wants to know if you are particular," Hektor probed. "For instance, are you looking to be a Battle Commander, or a Senior Tribune? Or even a Maniple Tribune."

"I was a Maniple Tribune with Flaminius Legion," he replied. "But I'll take any assignment as long as it's with a marching Legion."

"In that case, come alone to Villa Sisera at sundown," Hektor instructed. "Good day, gentlemen."

The Greek faded quickly into the crowd, leaving Cornelius shaking his head.

"What's the problem?" Jace asked.

"Senator Sisera is a member of the white party," Cornelius answered. "He believes in trade treaties and a strong military to protect the agreements. On the other side, the Dictator is a traditionalist and wants to retreat to the Latin borders. And the Master of Horse is Mars' red. He believes in the destiny of Rome and wants to expand the Republic in every direction. I don't know their connection to Senator Sisera."

"I guess you'll find out this evening," Jace offered.

31

"As long as it's in a Legion going against Hannibal Barca, I'll be satisfied."

From the floor of the Senate, Marcus Minucius exclaimed, "I accept the position of Master of Horse and swear my allegiance to Director Quintus Fabius."

Polite applause followed the short speech. Some of the Senators were not happy with Quintus Fabius as Dictator, and an equal number were not pleased with Marcus Minucius as Master of Horse. Yet, as displayed by the majority, the Roman Senate was very comfortable with the division of power.

Act 2

Chapter 4 – Fifteen Hundred from Glory

The sun rested on top of a low building and glowed as if it was a giant lantern. In moments, the orb would sink, descending the city into darkness. Cornelius guided his horse off the boulevard, trotted down a road, and entered an area of estates. Unlike his father's villa, the newer villas lacked a view, but made up for the loss with more land.

At the gate to Villa Sisera, he halted.

"Can we help you, sir?" a household guard asked.

"Cornelius Scipio to see Senator Sisera," he replied. "I am expected."

"Yes, Tribune," the guard replied. "Please ride to the main entrance."

The gate swung open and closed immediately after Cornelius rode through. To his surprise, guards positioned along the driveway saluted him as he passed. By the time he reached the main house, he'd counted five armed men.

"Welcome to Villa Sisera," Hektor Nicanor greeted him from the front stoop. "Leave your horse. A groom will take care of it."

Most villas had an image, or a symbol of the household's protector. Cornelius saw nothing of a God or Goddess at the entrance. Although there was a rough-cut piece of travertine.

The stone reclined beside the entrance, almost as if carelessly tossed aside.

Cornelius slipped off the horse and a young man took the reins. As he approached Hektor, Scipio glanced down. Chiseled in the travertine were the words, *Memento mori*.

"Remember, you too will die," Cornelius read. "That's a very ominous sentiment."

"It relates to the Senator's personal deity," Hektor told him while holding the door open. "The actual Goddess is very personal to him, and he chooses not to share his devotion."

"I can appreciate that," Cornelius remarked.

He and the assistant walked down a corridor. At a doorway, Hektor knocked on the frame but didn't pause.

"Sir, Master Scipio," Hektor announced while waving Cornelius into an office.

Most important men used the walls of their office to display trophies and memorabilia. Not so Senator Sisera. His walls were adorned with a few items and a couple of mostly empty shelves. Cornelius caught the impression of its sparseness as he walked to a desk.

"Thank you for seeing me, Senator," he said.

"Sit, Cornelius. Hektor, bring us some refreshments," Alerio Sisera instructed. "And make it the full-bodied wine. Not that watered grape juice my wife insists on."

"I'll bring the uncut wine for Master Scipio," Hektor acknowledged. "As for your beverage, Senator, I refuse to challenge Lady Gabriella."

"Probably, a wise choice," Alerio admitted. "Now Cornelius, to your problem as a cursed Legion officer…"

"Sir, I beg to differ. I'm no more cursed than," Cornelius hesitated, trying to think of an example. Then he remarked. "Ah, that stone at the entrance to your villa."

Senator Sisera dipped his head in either embarrassment at the accusation or in prayer, Cornelius couldn't tell which. But the crescent shaped scar on the crown of the Senator's head and the blade scars on his hands and arms let the young man know he was talking to a combat veteran. He quickly scanned the walls of the office again and a realization came to Cornelius. The Senator wore his trophies and memorabilia on his body, not on display shelves in his office.

"My apologies, sir, please forgive my impudence," he begged.

"We'll call it whatever you want," Sisera granted. "But in essence, you are as unwanted as a broken toe on a long march. Agreed?"

"Yes, Senator. Unfortunately, that's true."

Hektor came into the room, placed a glass in front of Cornelius, and one an arm's distance from the Senator. They watched as the assistant headed for the exit. Before he left, Hektor stopped and wiped dust from a shelf.

Cornelius inhaled sharply. A medallion suspended on a silver chain dangled below the shelf. He recognized the image of a she-wolf baring her teeth stamped into one side.

"Do you mind, Senator?" Cornelius asked while pointing at the medal.

"Be my guest," Alerio allowed. "It reminds me of a mystery and a sad story."

Cornelius lifted the chain from the shelf and allowed the medallion to spin for a moment before catching it in his fingers.

"The Romiliia Household with bravery and the fierceness of wolves," he recited before turning the bronze disk over.

"How did you know what was stamped on the medal?" Alerio inquired.

"A Cretan Archer has one exactly like this," Cornelius said. He placed the medal on the desk and sat. "As you said, there is a mystery about what the medallion represents."

"That's not the mystery I referred to," Senator Sisera replied. He straightened his back, took a drink of his wine, and slammed the glass down. "Tell me about this archer."

"Jace Kasia didn't graduate from the archery agōgē on Crete," Cornelius described. "He arrived on the island after a shipwreck. Washed ashore, he grew up on a farm and his training came from a disgraced master archer. Why are you so agitated, Senator?"

Alerio Sisera picked up the medallion and allowed it to swing in front of his face.

"So that's where you went," he commented.

"Excuse me, Senator, where who went?"

"Not just who. I'm thinking about my warship, my captain, my crew, and a friend and his family," Alerio corrected. He wrapped his fingers around the bronze disc. "Found on the Island of Crete you said?"

36

"Yes, sir."

"I'd like to speak to this Greek bowman."

"He is a Cretan Archer, Senator. But, Jace is Latin from his complexion to his build, to his features."

"Hektor! Send two riders to Villa Scipio," Sisera called through the doorway. "Have them escort a Jace Kasia here."

"Tonight, Senator?" the assistant asked from the hallway.

"Yes, tonight. And have Lady Gabriella organize a meal for two hungry young men," Alerio told the assistance. Then to Cornelius, he remarked. "When I was your age, I was hungry all the time. Can you eat?"

"As you said, Senator, I'm hungry all the time."

Alerio Sisera leaned on the desktop and, using his arms, he struggled to his feet.

"A lifetime in the Legions takes a toll on the body," he groaned, taking a step from behind the desk.

Cornelius assumed the wealthy Senator had been a man of business. But looking at the old man shuffle, and remembering the prominent scars, he realized Sisera had been a military man.

"We'll adjourn to a sitting room and talk," Alerio offered, "while we wait for your friend."

Cornelius wanted to protest the naming of Jace Kasia as a friend. But without a better description of a relationship between a Legion officer and a Cretan subordinate of the same age, he let the friend remark pass.

***

They walked down the hallway and strolled through a great room. Here, unlike the office, the walls and shelves held works of art. An older, but still beautiful woman waited at the entrance to a side room.

"Lady Gabriella, may I present Tribune Cornelius Scipio," Alerio introduced the youth.

"A full Tribune at such a young age? Your rank tells the tale of your bravery, Master Scipio," Gabriella greeted Cornelius. Gold flecks in her brown eyes caught the candlelight as she curtsied. "We've provided snacks and beverages for your conference with my husband. But if there's anything else, please ask."

"Thank you, ma'am, for the kind words and the hospitality."

Gabriella threaded her arm into Alerio's. The Senator leaned against her as they entered a room with short tables and three couches.

"Hektor said you needed seating for three, husband of mine," Gabriella remarked.

"Indeed, we have a mystery man joining us," Alerio told her. "But Cornelius and I need to talk first."

"I'll be sure to send in only the quietest server with your food," she teased.

A hint of anger distorted the Senator's features but vanished quickly when he noted her expression. Then a softness touched the wrinkles on his face, and he returned her smile.

"Whatever you think is best," he allowed. Lady Gabriella left the room and Alerio motioned to a couch as he reclined on another. "Now Tribune, we need to discuss your assignment."

"I appreciate that, Senator."

"You can't go into a Century, not heavy infantry, or light infantry for two reasons. No citizen will serve under you and no Legion officer will serve with you."

"Sir, two reasons?"

"One is you're unlucky. But you know that," Alerio listed. "The second is the perception that your father and uncle have deserted the Republic."

Cornelius jumped off the sofa, balled his hands into fists, and jutted his chin in the direction of the Senator.

"They have not deserted the Republic," Cornelius insisted. "Iberia is the source of Hannibal's reinforcements, supplies, and funding. My uncle, and soon my father, will continue to deny the Punic General those things. They have not deserted. Rather, they fight for the Republic where they can do the most good."

"Are you trying to convince me or yourself?" Alerio questioned. "Because from what I hear, Hannibal is here and not in Iberia."

"I, I mean. It's what I said," Cornelius stumbled over a response.

"Sit down, Tribune," Alerio invited. "We're discussing you, not your father."

Cornelius paced for several steps before returning to the couch.

"Forgive my outburst, Senator Sisera. I came to you for assistance then I slapped at the helping hand you extended."

"Nice recovery. Much better than I would have managed at your age," Alerio noted. "I take it from the fire in your belly that you aren't interested in a quartermaster posting, or an assignment as the staff officer for transportation."

"I want to fight, Senator," Cornelius assured him. "But I will take any position as long as it's in a marching Legion."

A servant came in with a tray of sliced pork, a bowl of mint sauce, a stack of flat breads, olives, and grapes. She placed the tray on a table between the couches.

"Will there be anything else, Senator," she inquired.

"We require vino to grease the wheels of negotiations."

Lady Gabriella announced from the doorway, "Your beverage, my husband will go on the table. A separate pitcher will go on the far side of the Tribune's seat."

Senator Sierra huffed and blustered.

"As a Battle Commander of a Legion on the Punic coast, no one measured out a daily ration of vino for me," Alerio complained.

"When you were a prisoner in Carthage, no one cared enough about you to watch out for your health," Gabriella reminded him.

Alerio deflated and a grin touched his lips.

"She's right you know," he told Cornelius. "During my career in the Legions, more people wanted me dead than cared about my wellbeing."

Cornelius Scipio's breath caught in his throat. Here he reclined in a villa where historic and heroic deeds were tossed around as if everyday occurrences. Standing, he faced Alerio.

"Senator Sisera, I apologize for bothering you. I'll take my leave."

"What's wrong?" Alerio inquired.

"I feel badly about burdening you with my challenges."

"Sit down, we aren't finished." After the youth reclined on the couch, Alerio told him. "There is one assignment, actually two, that no son of a Patrician household wants. One being the latrine officer for a Legion."

Cornelius swallowed hard, then commented, "You did mention there was another position."

"I did. Few noblemen want to command foreign troops," Alerio stated. "They are unruly, almost never in the center of the battle, and few of their commanders gain notoriety or fame. But they are in the fight from start to finish without glory."

"I worked with the Cretan Archers to pull my half Maniple off the banks of Lake Trasimene," Cornelius informed the Senator. "And again, during the escape from the Tiber River Valley. It's how I know Jace Kasia."

"For the last two years, I've help Marcus Minucius get his stables in order for the chariot races," Alerio told him. "It may not sound like much, but it amounts to a heap of gold coins. How would you feel about commanding five hundred Cretan Archers and a thousand Peltasts?"

"A thousand what?" Cornelius asked.

"If you don't want the assignment…"

"No, sir. I mean yes, sir, I want the job," Cornelius blurted out. He rushed his words as if the posting would vanish as quickly as it was offered. "If you would speak to the Master of the Horse, I will be in your debt."

"Now you're dealing in a currency I can use," Alerio warned. "When I call on you, I expect you to return the favor. Is that clear?"

"Yes, Senator, I understand."

"Peltasts are light infantrymen from Thrace," Alerio told him. "They're reputed to be as good with their javelins as Legionaries. I don't know how, but that's the lore. Between them and the archers, you'll be in command of fifteen hundred auxiliary troops. That's three times the number of infantrymen a Maniple Tribune controls. Are you up for the challenge without the glory?"

"I am, Senator."

"Then the job is yours. Report to the Central Legions within the week. That's where the new Legions are being formed."

"I thought you needed to speak with Senator Minucius."

"I did that as soon as your father finished bragging about your heroics at Ticinus," Alerio informed him. "While we wait for Jace, tell me about Hannibal's tactics. Is it true he shifts units around faster than Mercury delivers messages?"

"While the messenger of the Gods is fast, he is late when compared to the Punic General," Cornelius described. "Because Hannibal has already pre-planned his maneuvers. Be it an ambush, feeding soldiers into a battle, or covering escape routes, he makes his decisions before the battle begins."

"You think his weakness is inflexibility?" Alerio questioned.

"I never thought of it in that way," Cornelius admitted.

"Well, you better," Alerio coached. "I know Quintus Fabius. This fight against Hannibal will go on for at least a year. You'll have ample opportunity to test your theories."

"But the Dictator was elected to end the war."

"Was he? Or, maybe Fabius was elected to end the deaths of Latin boys?" Alerio suggested. "There is a difference."

They talked about battles and tactics until Hektor appeared at the entrance.

"File Leader Kasia of the Cretan Archers is here, Senator," Hektor Nicanor announced.

"Send him in," Alerio instructed.

Jace Kasia marched into the room and Alerio Sisera shouted, "Stop. Stop right there. Don't move. Hektor, ask Lady Gabriella if she is free."

The only sound in the room were feet rushing through the door to the great room. Moments later Hektor's sandals and much softer footfalls marked his and Gabriella's return.

She came in fast eyeing Alerio to be sure he wasn't in distress of some kind. He seemed fine, but his arm extended and pointed to a youth standing just inside the doorway. Spinning, Gabriella Carvilius DeMarco Sisera put her knuckles to her mouth to cover a screech of surprise.

"Lucius. He looks just like Lucius when he was a young man," she gasped.

"I'm sorry, ma'am. But who is Lucius?" Jace questioned.

"Archer Kasia, show her the medallion," Alerio instructed.

Jace fished out the silver chain, slipped it over his head, and extracted the bronze disk from under his hooded doublet. Before he could offer it, Gabriella snatched it from his hand.

"His name was Lucius Romiliia, and his wife was Otacilia Romiliia," Gabriella breathed out while pressing the disc between her palms. "She was a friend of mine and a Samnite Princess. They vanished, along with one of my husband's warships, thirteen years ago. Now, let me ask you, young man, who are you?"

Jace replied while lowering his head to show his sincerity, "Ma'am, truthfully, I don't know."

Chapter 5 - Found, but Unwanted

"Even in a night deepened by Nyx, you couldn't be mistaken for anyone except the child of Lucius and Otacilia," Gabriella exclaimed while hugging Jace.

"The Goddess of Night aside, Lady Gabriella," Jace remarked as he stepped back, glowing from the recognition and the embrace, "if I'm that son, how did I end up on the Island of Crete."

"The God of the Sea must have plans for you," Gabriella guessed. "But what Poseidon's plans are for anyone, no one knows. Except maybe the Oracle of Delphi. As for what happened before, I'll let my husband tell the story."

Alerio sipped from his watered wine, scowled at the weak beverage, before starting the tale.

"Two years before the first war with the Punics ended, the Republic had no reserves," Alerio told them. "With the coffers empty and the fighting going offshore, we needed a new fleet. But we had no funds to build the ships."

Jace and Cornelius rested on the edges of their couches while Lady Gabriella and Hektor remained standing. No one ate or drank while the Senator talked.

"After a debate, the Senate asked wealthy noblemen to fund the building of one warship each. Together, we build a fleet of two hundred warships," he described. "Lucius Romiliia, against my advice, sold his family's villa and invested the coins in a quinquereme."

"Oh no, did it sink?" Jace inquired.

"I advised against selling the villa because Lucius, although a Patrician, was low on funds and had a young wife. His gamble on the five-banker seemed too risky. Nevertheless, he became the warship's senior officer and lucky for him, the recruitment officer brought him a crew of Ligurians from the area around Genoa. Those men knew the sea and took to the warship immediately. At the final battle off the coast of Sicilia, Centurion Romiliia distinguished himself and captured two enemy ships-of-war. Between the coins for the prizes and his share of the peace fee from Carthage, Lucius became a wealthy man."

"If he recouped his coins and turned a profit," Cornelius asked. "How did he end up on your warship off the coast of Crete?"

Alerio sipped a mouthful then spit the watery vino back into his glass.

"After the war, Lucius and Otacilia bought an estate on the border of Liguria. It seemed like a reasonable choice, seeing as his crew came from the area. He even hired some of the men to work the farm. But that proved his downfall."

"How can owning land and hiring locals be bad?" Jace questioned.

"Seven years after the war ended, the Ligurians broke their treaty with the Republic," Alerio answered. "Consul Lucius Albinus sailed up the coast with his Legions and quickly put down the rebellion. Then leveling murky charges, the Consul and a few Senators claimed Lucius Romiliia had armed and incited the rebels. Lucius, his wife, and a newborn son returned to Rome to face the charges."

"The whole affair stunk," Gabriella declared. "It was a land grab, pure and simple. They tried Lucius for treason, found him guilty, confiscated his property, and sent him into exile."

"Even if I was the son of Lucius Romiliia," Jace stated, "I'd still be a coinless archer from Crete."

"Would Jace, at least, be a citizen of the Republic?" Cornelius inquired.

"In any other era, the answer would be yes. But with General Hannibal running amuck and everyone wanting personal fame and glory, no one wants the competition of a new nobleman," Alerio answered. "Until the Punic's demise, few Senators would vote to reinstate the son of Lucius Romiliia into the Patrician class."

"What they did to Lucius and Otacilia was just wrong," Gabriella complained as she started towards the doorway. Then she stopped and added. "And what happened to you, Lucius Jace Otacilia Romiliia Kasia is a travesty."

"Yet, I feel as if I've been found," Jace exclaimed.

"But you're unwanted," Cornelius reminded him.

"To have a name, even without a position or means, fills my heart," Jace explained. "I've always been an orphan, not like you, a descendant of a famous family. Now I have a connection to Rome and maybe relatives in the Samnites Tribe."

"What will you do with the information?" Cornelius asked.

"Not a thing," Jace admitted. "Can we eat now?"

"Please, while you dine, tell me about your archery training," Senator Sisera invited the youth. Then to Cornelius, he promised. "And afterward, we'll talk about the Thracian light infantry."

***

Jace gave a brief history of his longs days of being a stick, which brought a laugh from Cornelius and a wise nod from Senator Sisera. After details of holding a bowstring, until his fingers bled, before being allowed to shoot the arrow, the archer turned to Cornelius.

"You've seen some of what the Cretan Archers can do, Tribune Scipio," Jace mentioned. "How will you use the Thracians?"

Before Cornelius had a chance to answer, Hektor cleared his throat. Then as if delivering a curse, he uttered, "They honor Ares in barbaric rites."

"Why the hostility towards the Peltasts from Thrace?" Alerio questioned.

Hektor Nicanor went to a pitcher of the full-bodied wine and poured a glass.

"The Thracians worship Ares, the God of Courage and War," the Greek assistant answered. He took a long pull on the wine before continuing. "To you Latians, he is known as Mars. Mars the protector of Rome and the Republic. And Mars is honored before battle by Legionaries in hopes that the God will share a blessing of courage. But in Greek lore, the rebellious God Ares is viewed differently. For us, Ares means trouble."

Hektor drained the glass and hammered the vessel down on the tabletop.

"When Hephaestus, the God of Craftsman discovered his wife was having an affair with Ares, he trapped the lovers in a net. Then he displayed them to the other Gods of Mount Olympus so Aphrodite and Ares could suffer ridicule. In another legend, during the start of the Trojan War, Aphrodite, protector of Troy, persuaded Ares to take the Trojan's side. However, his sister, Athena, aided the Greeks. After the Trojans lost the war, the troublesome God Ares was blamed for the conflict."

Hektor paced the floor. Senator Sisera, Jace, and Cornelius watched and waited as the emotional assistant worked off some of his agitation.

"Even the Spartans, as warlike as they are, have the statue of Ares in their temple in chains," he informed them. "War destroys, allows for famine, disease, and causes heartbreak. Any group that reveres Ares, the God of War, is cursed. Some men consort, forgive, and cuddle the Thracians. But that's wrong because it is immoral to pity the rebellious."

"I don't have much choice," Cornelius remarked, "if I'm going to be their commander."

"You, Master Scipio, would be well advised to shun the Thracians at every opportunity," Hektor told him.

"You've neglected a small part of the story, Hektor," Alerio advised.

"If I've overstepped my place, Senator, I apologize."

"Consultation is always appropriate," Alerio assured him. "What I meant was, this is a time of heartbreak, loss, and possibly famine. And it will be for as long as Hannibal roams free on the shores of the Republic."

"And for that, you would freely release the blessings of Ares?" Hektor inquired.

"As long as the Peltasts from Trace are facing away from the Legions," Alerio described. "And targeting the enemy, while under the command of Tribune Scipio, I say take the chains off the God."

"And I repeat, sir, with all due respect, one should not pity the rebellious."

"I don't want pity," Alerio said with fire in his eyes. "I want to be twenty years younger and in command of a thousand Thracians and five hundred Cretan Archers. I want

49

to run my gladius into Hannibal's chest and feel Goddess Nenia take his soul from his dying body."

No sooner had he finished speaking, then the Senator grabbed at his back, let out a groan, and fell off the couch. On the floor, Alerio kicked his legs, contorted in pain, and cried out.

Hektor dropped to the Senator's side and Gabriella rushed into the room.

"I have the stones being put in the fire," she said while placing her hands on Alerio's back. Then she explained. "The Battle Commander suffered trauma to his back in Messina. When he overdoes any activity or gets too lively, the bones, muscles, and flesh of his back remember the incident. We'll put stones, warmed in a fire, on his spine until the memories fade."

"We should take our leave," Cornelius announced.

He and Jace stood but Alerio lifted an arm to Cornelius.

"I want to do all that," Alerio said while grinding his teeth, "but I can't. Give me your word, Scipio, that you will."

"Senator Sisera, as Mars is my witness, I will not stop until I've destroyed Hannibal Barca."

Alerio nodded his head and just before releasing the youth's arms, he whispered, "Don't be afraid. *Memento mori.*"

While servants lifted Senator Sisera off the floor, Jace and Cornelius passed through the great room and out the front door. As they stood waiting for their horses, Cornelius took a shielded candle from the wall and bent over the piece of travertine.

"*Memento mori,*" he read the carved letters by candlelight. "Now I understand."

"Understand what?" Jace asked.

"Why there's no image of the Sisera's household deity on display."

"Tell me," Jace encouraged him, "why is the protector of this villa not represented?"

"Because the personal Goddess of Senator Alerio Sisera is Nenia, the Goddess of Death."

"I would imagine a figurine honoring death might put a few visitors off," Jace remarked. "But, by the Gods, Senator Sisera is an interesting man."

Their horses arrived and the two youths mounted and rode away from Villa Sisera. With them, they took aspirations. One to find a way to win battles, and the other to find his heritage. They would discover that neither was an easy path.

Chapter 6 – Discarded Normal

They would have left Rome days earlier, except Cornelius visited several families who lost sons or husbands on the banks of Lake Trasimene. In his mind, he would arrive, deliver words of comfort, then quickly leave. It didn't turn out as he imagined.

"We had to bury a proxy body," many of the grieving families informed him. "Now that we know the circumstances of his death, we can lay to rest his memory.

Tribune Scipio, come witness our sacrifice to the Gods, then join us for a feast."

The extended stays at each villa limited his bereavement visits and delayed the departure from the city. On the day his father left for Iberia, Cornelius collected a much wealthier Jace Kasia.

"Where did you get the pack mule?" Cornelius inquired.

He snapped the reins at his mount. Both horses and the two pack mules moved. At a leisurely pace, the caravan wandered off Palatine Hill and crossed the city, heading for the southern gate.

Taking in the sights of Rome and half listening, Jace replied, "I needed the beast to carry the packages."

"I meant where did you get the coins for the mule," Cornelius said refining his question. "And while we're on it, what's in the packages."

"According to the ethos of Crete, every citizen must strive to make a profit," Jace explained. "The packages are gifts for my archers, my second file leader, Lieutenant Gergely, and Captain Zoltar."

"Very admirable of you," Cornelius allowed, "but the coins?"

"While you were off doing noble acts, I walked to the agora."

"The agora?" Cornelius questioned. Then he thought for a moment and suggested. "You went to the Forum."

"If you're talking about the marketplace with vendors buying and selling products and people looking for entertainment, yes," Jace told him. "Did you know most Roman's don't know the Goddess Artemis?"

"To us Latins, the Goddess of the Hunt is Diana."

"Much to my disappointment," Jace remarked. "It took a few verbal gymnastics to recover, but finally I convinced a crowd that Artemis was Diana in Greek."

"That must have been an interesting day."

"Oh, I did the talk over four days, at least three times a day."

"Whatever for?"

"Well, some of my arrows have an 'A' stamped into the glue at the fletching," Jace described. "I would shoot and almost miss a target. Then after pulling one of the arrows blessed by the Goddess from my quill, things changed. I hit the target dead center and was able to perform an amazing archery demonstration. You'd be surprised what people will pay for an arrow blessed by the Goddess of the Hunt. The price went up after each validation of her involvement."

"You're trained to the bow," Cornelius asserted. "There's nothing magical about those arrows, except they're shot by a master archer."

"I know that, and you know that, Tribune," Jace stated. "But the citizens, shoving coins into my hand after every trick shot, didn't know I was a Cretan Archer."

"I'm surprised a professional bowman and a bowmaker would stoop to circus tricks," Cornelius questioned. "Isn't there an obligation of nobility in the title of Cretan Archer?"

"Certainly," Jace assured him, "it's to make a profit."

***

Fourteen miles southwest of the Capital, large estates with massive villas appeared on the hills above the road.

"The headquarters for the Legions of the Master of Horse are in Ariccia, up there. This is where I leave you," Cornelius announced. Then he directed. "Stay on the Via Appia until you find the turn off. Three mile southeast of here, you'll run into the Central Legion's training camp."

"How will I know if it's the correct turnoff, Tribune?" Jace asked.

After the relaxed familiarity of the holiday, they easily slipped back into the hierarchy of the Legion.

"Look for the roadway with a topcoat of dust as deep as your fist."

"How do you know these things, sir?" Jace questioned.

"Ever since I was a little boy, my father and uncle have taken me on tours of Legion camps," Cornelius told him. "They wanted me to know my way around the military. The dust you find is from years of Legionaries marching or jogging to and from the camp."

"Thank you for my name, Tribune Scipio," Jace said acknowledging the conversation at the Sisera Villa.

He reached into a bag, pulled out an object wrapped in cloth, and handed it to Cornelius. Then the archer saluted and headed the horse and mule away from Ariccia.

Cornelius watched him for a few moments, speculating how his life would be different if he didn't have a family. Maybe he could turn a profit at the Forum with tricks. The thought was freeing. And the idea of no longer dealing with the politics of navigating life with the name Scipio seemed appealing.

Slowly, he pulled back the folds of the cloth until a Legion dagger appeared. In shape and sharpness, it resembled any normal pugio. Except lengths of silver thread adorned the pommel and the guard. He had seen daggers with more extravagant embellishments. But they made the owners seem pretentious. The gift from Jace Romiliia Kasia projected taste while staying true to the purpose of a wide-bladed dagger.

For a heartbeat, Cornelius pondered doing circus tricks at the Forum for a living. But his envy of the orphan ended quickly. Bred for duty to the Republic, Cornelius turned his horse off the Via Appia.

Several strides later, the horse headed up the roadway to Ariccia. Home to country estates, the headquarters for Legion command staffs, and the gateway to Cornelius Scipio's future.

***

"What am I supposed to do with a Scipio?" Colonel Pantera asked. "I've no staff officer or combat officer who wants or needs anything to do with you. The Legions have been cursed since that Punic General arrived. And Scipio, you've been there every time."

Cornelius stood in front of the Battle Commander's desk feeling ill. Often when important men made agreements, they neglected to notify their underlings. The Colonel for Minucius Legion North was subordinate to the Master of Horse and obviously had not been told of the agreement between Senator Sisera and General Minucius.

But Cornelius grew up around powerful men. He understood the use of a bluff to get want he wanted.

"Sir, I'm not asking for a job," he explained to the Battle Commander while leaning on the desktop. "I'm here to inform you that I'm assuming command of the Thracians and Cretans."

"You what?" Pantera roared. "You're just a boy. And a bad omen."

"I'm a full Tribune of the Republic. And as you've pointed out, I have more combat experience than almost anyone in your Legions," Cornelius countered. Then before the Colonel could think, he added. "Now, sir, please advise your Senior Tribune that I will be protecting your right flank."

"The toughest wing of a combat line," Pantera sighed.

"Yes, sir. Where your shields are open, that's where you'll find me."

"But the Cretans are archers," Pantera tested. "What do you know about directing archers."

"I used them to link up our Maniples at Trasimene and to organize a breakout," Cornelius responded. "You must agree, sir, that I am the best qualified staff officer for commanding the right-side auxiliary."

The veins on Vibius Pantera's forehead pulsed under his skin. In what could only be an internal struggle, the Battle Commander's lips quivered as he worked through the alternatives to young Scipio. But, as everyone knew, few staff officers wanted the responsibility of commanding unruly troops who might break at the first sign of pressure.

"We start field maneuvers in four days," the Colonel told him. "Once we begin drilling the Legion, if you fail, for your insubordination, I'll send you back to the Capital with lash marks on your back."

"Yes, sir," Cornelius acknowledged. Inhaling deeply, and in a voice that filled the office, he bellowed. "Colonel Pantera. Tribune Cornelius Scipio reporting in to assume command of your right flank."

"Welcome to Minucius Legion North, Tribune. See Timeus Opiter, your right-side Senior Tribune and get on the payroll. And although I hate to, but I will ask. What do you need?"

"I need a Junior Tribune who would be better off on a construction site than on a combat line," Cornelius answered. "A pair of Optios who know how to keep order. And two Centurions with drunk and disorderly charges pending against them."

"What are you going to do with the Thracians and Cretans, build them a pub and stock it with drama girls?"

"No sir, I'm going to communicate with them in their language about a universal truth."

"What truth?"

"Learn to fight beside the Legion heavy infantry. Or become so much butchered meat after the Punic cavalry finishes chewing you up."

A short while later, Cornelius marched out of the room. Once the door closed, Timeus Opiter stepped to the Battle Commander's desk.

"He did us a favor, sir."

"What favor?" Pantera inquired of the staff officer.

"He told us how to get rid of him," Senior Tribune Opiter snickered. "Men always say their biggest fear when boasting. And Tribune Scipio mentioned his fear of cavalry."

"Maybe," Colonel Pantera allowed. Then while rubbing his forehead, he asked. "But why an engineer for a second in command, two drunk Centurions, and only two NCOs for discipline?"

"Sir, I wouldn't know," the Senior Tribune admitted.

***

At the Legion camp, Jace Kasia rode by a supply building, and a large structure with Legion staff officers idling away the day in chairs. The archer kept his head forward, intentionally not making eye contact. Farther down the street, he reached a group of men in long tunics and pulled up.

"Yes sir, how can we help you?" one asked.

Jace paused for a moment trying to understand the use of 'sir'. In the space while he thought, three of them slipped away as if avoiding a work party.

"I'm looking for the camp of the Cretans," he said.

"It's on the far side, next to the Thracians," a second man told him while pointing to the south. "Is that all, Centurion?"

"Not a Centurion," Jace remarked. "Not even a citizen of the Republic."

"You look like an officer."

"I'm an archer from Crete," Jace insisted. "Where are you from?"

"We're Samnites," another answered. He pointed at the mountains to the east, "from over the hump."

Seizing the opportunity, Jace asked, "If I said Princess Otacilia, would the name mean anything to you?"

"Why? Should it?" the second man inquired.

"No, it's my mother's name," Jace told him. "She was a Samnite Princess, or so I've been told. There was little chance, but I thought…"

"Otacilia is a Hirpini name," the first Samnite declared. "You'll need to speak with the Wolf."

"Speak with who?"

"Lieutenant Papia. He's the war chief of the Hirpini infantry," the man answered. "We call him Wolf because Hirpini in the old language means 'those who belong to the wolf'."

"The Wolf. It's a joke," the second Samnite stated.

Jace didn't acknowledge the humor. He was too busy touching the medallion through his doublet and remembering the writing, *'The Romiliia Household with bravery and the fierceness of wolves'*. It wasn't just a slogan honoring the Roman wolf. The words had significant meaning for his mother's tribe, as well.

"Thank you," he said offhandedly before urging the horse and mule forward.

***

For most of the trip across the sprawling Legion camp, his mind turned over the possibility of meeting someone from his mother's tribe. When the straight lanes and even rows of Legion tents ended, he came back to the present.

Almost as if mimicking the uniformed squares of the Legionaries, these tents were arranged in wavy lines and the roads deadened before curving around islands of misplaced tents.

Men with long hair sat or strolled between campfires. The hair caught Jace's attention. No Cretan Archer allowed his hair to grow over his neck. Long hair flying around in the wind could interfere with the bowstring, the arrow, and the archer's aim. He decided they must be Thracians because a few hundred feet away, he spied the familiar circles of a Cretan camp.

With a sense of being home, Jace relaxed. From a battlefield to the biggest city he could imagine, and now the sight of a massive training camp, he needed a few days to digest it all. Being around other archers would allow things to return to normal.

"Bower, where have you been?" Lynceus Inigo exclaimed. Following the big youth, three archers walked as if in a formation. Some things never changed. One being Lynceus' need for an audience of supporters when he abused an underling. "I've been waiting for you, Kasia."

A memory washed over Jace. His outstretched arm pinned against a target while log sized arrows struck around the limb. Then the threat of being murdered followed the humiliation. A smile touched Jace's lips because the situation had changed since the days at the archer academy.

"Lynceus. Come around here," Jace invited him. "There's something you should know."

Lynceus strutted to the far side of the horse and stuck his chin out.

"What bowmaker?" he demanded as he approached.

"Just wanted you to know, I'm a File Leader."

After saying the words, Jace kicked Lynceus Inigo in the chest. Then he nudged the horse into motion. Behind him, the three sycophants rushed to help Inigo to his feet.

A few turns later, Jace reached a groups of tents with archers he recognized. Reining to a stop, he called to Archer Hali Adras. Before leaving Rimini to accompany the Tribune to Rome, Lieutenant Gergely assigned Hali as his assistant File Leader.

"Hali, take the mule, I've got to get the horse back to the Legion stable," he told the archer.

"Leave the horse for Eachann. You've got to see the Lieutenant."

"That's good, I have a gift for Gergely, and one for you as well," Jace informed him while sliding off the mount.

"Because of his injuries, Gergely's been moved to supply," Hali told him. "You're to report to our new Tail Leader, Lieutenant Inigo."

Jace wobbled. If not for Hali's hand on his shoulder, he might have fallen against the side of the horse.

"Great. I'll give him Gergely's gift," Jace stated. "Not that it will do me any good."

"Did I miss something?" Hali inquired.

"You'll catch up soon enough," Jace promised while untying the packages and lifting them off the mule's back.

Act 3

Chapter 7 – From the Grave

"File Leader Kasia, reporting in, Lieutenant," Jace announced as he stepped under an overhang.

The awning extended from a large tent located in the center of Lieutenant Inigo's cluster of Files. Attached like concentric rings, Capitan Zoltar, his command staff, and the supply tents joined Inigo's Files. On the other side of Zoltar's area, Lieutenant Ladon Stavros' tents abutted the headquarters cluster. By design, the layout of the Cretan camp resembled an ouroboros. But rather than the horizontal symbol for infinity, the snake eating its own tail was in a vertical pose. In addition to the mystical power of the shape, the position of the tents provided anonymity for the Lieutenants and easy access to the Files for the Captain.

Stavros usually handled logistics. But due to his injuries, Gergely became the supply officer for the Cretan expedition. Unfortunately for Jace Kasia, Ladon Stavros assumed command of the experienced Files leaving the junior Files for Inigo.

"I don't like my File Leaders running off in the middle of a troop movement," Hylas Inigo scolded.

"Sir, I had permission from Lieutenant Gergely," Jace informed his new boss.

"Wait, let me check," Hylas said. In an exaggerated manner, the Lieutenant twisted his face from side to side. "Nope, I seem to be the only officer in the area. And I still don't like my inexperienced File Leaders disappearing when we have a Company to move through enemy held territory."

"Yes, sir. I apologize and will take any punishment you feel is appropriate."

"I'm glad we agree…"

A big voice boomed from between the tents.

"Hylas. Where in Zeus' name are you?"

Hylas Inigo jumped to his feet and called back, "at my tent, Captain Zoltar."

"When I was a Lieutenant, you'd rarely find me at my quarters," the Captain said while emerging from between a pair of tents. "I was too busy checking on my Files and preparing the archers for combat."

"Sir, I just arrived here. There was a discipline issue and I thought it best to use my tent," he lied. "You know, to provide privacy for the accused."

"Not a bad tactic," Pedar Zoltar concurred. "How bad was the infraction?"

"File Leader Kasia vanished while we were moving from Rimini," Hylas gave the Captain a shortened version. "I was going to…"

Zoltar shot a hand up and Hylas froze in mid speech.

"He is young. Perhaps too young to be a File Leader. Although Acis Gergely speaks highly of him," the Captain said after studying Jace. "Let's just take the title, leave him in the File, and call it good. No reason for additional punishment, don't you think?"

"Yes, sir, a satisfying decision," Hylas allowed while squeezing his hands into fists. "You're dismissed, Archer Kasia."

"Thank you, sir," Jace said. Then he smiled and announced. "I've brought gifts for you both from Rome. I'll run and get them."

"Excellent. Everyday I make a profit is a good day," Zoltar stated as Jace marched away. Then he warned. "Keep an eye on him, Hylas. He didn't attend the agōgē and I'm suspicious of any bowman without proper training."

"Yes, sir," Lieutenant Inigo acknowledged. "Did you come over here for a reason?"

"Yes. We begin field drills with the Legion in four days," Zoltar informed him. "Make sure your archers are ready."

"Yes, sir."

The Captain ducked from under the awning and soon vanished between a pair of tents. Once he was alone, Hylas Inigo looked at the flap to his tent.

"You can come out," he instructed.

He brother pushed the goat skin aside and stepped clear of the tent.

"You were supposed to punish Kasia," Lynceus complained.

"I'm not about to threaten my position for you, little brother," Hylas explained. "He's no longer a protected File Leader. If you want more, challenge him. But leave me out of it."

64

"I'll challenge him," Lynceus exclaimed while rubbing the sore spot on his chest. "And I'll kill him."

"You do that, and Captain Zoltar will ship you back to Crete," Hylas cautioned. "Just hurt Kasia and be done with it."

Lynceus Inigo stomped off. Alone, Lieutenant Inigo wondered if he cared too much for his little brother and covered for him too often. He picked up a wineskin, sat under his awning, and took a long, long stream of wine.

***

Before the trip to Rome, the loss of the File Leader position might have carried more disappointment. Being a leader of archers still mattered, but Jace's quest to discover more about his mother overrode the hurt of the demotion.

Hali Adras wasn't happy about his promotion. But the second File Leader agreed it was better to be the leader then to follow someone less qualified.

Jace collected the gifts and delivered one to the Captain and another to Lieutenant Inigo. Both officers asked how they constituted revenue. Jace told them of the Forum and his trick shots. He left out the part about using the Goddess of the Hunt to increase his profit margins. While a trader like his Uncle Dryas would understand, Jace wasn't sure Cretan officers would have the same attitude.

"In the best tradition of Crete," Hylas Inigo avowed, "I commend you on earning a profit."

"My pleasure, Lieutenant," Jace replied.

As he strolled back to the File area, he contemplated the change in Hylas. When he got back from the Capital, the officer appeared angry. But when he accepted the gift, Hylas was gracious. Although that could have been the wine talking as the Lieutenant had two empty wineskins on the table.

Maybe Jace had the Inigo brothers wrong. Then, as he approached the tents of his File, he noted Lynceus standing on the case containing his war bow.

"Not both of the brothers," Jace muttered before yelling. "Get off my war bow, you ignorant feather merchant. If you want a challenge, you don't have to disgrace yourself, just ask."

Hali Adras, who had his back to Lynceus, spun at the insult. Seeing an archer standing on another man's war bow, the new File Leader charged. But Lynceus was bigger and stronger. He caught Hali, jerked him off the ground, and flung him into the air. Flipping and clawing, Hali landed hard and wrong. The snap of his shoulder bones shattering brought the rest of the File to their feet.

Lynceus and his three cohorts formed a wall and began to back out of the camp.

"Stop," Jace ordered. The four intruders halted, and the archers of the File formed a protective barrier around Hali. "You want me, Inigo? Fine, knives and shields in the fighting circle at the range."

"I'll see you there," Lynceus confirmed.

He and his gang strutted away. Jace knelt beside his File Leader.

"This is going to hurt," he warned.

Two archers took the uninjured side to stabilize Hali. Jace gripped the other arm and pulled it away from the shoulder. When a grinding notified him that the bones had separated, another member of the File wrapped a long cloth around the shoulder and the arm.

"It was fun while it lasted," Hali Adras admitted. Then he told Eachann. "Run and tell the Lieutenant that I resign the position of File Leader. If he asked, tell him, it's too dangerous. Jace, it appears you'll have your job back."

"Not yet," Jace said before asking. "Are you alright now?"

"I won't be pulling a bow for a while. But I'll heal."

"I'm sorry that my mud splashed over on you," Jace apologized. "If you'll excuse me, I need to check on my bow and get ready to settle this once and for all time."

"Archer Jace Kasia," Hali warned while clinging to Jace's arm, "don't kill him. You'll get discharged from the Company. And in the end, Lynceus Inigo will have won."

"Even though he'd be dead?"

"Vengeance from the grave may not be satisfying for the deceased," Hali informed Jace. "But, it's revenge just the same."

***

Word of the challenge spread. By the time Jace, the wounded Hali Adras, and the archers of their File arrived, they had to push aside spectators to reach the fighting circle. Moments later, Lynceus Inigo, his File Leader and his fifteen archers arrived.

"Kasia, I'm going to cut you," Lynceus shouted over the circle and noise of the crowd. "Cut you deep."

The archers who came to watch the fight, cheered the boldness of his statement. Then, they turned to see how his opponent would respond.

Jace pulled his doublet off and tossed it to Eachann.

"Watch that for me," he said to the archer. After sliding the silver chain and medallion over his head, he told Eachann. "If I die, get this to Senator Alerio Sisera in Rome. Tribune Scipio can send it for you. And keep my war bow for yourself."

"That's great," the young archer said. "But now I don't know if I should wish you good luck, or safe journey?"

"Just guard my stuff until this is over," Jace advised.

From a pouch, he pulled a small round shield. Across the circle, Lynceus did the same. While they strapped the shields on their forearms, a few archers in the crowd chuckled. Where Inigo's glowed almost mirror like, the bronze face of Kasia's shield showed dents and long slits from heavy blows from swords strikes.

"Hey Kasia," someone shouted, "to find a shield that old, did you have to rob a grave."

Jace glanced around at the faces while holding up the shield so everyone could see it.

"I could have hammered, sanded, and buffed them out," Jace exclaimed. "But the scars on my shield were installed by Master Archer Zarek Mikolas. I am not worthy to erase my teacher's work."

Realizing that he'd revealed his secret, Jace clamped his lips together. But a commotion in the back of the crowd rolled forward as Ladon Stavros shoved bodies out of his way.

"Who mentioned Zarek Mikolas?" the Lieutenant demanded. Most archers in the crowd had no idea who Mikolas was, and those who did, kept it to themselves. When no one answered, Ladon said. "Zarek Mikolas cheated his archers and put their lives in danger for gold. When the son of the Archon discovered the truth, Mikolas murdered Archer Sim Admetus in a drunken rage."

"I did," Jace said. Then in a louder voice, he proclaimed. "I said the name of my teacher, Zarek Mikolas."

"Leave. Leave now," Stavros commanded. "Pack your belongings. You are discharged from this Company."

"You got off easy, Kasia," Lynceus Inigo cackled. "Banished before I could make you suffer."

Then the voice everyone knew and feared rolled over the assembled archers.

"Make a hole," Captain Zoltar roared. When the archers moved too slowly, he added. "Make it wider or I'll have the lot of you on the range overnight."

After the threat, the crowd parted leaving a double wide path to the fighting circle. Taking advantage of the opening, Lieutenant Acis Gergely limped behind the Captain.

"What is this?" Pedar Zoltar demanded.

"The name of Zarek Mikolas has been invoked," Stavros volunteered. "I've put a stop to it by dismissing Archer Jace Kasia for praising the disgraced archer."

"You did?" Zoltar inquired with an amused expression on his face. "Are you officiating at this, this whatever it is?"

"No, sir. I just followed the crowd."

"You followed the crowd to a fighting pit, but don't know what's happening?"

Chuckling leaked from the archers at their Captain's question. Or maybe at the supply Lieutenant's inane response.

"There was a challenge made and accepted," Lynceus boasted. "Archer Kasia and I are resolving private issues."

"Ah, finally someone who knows why we're gathered together," Zoltar exclaimed. "But Stavros isn't mediating the circle. And Lieutenant Gergely was with me, so we aren't facilitating the challenge. That leaves one other officer? Where is Lieutenant Inigo?"

"Sir, when I told him Archer Inigo shattered File Leader Adras' shoulder," Eachann informed the Captain, "he groaned, took a drink of wine, and said, tell Kasia, he has his job back."

"Is that true?" Zoltar questioned Hali Adras.

"Jace hasn't accepted the position yet," Hali responded.

Laughter of anticipation rolled through the crowd. To keep order in the Company, no File Leader could fight an archer or accept a challenge from one. Because Jace hadn't acknowledged the position as File Leader, the fight could continue.

"That's not what I meant," Zoltar exploded. "Did Archer Inigo do that to your shoulder?"

"Let me put it this way, Captain," Hali replied. "My shoulder and I really want this fight between Kasia and Inigo to happen."

"What if Kasia loses?"

"He won't," Acis Gergely said while limping to the edge of the circle. "He was trained by Zarek Mikolas, an old master. A teacher who believed in pain before precision, and exhaustion before practice."

"And who will referee the challenge?" Zoltar inquired.

"I will," Gergely announced.

"But you're injured, Lieutenant," the Captain noted. "What if the fight gets out of hand?"

To keep from stepping with his injured leg, Gergely twisted around and called to Jace.

"Archer Kasia, on the memory of your teacher, Zarek Mikolas, do you swear not to end archer Inigo's life?"

"I do, sir," Jace replied.

"This is almost an embarrassment," Captain Zoltar remarked. "All the procedures have been ignored. However, there are personal issues to be resolved. Let the challenge proceed."

In the center of the cheering crowd, Jace rested his hand on the hilt of his knife and stepped forward. On the far side, Lynceus drew his blade and entered the fighting circle.

Lieutenant Gergely rested the head of his crutch against his side, lifted his arms overhead and, bellowed, "Let the challenge begin."

***

Lynceus Inigo shuffled to his left, keeping his blade beside his shield. The combination would allow for a stab followed by a block of any counter strike.

While the big Greek stayed tight and ready for the first clash, Jace Kasia moved with his arms suspended at chest level and his hands wide apart.

Before the combatants came into contact, a murmur replaced the cheering. Jace's open stance wasn't unusual, fighters good at hand-to-hand combat often used it. The buzzing resulted from Jace not drawing his knife. His right hand was empty.

"Hali, you won't be needing that bush knife," Jace called out, "sell me the scabbard."

"Feeling inadequate?" Lynceus asked.

Jace shuffled his feet quickly and jerked his arms. Lynceus jumped back to avoid an attack that didn't come. Some in the crowd cheered the feigned assault.

"But you have a knife," Hali pointed out.

The crowd grew silent, trying to figure out Kasia's reasoning for not pulling his blade.

"I use a small skinning knife," Jace said as he continued to circle with Lynceus. "Until now, I forgot I wasn't using my war hatchet."

Chuckles broke from the attendees when they observed the different sized blades. Lynceus Inigo carried a heavy camp knife suitable for chopping wood or severing limbs.

"You can have my knife," Hali offered.

"Not the knife, I want to buy the scabbard."

Lynceus charged forward, his shield out front, and the knife positioned for a thrust. Jace squatted under the big Greek evading the smash and slash. Then, the Latian rolled forward. At the end of his tumble, he inserted a leg between Lynceus' legs. Using momentum and a bent knee, Jace tripped his opponent, sending Inigo to his back and putting Jace on his face.

The momentary sprawl provided an opportunity for the quickest to recover. But Jace didn't have his knife out and Lynceus was stunned. Instead of finishing the contest, the fighters untangled their legs, came to their feet, and resumed circling each other.

"Sheath?" Jace inquired.

"Here," Hali alerted Jace.

With an underhanded pitch, he tossed the scabbard.

The leather casing for the bush knife arched into the air. Jace crossed his feet at the ankles, while trying to move laterally. Stumbling, he almost fell. In an awkward grab, his left hand rather than his right ended up positioned under the flying sheath.

After barely catching it, Jace extended his left hand as if to pass the sheath to his right hand. However, instead of passing it off, Jace flipped the scabbard from behind his shield.

Although the forearm shields used by the archers were small compared to infantry shields, up close they created a blind spot. And with two shields in line, Lynceus didn't detect the heavy piece of leather until it smacked him in the face. In a reflex action, he jerked back and swiped at the flying scabbard with the back of his knife hand.

Without a blade between them, Jace jumped forward into the gap behind Lynceus' shield while hammering the Greek's head with his shield. Lynceus dropped and Jace followed him to the ground. In a series of blows that broke or bruised selected sections of his rib cage, Jace Kasia pounded until Lynceus Inigo curled into a ball and began crying.

***

Cornelius Scipio reined in his horse and raised a hand to stop the wagon that followed him. The mule team settled, and the occupants stood to peer over the crowd.

A Junior Tribune eased his horse up next to Tribune Scipio. They both gawked at the fighting circle.

"That one archer seems to be in bad shape," the Junior Tribune noted. Then he inquired. "What is the Latin doing there?"

"Apparently, he's winning," Cornelius answered.

Chapter 8 – Madness and Fears

After spotting the Tribune on the far side of the crowd, Pedar Zoltar bellowed, "That settles the issue between Kasia and Inigo. If anyone disagrees, come see me at moonrise. And bring your long pack."

The thinly vailed threat of being dismissed in the middle of the night and sent to Rimini to catch a boat to Crete wasn't lost on the attendees. Most scattered, leaving the injured Lynceus and untouched Jace in the circle. Their Files, on opposite sides, waited for the crowd to clear.

Once Inigo was scooped up and taken away, Kasia's File charged into the circle to celebrate. Before his archers surrounded him, Jace acknowledged Cornelius with a salute. Then he was swept away among cheering and back slapping.

"Lieutenants Gergely, how are the wounds?" Cornelius inquired as he and a junior staff officer rode forward.

"I'm healing, sir. Thank you for asking," Acis Gergely said. "My I present my Captain, Pedar Zoltar. Captain, this is Tribune Cornelius Scipio. If it wasn't for the Tribune, we wouldn't have gotten any of our people off the bank of Lake Trasimene."

"With help from the Cretan Archers, I was able to collect trapped infantrymen during the fighting. And your archers were instrumental in the breakout," Cornelius added. "This is my assistant, Junior Tribune Pluto Manius."

The thin young man had a puzzled expression on his face. As a junior staff officer, he assumed his job was running messages between units. To be noted as an assistant to the commander of an auxiliary was a big step up in responsibility.

"You should say something, sir," Optio Caeso advised.

"It's a pleasure to meet you," Pluto acknowledged the Captain of the archers.

"In four days, we'll be joining the Legion for maneuvers," Cornelius told the group. "To help us coordinate, I'm inserting one of the Legion's finest in your Company. He'll go where your Files go, or where you tell him. His task is to learn the capabilities of your archers in order to better use them in battle. Is that agreeable, Captain Zoltar?"

Optio Caeso, one of the NCOs, dropped from the tailgate, snatched his pack from the wagon bed, and stood waiting to be called forward.

"It's fine with us," Pedar said. "But Cretan Archers start every morning with a run. Then we do exercises to keep our muscles flexible and run practice sessions in the fighting pit before archery practice. Is that a problem?"

"That's not a problem for a Legionary," Cornelius bragged. He twisted around and looked at the wagon. Optio Caeso took a step forward but stopped when the Tribune waved him off. "Centurion Restrictus, front, and center. Bring your gear."

An overweight Legion officer scooted from the back of the wagon and huffed when he bent to retrieve his pack.

"Captain Zoltar, this is my liaison to the Cretan archers," Cornelius introduced the representative. Jaws dropped as Restrictus waddled to the Tribune. "I have it on good authority, that despite his appearance, the Centurion is looking forward to participating in every activity. Isn't that right, Centurion?"

If there was any pity for Restrictus it faded when he burped, spit up red wine, and blinked with bloodshot eyes.

"We are happy to accommodate the Legion of Rome," Zoltar professed. "Lieutenant Gergely, I'm assigning the Centurion to your Files."

"But you relieved me," Gergely reminded the Captain.

"Well, I'm reinstating you. From the looks of it, you'll be moving at the Centurion's speed," Zoltar explained. "And as you mend, I expect to see a drastic increase in mobility from both of you. Is that what you had in mind, Tribune?"

"Centurion Restrictus has two days to learn about the Cretan archers. Then I expect a complete report," Cornelius stated. "Thank you, Captain Zoltar."

He saluted, guided his horse around, and led the wagon and the junior staff officer towards the Thracian camp.

***

Restrictus blustered, uttered something uncomplimentary about young Tribunes, then demanded, "Who is my porter?"

Lieutenants Gergely and Stavros stiffened. Because everyone carried bows, arrows, their hands weapons, and personal kit, Cretan officers took pride in hauling their own belongings. They didn't know how to deal with a Legion officer.

The situation didn't faze Captain Zoltar for long.

"You are part of my command," he said in a soothing voice. Then he punched Restrictus in the gut. When the Centurion bent forward, Pedar Zoltar clubbed him in the back of the neck with his elbow. "You are part of a Company of archers. Now, you can challenge me, and we'll step into the fighting circle. I wish you would, I need the exercise. If not, pick up your gear and get your fat butt out of my sight."

Restrictus whined what might have been a curse.

"What?" Zoltar asked while bending down so he was cheek to cheek with the overweight Legion officer. "Was that a challenge? I choose war hatchets."

"No, Captain," the Centurion assure him. He hoisted his gear and looked at Gergely with pleading eyes. "Where's our tent, Lieutenant?"

Before Acis Gergely could reply, the Centurion waddled by him.

"Sir?" Gergely asked.

"You are dismissed," Zoltar said. "Make sure your pet *ageláda* makes morning formation."

After acknowledging the instructions, Gergely pivoted on his crutch and limped after Restrictus.

***

Cornelius didn't know much about the Thracians. His only guide came from Hektor Nicanor's warning speech. And if he followed that advice, he'd accomplish nothing. As a result, the young Tribune sat upright, held his head high, and his neck stiff. It was uncomfortable, but he figured it was what the Thracians expected from a Legion officer.

"I'll have the name and location of your Captain," he demanded when he spotted four men with pelta shields and javelins.

"Captain Ignatius is in his tent," one replied. He indicated several goat skin structures at the end of the street.

"The big one, I presume," Cornelius offered.

"You can presume all you like," another of the light infantryman said in a tight voice as if mimicking an educated Latian. "But you better bring an offering to Ares.

78

That's the temple dedicated to the God of War. The Captain's quarters are on the right."

"You know, sir," another chimed in, "like the sword hand of Ares. That's our Captain."

Catching a movement from the corner of his eyes, Cornelius waved down Optio Quaesitus. Coming no doubt to teach the infantrymen some manners, the veteran NCO scowled at the signal to stand down. It went against his nature, but he sat back in the wagon.

"Thank you, gentlemen," Cornelius said while nudging his horse forward.

"He called us gentlemen," one light infantryman remarked.

"After you, gentleman," another commented before shoving the first in the back. "Please. Be my guest."

The four crossed the street teasing each other and bowing to everyone they passed.

"They are uncouth barbarians," Pluto observed.

"Maybe so, Junior Tribune Manius," Cornelius admitted. "But never forget, those are the only troops we have to hold the right flank of the Legion."

"May the God Kratos grant us the strength to protect the Republic," Pluto Manius prayed.

"Exactly," Cornelius agreed.

Tribune Scipio wouldn't have agreed so quickly if he knew Kratos heard the prayer. Because like all deities, the God of Strength, Might, and Sovereign Rule decided to test the young staff officer to see if he was worthy of the blessing.

***

"Tribune Scipio? Why, you're no more than a boy," a big Thracian exclaimed.

The man stood in front of the tent flaps, blocking the entrance to the Captain's tent.

"Optio Caeso. Optio Quaesitus, come up here please," Cornelius called back.

The two muscular NCOs jumped from the wagon and marched to him.

"Would you like us to remove the barbarian, sir?" Caeso inquired.

"That won't be necessary," Cornelius assured them. "I do however require that you maintain discipline on the street."

The Sergeants glanced at each other, then up and down the empty street. Puzzled, they thought again that the young Tribune was either totally incompetent or quite mad.

"Yes, sir, we will," Quaesitus confirmed.

"Good to know," Cornelius replied before savagely kicking his mount in the ribs.

The horse didn't rear back or squat to gather its strength. In a leap, the beast vaulted the three steps, plowed into the Thracian, and drove him across the narrow porch. In a heartbeat, the belligerent barbarian, the horse, and Cornelius were inside the tent.

As quickly as the chest of the horse pushed him back, the Thracian came off the floor and charged at the Legion officer. Then he stopped. The sharp edge of a cavalry sword rested against the side of his neck.

"Is this the quarters of Captain Ignatius?" Cornelius inquired. He kept light pressure on the man's neck with the spatha. Just enough to let the Thracian know, if he dared to more, he would die.

"I'm Alick Ignatius," a man with long hair and a bushy beard replied. He leaned back in his chair with a bemused expression that creased the lines around his eyes. "And who are you?"

"That wasn't the question," Cornelius said pleasantly. With a tiny move, he opened a cut that dripped blood down the Thracian's neck. "The question was. Is this the quarters of Captain Ignatius."

"It is, Tribune," Alick stated. Then with a laugh, he questioned. "Why, don't you know where you're riding your horse?"

"I just wanted to be sure," Cornelius responded. "I didn't want to kill this interfering pig in the temple of Ares. Unless, I could consider it a human sacrifice. But as we're not, this is simply justice."

He swung the blade out as if to chop the Thracian's neck.

Alick Ignatius jumped out of his chair, holding both hands out while screaming, "Please no. He's my sister's boy. He gets a little full of himself. You know how family is?"

"My family is in Iberia fighting the Carthaginians," Cornelius told him. "But seeing as we need to work together, I'll reserve judgement. But keep him out of my way."

"Yes, sir. What can the Thracians do for you?"

"I want to place a man with your squads," he explained. "In four days, we'll do maneuvers with the Legion. And I need to know your capabilities."

"We're Thracian Peltasts, born to the shield and the javelin," Ignatius boasted. "All you need to know is our enemies fear us."

"Tough, are you?" Cornelius asked. Then he swung the spatha back but rotated the sword. He struck the Thracian with the flat of the blade and Alick Ignatius' nephew dropped to the floor. "Like this one?"

The big man landed hard and bounced once before coming to rest as limp as a woolen blanket. Ignatius ran his eyes over the unconscious form.

"I'll accept your man onto my staff," the Captain granted.

"No, he needs to be in with the infantrymen," Cornelius informed him. Then he yelled. "Optio Caeso. Escort Centurion Situs in here please."

A short while, but longer than it should have taken, the NCO shoved a thin Legion officer into the tent.

"I apologize for the delay, sir," the Sergeant remarked. "But the Centurion had some reluctance."

Situs was so lean that he boarded on frail. Obviously, he was a man who preferred taking his meals from a wineskin while forgoing solid food.

"This is the man?" Ignatius asked. "He won't last a day with my Peltasts."

"Only two days," Cornelius corrected. "Then he needs to report to me on the best use of your light infantry during a battle."

"You can't do this to me," Situs bellowed. "I'm a Legion officer and a citizen of the Republic. Not a slave you can shove around. I'm leaving."

Caeso took a half pace when Cornelius hopped off the horse.

"I've got this, Optio," he said. "I recently received a gift. Look here Situs, see the fine silver threads around the hilt and guard. Come closer, take a good look at the last thing you will ever see."

"Your mad," Situs screamed while jerking away from the Legion dagger. "I'll stay. And I'll give you're a report. But then I'm going straight to Senior Tribune Opiter and report this abuse."

"That is, of course, your right," Cornelius allowed before he swung up into the saddle. He pulled the reins to turn the horse to the exit, then said. "Come Optio, we've work to do."

"Yes, sir," the totally confused NCO replied.

Outside, Caeso walked beside Quaesitus. Before they reached the wagon, he whispered, "The boy Tribune might be mad. But he's not soft."

"He has that in his favor," Quaesitus said. "Where to now?"

"All I know is he said, we were going to work."

"What have we been doing all afternoon?"

"It seems, Legionary, according to Tribune Scipio, not working."

***

Junior Tribune Pluto Manius, and the wagon hauling Optios Caeso and Quaesitus rode into a square of tents. The Tribune's horse was tied in front of the biggest. Not far away, the straight roads of Minucius Legion North began.

"Where did this come from?" Quaesitus asked.

"I don't know," Caeso answered.

"I heard Tribune Scipio has loyal Centurions from his father's time as a Consul," Pluto said. "It seems logical that they built this compound."

Cornelius appeared at the entrance to the command tent.

"We've got food," he announced. "Afterward, we'll get to work."

When the four men had platters heaped with food and glasses of wine nearby, Caeso inquired, "Sir, can I ask you a few questions."

"After what we accomplished this afternoon, I'm open to a discussion."

"About this afternoon, Tribune. Why did you place the very worst examples of Legion officers with the Cretans and Thracians?"

"You and Optio Quaesitus would seem to be the better choices for the positions," Cornelius admitted. "Fine examples of Legion leadership, organized, tough, and knowledgeable. But, you see, that is exactly the type who the Cretans and Thracians deal with now. Do you really think they would take either of you into their confidence?"

"But sir, we could have examined their tactics and presented a comprehensive and detailed description for you," Quaesitus insisted.

"I've worked with the Cretan Archers, so I know them," Cornelius informed the junior officer and the NCOs. "And at Trebia in the Po River Valley, I watched light infantrymen die by the hundreds because none of their officers could figure out how to use them properly."

"Sir, that's a harsh indictment," Pluto Manius suggested.

"You won't ask Junior Tribune Manius, but I'll tell you why you're here," Cornelius said. "I want the ideas of an engineer and that of the Optios on how we can protect the right flank of the Legion with what we've been handed. For that, I need experienced views on the standard procedures. And your fresh ideas. But there is one piece of information I need before we can get our arms around a final tactic."

"And what's that, sir?" Optio Caeso inquired.

"I need to know what would make the Cretans fold, and the Thracians run," Cornelius replied. He stood and walked to a large, covered table. After pulling a tarp off a table map, he concluded. "In short, I need to know what they are afraid of."

"And the misfit Centurions are going to hear about that?" Quaesitus asked.

"When people brag, they always boast about conquering what they fear the most," Cornelius answered. He set up blocks in lines as if positioning Legionaries in combat Maniples. "Now, finish your food, and let's get to work."

Chapter 9 – Tactics from the Tactless

The morning of day three found Cornelius and Pluto stooped over the table map.

"If we set the edge as a solid line, our forward element will be too weak," Cornelius complained.

"Tribune Scipio, with all the talk of positioning and what people fear," Pluto brought up, "what are you afraid of?"

After straightening and stretching his back, Cornelius looked at the side of the tent. But he wasn't gazing at the goatskin, rather the young staff officer was seeing through to the past.

"At the Ticinus River, our scouts retreated through the center of our cavalry," he answered. "Although it caused a disruption, our center held. But it soon fell into disarray when Numidian light cavalry slashed into our flanks. With the erosion of our left and right defenses, military order vanished."

"Your fear is a shattered flank," Pluto summed up.

"It's why I keep trying to make a solid formation from the Thracians along our right side. But the placement reduces the number of light infantry at the front."

The sound of a wagon stopping outside ended the conversation. Both Legion officers faced the entrance and waited to see how fast the situation could deteriorate. It didn't take long.

Situs smacked the tent flap aside and stumbled in seething with rage.

"I am done with you," the thin officer stated. "Those Thracians are animals."

"Not a pleasant experience?" Cornelius questioned.

"They spend all day bashing each other with their shields and throwing javelins at each other," the Centurion grumbled. He held up a deeply bruised arm, no doubt from shield drills. "I'll give them credit for courage but none for common sense or discipline."

"Interesting. Tell me what they talked about around the campfires in the evenings."

"Why do you care about gossip?"

"Let's just say I have a fascination with Thracian mythology," Cornelius offered.

While he chatted with the angry Legion officer, Cornelius noted the absence of his Optios and the other Centurion. It didn't bode well for his second interview.

"They talked about women and the God Ares a lot," Situs said with an evil laugh. "They miss home. Oh, and they comb their long hair all the time. It's annoying when grown men play with their locks."

"Sounds unhygienic," Cornelius proposed.

"Their camp might as well be a sheep ranch. There is hair everywhere," Situs described. "Before battle, they tie it into a topknot and stuff the hair under their helmets, so it doesn't fly into their eyes. Now, I'm leaving to report you to Senior Tribune Opiter. You can't threaten me with your pugio and abuse your authority by throwing me to the barbarians."

"Two things before you go. Have a glass of vino with me to celebrate your successful mission," Cornelius remarked.

He poured a half glass for himself but topped off a mug for the Centurion. "And while we drink, tell me what tactics they discussed in the evenings."

"What tactics? The Thracians claim to run towards the clash of shields and swords," Situs said between long, hard pulls on the wine. Then almost as if he'd been stranded in a desert, he downed half the glass before commenting. "One thing struck me as odd. For all their bluster about seeking combat, they talked about a tactic of opening their ranks to avoid fighting cavalry. It seems they have a tradition of stepping aside and allowing riders to pass through their formation. Now, I'm going to headquarters and do my duty."

"You've done an excellent job, Centurion Situs," Pluto complimented him. Reaching to another table, the junior staff officer picked up a full wineskin. "The Tribune would like you to have this as a token of his appreciation."

"It's not enough to compensate me for the disrespect shown to my rank," Situs declared while snatching the wineskin from Pluto. "I hope to never see the two of you ever again for as long as I live."

He swaggered to the exit while pulling the cork from the wineskin.

"That was really good vino," Cornelius protested.

"It was well worth the cost, Tribune," Pluto suggested. "He'll never make it to headquarters. And even if he does, no one will believe charges lodged by a drunken combat officer."

"In that light, I agree, it was worth the cost," Cornelius said. He faced the entrance and called for the fat Centurion. "Restrictus. Care to join us?"

He didn't expect a reception any more pleasant than he received from Situs. In preparation, Cornelius poured another mug of wine and waited.

***

Quaesitus came in first. The NCO balanced an arrow on the palm of his hand. With a look of awe on his face, he glanced up and said, "Good morning, Tribune."

Next, Optio Caeso walked through the flap, also holding an arrow.

"Is there a Centurion out there?" Cornelius inquired. "Because you were sent to collect two of them."

"Yes, sir. Centurion Restrictus wanted to see his quarters in the compound," Caeso replied. "And to get cleaned up before reporting to you."

"That's unexpected," Cornelius admitted. "What's that you're holding?"

While the NCOs contemplated how to answer, Legion Centurion Restrictus marched in and saluted. Where he had been drunk and slumped in defeat two days ago, a different officer walked into the command tent. Standing erect, the still fat man displayed a new attitude. And the ruby wine blush had been replaced by a complexion kissed by the sun.

"Those, Tribune Scipio, are arrows blessed by the Goddess of the Hunt," Restrictus explained. "Of course, we call her Diana, but the Greeks know her as Artemis. I bought one for each of us."

Cornelius blinked several times, trying to recall where he had heard that tale before. When Restrictus handed him an arrow and pointed out the 'A' stamped near the feathers, he remembered Jace's scam in the Forum.

"Thank you. Now, what can you tell me about the Cretan's biggest fear," Cornelius questioned.

"That's easy, sir. They attend an archer's academy from the age of eight," he explained. "In Herds and later in Troops, they were always surrounded by companions. It's understandable that they fear being left alone. In short, the archers fear isolation more than death."

Cornelius paused to think about the information. Pluto Manius didn't.

"If we extend that to being left wounded on a battlefield," the Junior Tribune projected, "we have a workable solution."

He moved blocks on the table map, breaking the auxiliary units into three parts. The junior staff officer fit each part beside markers representing one of the Maniple lines.

"You're leaving gaps in the flanking formation," Cornelius observed. "Is that a nod to the preference of the Thracians?"

Restrictus went to the table. He shifted a few blocks of archers until they were positioned to the far right and located between markers signifying Thracian infantry units.

"Will that stop a cavalry charge?" Cornelius asked.

Caeso and Quaesitus selected shields from a stack in the corner. One Optio held his low while the other raised his shield above the first.

"If the Thracians hold their shields like this," Quaesitus lectured, "no horse will approach, but they'll still have to deal with javelins thrown from horseback."

Cornelius circled the table examining the formation.

"We instruct selected units of light infantrymen and archers to hold the side against cavalry attacks," he described. "The Thracians create a wall, and the Cretans provide offense to keep the cavalry away. It seems everyone is pleased."

"Except, Tribune," Restrictus pointed out, "the formation does not address the Cretan's fear of dying alone. In fact, it isolates whole Files of bowmen."

"I have a solution for that," Pluto Manius offered. "Both auxiliary forces require resupply, one with arrows and the other with javelins."

"They already have systems in place for the resupply of their missiles," Cornelius challenged.

"Yes, sir, that's the problem," Pluto said. "They both use large wagons as central distribution points."

"And as rally areas for their wounded," Restrictus ventured. "However, if you changed the distribution points."

The combat officer's voice tailed off as he thought about the solution.

"Exactly what I had in mind, Centurion," Junior Tribune Manius exclaimed. He ran for the exit and vanished.

"Where is he going?" Cornelius asked.

"To find a wheelwright and a carpenter," Restrictus answered. "Quite possibly, Tribune, more than one of each."

"Wine," Cornelius offered.

"No, sir. I need to go for a hike if I'm going to keep up with the archers."

***

Squads, Centuries, and Maniples had jogged or marched out of and back to the Legion camp, individually. All the elements of Minucius Legion North drilled, trained, and sorted out their equipment on those sorties. Their actions came to a head four days after Centurion Scipio reported to Battle Commander Pantera.

Forty staff officers, and as many Centurions marched three thousand heavy infantrymen out of the Legion camp. On either side of the heavies, eight hundred Legion skirmishers flowed over the landscape.

The staff of the Battle Commander rode at the head of the marching Legion.

"Well? Where are my auxiliaries?" Colonel Pantera questioned.

"Sir, I sent word to Scipio to remind him about today," Senior Tribune Opiter assured the Battle Commander, "and another messenger went to the Samnites."

Because some of the Samnite tribes were part of the Republic, the mountain people held a unique position. In addition to the infantrymen enlisted in the ranks of the Legion, the Samnites supplied a separate auxiliary force.

"Dismissing Scipio may be easier than you thought," Colonel Pantera suggested. "If he doesn't show up, he's gone."

"Would you really have had him whipped, sir?" Opiter questioned.

"Great Jupiter, no," Pantera professed. "Do you know who his father is? Touch that boy and you'd kill your political career."

They topped a hill and on either side of an open field, his auxiliaries waited.

"It seems he got your message," Pantera mentioned. "Okay, Senior Tribune Opiter, send a courier and execute your plan."

"Yes, sir," the right-side Senior Tribune acknowledged.

***

Cornelius spied the Legion command staff when they appeared on the hill.

"Captain Ignatius. Have your Peltasts stay together until the Legion breaks into Maniples," he directed. "Then, fall in beside the segments of their heavy infantry."

"For a day and a half, you've had us group together, break apart, split off, then regroup. I think we understand the drama," Alick Ignatius remarked.

"That's true. But this time, the Colonel will be watching," Cornelius reminded him. "Captain Zoltar, can I get scouts out front and to the side of the Legion, please."

"Tribune Scipio for one so young, you are good at commanding men," Pedar Zoltar offered. "You'll have your scouts."

Ignatius and Zoltar rode away to issue orders.

"Now, Tribune Scipio?" Pluto Manius inquired.

"Not yet," Cornelius replied. He raised a hand and signaled Restrictus. "Let the Centurion get his people into place first."

Attached to the lead group of archers, the overweight Legion officer struggled to keep up with the bowmen. Although he fell behind, the Centurion didn't stop. But he did muster a brief return wave in answer to the signal.

"He is game," Pluto commented. "I knew he was serious when he refused the horse."

"It's actually smart," Cornelius told the Junior Tribune. "In real combat, you don't want to be mounted near the attack line. It makes you a target for enemy missiles and puts undue pressure on that section of your line."

Individual Cretan Archers raced away from the formation. As if a splash of water, they radiated out from the auxiliary force. With his security out and his troops falling in beside the marching Legion, Cornelius made a circle in the air with his hand.

Behind and off to the side, Optios Caeso and Quaesitus spoke with four teamsters and six porters. Shortly after receiving the signal to move out, the pedestrians and four wagons rolled in behind the Thracians.

"Now, Tribune?" Pluto Manius questioned.

"Not, yet," Cornelius told him.

The Tribune didn't look at the junior staff officer when he answered. Not that he was displeased with the eagerness of the younger man. But the hills to the right occupied Cornelius' attention while he prayed.

"Goddess Apate, please bless the cavalry remark I made to Colonel Pantera and Senior Tribune Opiter," he whispered to the Goddess of Deceit. "If you allow them to be smart enough to identify my weakness and send cavalry, this evening, I will sacrifice a ram to you."

In the center of the military movement, the Legion stretched like a soft piece of lamb skin. Far from chaos, the dismantling of the tight ranks came from orders shouted by the Colonel's staff. Rapidly, they got passed down through the chain of command until his instructions were known to every Legionary.

Nine hundred sixty heavy infantrymen, twenty-four NCOs, and twelve Centurions marched forward in an ever-widening triple line. The First Maniple had deployed. Behind them, the Second and Third mimicked the First until the three Maniples took up a much larger footprint than a marching Legion.

Far to the right, a single archer sprinted to the top of a mound and waved his bow case. Thicker than an arm and longer than a leg, the case made the signal clear over the distance.

"Thank you, Goddess Apate," Cornelius said before turning to Pluto. "Now, Junior Tribune Manius."

Pluto Manius saluted, kicked his mount, and charged towards the wagons and his NCOs.

Cornelius pulled a waterskin off a saddle horn. He had formalized a response and built formations to satisfy the needs of his units. If everything worked, Battle Commander

Pantera would have to acknowledge him as the right flank commander. If his plans failed, Cornelius Scipio would be on the next ship heading for Iberia. His dream of defeating Hannibal Barca dashed before he even reached a senior command position in the Legions.

After taking a stream of water, he watched the division of the Thracians and Cretans. They formed three groups, mirroring the heavy infantrymen. At the supply transports, Junior Tribune Manius directed the removal of tarps from two of the wagons.

"Cavalry, defensive formation," Cornelius shouted the alert.

His warning echoed through the light infantrymen and the archers. In an orderly manner, Files of archers and squads of Peltasts broke from the clusters. On the far right, they created a wall of shields interspersed with Files of Cretans in their shooting formation.

As a commander, Cornelius had done all he could. The rest was up to his troops.

***

Junior Tribune Manius was so excited that he slid off his mount and helped unload the small carts from a wagon. Then, while grabbing another, a rough hand landed on his shoulder.

"Sir, don't you have other duties?" Optio Quaesitus inquired.

Pluto stood and glanced around. Six small carts were being loaded with baskets of arrows and stacks of javelins. The porters helped organize the loads while the teamsters passed around the missiles.

"I should be watching the result of the cavalry charges," Manius admitted.

"It's easier to see from horseback," the NCO recommended.

Pluto mounted and took a moment to admire his work. With six carts, a resupply of arrows and javelins could be rushed to the defenders on the side wall. In case of injuries, no archer would suffer alone. The carts would act as vehicles to rush the wounded to one of the four wagons.

Junior Tribune Manius lifted his eyes and watched four squadrons of cavalry gallop at the shield walls of the right flank.

They rode hard, yelling, and flashing their spathas for effect. Before they reach the flanking elements, the Thracians stacked shields creating a barrier. Where there was no barrier, Files of Cretans began a rotation.

Legion horsemen bent upon breaking the flankers' formation charged at the Thracians. The lead riders had open ground, then lines of shafts with feather ends sprung up in front of their horses. To protect the mounts from the arrows, the squadrons angled away from the Thracian shields.

One bold cavalry officer guided his squadron into a gap caused by the Maniple spacing. He and his riders were a horse's length into the space when the soil in front of them burst into bloom. Like stems on flowers in a garden, except these leaves were sharp javelins and well-aimed arrows.

When they realized they couldn't penetrate or panic the flanking Thracians or Cretans, the Legion cavalrymen rode away. While they fled in embarrassment, Pluto reined his horse around with pride and kicked the mount into motion.

"How goes the plan?" Colonel Pantera inquired.

They could see shields raised, hear some of the shouting, but their sense of understanding ended in the dust raised by the horses.

"Battle commander, I can't imagine but we'll be meeting the Centurion of Horse any moment now," Senior Tribune Opiter ventured. "With that much movement, Scipio's flank screen should collapse shortly."

A commotion with his veteran bodyguards drew Pantera from the battle on the right flank.

"What seems to be the problem?" he demanded.

"Colonel, this Junior Tribune is not one of your messengers," the Optio of First Century responded. "What do want me to do, with him?"

"I know you. Pluto Manius," Pantera said. "Let him through."

"You're not cavalry," Senior Tribune Opiter remarked. "Who are you?"

"Sir, compliments of Tribune Scipio," Junior Tribune Manius exclaimed. "We engaged with a force of forty mounted Legionaries on the flank. And I am pleased to report that the cavalry has been driven off. Battle Commander, the screen for your right flank is intact. On a personal note, sir, Tribune Scipio says, wherever your shields are open, he'll be there."

"Very good, Junior Tribune," Colonel Pantera acknowledged. "Please relay my congratulations to the Tribune and his staff."

"Yes, sir," Pluto said.

As the junior staff officer rode away, Pantera turned to Opiter.

"It seems our young Scipio is more capable than we gave him credit for," the Colonel remarked. "Get him a staff so we can keep our eyes on him."

Act 4

Chapter 10 – Bindings and Findings

After seven days of drilling and field training, General Marcus Minucius marched his two inexperienced Legions northward. Before reaching Rome, they angled northeast towards the mouth of the Anio Valley. The Master of Horse and the Dictator expected Hannibal Barca to burst forth from the valley on his way to sack Rome. In preparation for battle, they rushed Legions and auxiliary forces to the western edge of the Apennine Mountains. And they evacuated citizens from unwalled towns in the region and sent them to cities with defensive walls. At the center of the anticipated battlefield, the unwalled town of Tivoli gave rise to rumors in the ranks.

Within a day of starting out, the Velites in the vanguard of the Minucius Legions linked up with Centuries from Fabius Legion East. Farther back in the columns, Hali Adras rushed up beside his File Leader.

"I heard from guys in the second Maniple that Tivoli is lovely," Hali told Jace. "The Dictator removed all the residents. And the Legionaries are using the villas for their bivouac."

"Sounds delightful," Jace admitted. Then he asked. "Do you think they'll allow a bunch of Cretan bowmen to share a house?"

"Probably not," the second File Leader admitted after thinking for a few steps. Then he offered. "At least it'll be a nice place to camp."

As happened with gossip in most massive troop movements, the men of Minucius Legions North and South heard about the beautiful and deserted town on the edge of the valley. But, like soldiers since the dawn of time, they never reached the fabled town of Tivoli. Diverted to the south, they drew the assignment of watching the foothills. Legion command feared Hannibal would attempt to sneak forty-five thousand infantrymen and horsemen out of the wide valley and hike them through rocky gorges and over tree covered ridges.

"Jace, take the rear of our formation," Lieutenant Gergely directed. "We're heading south."

"Didn't we just come from the south?" Eachann questioned.

"A different south," Jace told him before replying to the Cretan officer. "Yes, sir. We are the tail file."

Hali, Eachann, and Jace stepped out of the line of marchers and wave the other fourteen archers out of the flow.

"We're covering the rear," Jace informed them. "Anybody know which Century is back there?"

The friction between auxiliary units and Legion Centuries regularly required the attention of their officers. While an ongoing issue, the encounters for the most part were mild harassments and some punches. Yet, a few Legionaries had developed reputations for picking fights and slinging insults at Cretans and Thracians. Confrontations with Samnite light infantrymen were rare as the tribes had Legionaries in the ranks.

"I haven't heard of any trouble back there," an archer ventured. "Could be a friendly group."

"Let's hope so," Hali said. "I don't want to be watching my back for the rest of the day."

Lieutenant Ladon Stavros and the supply wagons rolled by. Jace braced and saluted the supply officer. In response, Stavros spit in the File Leader's general direction. He missed on purpose.

Archers carried side arms and could fight, thusly few people wanted to mix it up with the bowmen. Legion heavy infantrymen were different, they enjoyed a good skirmish. But the reason Stavros didn't spit on Jace was out of necessity. As a Cretan officer, he needed Jace to follow his orders if he took command. Plus, he was leery of losing an outright fight with the File Leader.

"He hates it when you exaggerate the salute and stiffen your posture," Hali mentioned.

"I know," Jace commented. "But Lieutenant Stavros considers me a subversive, anyway. So, there's no real harm done."

The trees kept the sun off the marching men, making it a pleasant trek. When Lieutenant Inigo's Files came by, Jace acknowledged the officer but held back on the grand gesture he used for Stavros.

"That's more like it," Hali remarked. "Inigo doesn't like you. But you two are civil to each other."

"The Lieutenant is afraid Jace will beat on Lynceus again," Eachann commented. "That's why he's nice."

"There's the last File," Hali announced. "And look, no Legionaries."

For a moment Jace couldn't make out the last archer. Their wool and leather clothing and the Samnites' were close in color and style. But the sight of a bow case, sticking over the shoulders of the archers at the end, identified the tail of the Cretan formation.

Jace fell in step with a middle-aged Samnite warrior. His File, after some disruption, settled down to the hike at the rear of the Cretans.

"Which tribe do we have the pleasure of marching with?" Jace asked.

"I'm Lieutenant Papia, War Chief of the Hirpini," the man answered. "And you?"

For a heartbeat, Jace almost replied File Leader Kasia.

But the word Hirpini tumbled around in his mind, and he replied, "Lucius Jace Kasia Otacilia."

The Hirpini officer stumbled and Jace reached out to steady him.

"Did you say Otacilia?"

"Yes, sir, that's my mother's name."

"A fine family name," Papia declared. "What region is your family from?"

"I don't really know. My mother and father died in a shipwreck off the coast of Crete," Jace told him. "He was a Latian, and she was a Hirpini Princess."

"So, you say," Papia uttered. "Do you know the tribe's motto?"

Jace shuffled stepped to untangle his feet while he thought. Of course, any imposture could claim to be a Hirpini. Why should the War Chief believe him? Then he fished the medallion out from under his doublet.

"I don't know anything about the tribe except this," he admitted, handing the bronze disc to Papia. "Hirpini means, those who belong to the wolf. And the medal says, the Romiliia household with bravery and the fierceness of wolves. My father was Lucius Romiliia."

"Once you're camped, come see me under the arch."

"What arch?" Jace asked. "Is that a secret code word of the Hirpini tribe?"

Papia laughed, pointed ahead with his arm elevated to indicate the sky above the trees.

Jace caught a red splash through the high branches. Then in several more steps, an enormous arch came into view. He stopped and Papia put out a hand to move him along.

"I didn't think there were that many clay bricks in the entire world," he stammered.

"It's the *Ponte della Mola* aqueduct," Papia explained. "What you see is only a small section. One end is in a lake in the Apennine Mountains. And, at the other end, a cistern in Rome. The aqueduct transports fresh water to the city on top of the arches. And every mile has thousands of bricks."

"How do you know so much about it?" Jace inquired while craning his neck to take in the structure.

"Fifty-five years ago, the Samnites helped build the aqueduct. They didn't want to. But when you lose battles, you do what you're told."

"You specifically said Samnites built it. Weren't the Hirpini involved?" Jace questioned.

They passed under the arch.

"I said tribes that lost in battle built the aqueduct," Papia clarified. "The Hirpini didn't lose. Until tonight, Jace Otacilia."

Word was passed for the Samnite auxiliary to set up for the night. They fell out of the march and began clearing brush while the Cretan columns marched forward. A mile to the south of the towering brick arches, the bowmen set up their camp.

***

Late in the day, Jace backtracked to the aqueduct. He located the Hirpinian sitting at a campfire under an arch. In front of the War Chief, a small copper pot hung over a fire. A thick substance steamed in the heat, and a strong aroma filled the air.

"*Castrid and deíkum maimas carneis tanginud ammíd fust tefúrúm or fust fratru'm,*" Papia said while splashing some of the liquid into a pair of clay cups.

He held one out for Jace and indicated a log.

"Thank you," Jace acknowledged. After pulling two arrows from his quiver, he took the cup of herbal tea, and sat. "What did you say when I walked up?"

"Just a statement, nothing for you to worry about," Papia assured him. He took a sip of the aromatic tea and encouraged. "Tell me about your mother."

"She and my father lived in Rome. But after the first war with Carthage, they moved to an area above the Republic and bought a farm," Jace responded. "They moved back to the city with me when political troubles started."

"Something to do with land holdings?" Papia suggested.

"I don't think so. My father was accused of rebellion. He was put on trial, found guilty, and exiled. On their voyage, the ship sank on the north side of the Island of Crete. That's where I grew up."

"And tried to become an archer?"

"I'm a Cretan archer," Jace shot back. He held up the finely crafted war bow with one hand and rested the other hand on the pair of arrows. "And, I am a File Leader of sixteen bowmen."

"You have a temper?" Papia noted.

"Only when I'm wronged or backed into a corner," Jace admitted. "Most days, I'm relaxed."

"And you claim the persecution of your family had to do with a rebellion?" Papia questioned. "And not land?"

Jace rested the bow across his knees and removed his hand from the arrows. His fingers never strayed far from the shafts.

"Lady Gabriella did suggest that powerful men coveted my father's estate," Jace offered. After a sip of the herbal tea, he scrunched up his face, thought for a moment, and questioned. "Wait, what made you mention land?"

"Who is Lady Gabriella?"

"My Tribune took me to Rome after Lake Trasimene as a reward for saving his life," Jace replied. "He introduced me to a Senator Sisera and his wife, Lady Gabriella. Turned out, they knew my parents and gave me a lot of my history."

"They welcomed you into the noble class of the Republic," Papia presumed. "Congratulation, Patrician Romiliia."

"I am a Cretan archer, trained and tested in the way of the bow," Jace boasted. "The idea that Latian nobles would welcome me into their villas, let alone into their ranks, is humorous."

Papia sipped the mountain tea and gazed into the fire. He and Jace sat until just before dark.

"Thank you for the tea, but I should be getting back to my File."

"Your pack," Papia whispered. He swung his head, looked Jace in the eyes, and proclaimed. "We are the wolf-men. Although you have Latian skin, I can see my people in your eyes and sense my ancestors in your nature. With confidence, I call you *fratru'm*."

"You used that word before. What does it mean?"

"In the old tongue, it means a brother," Papia told him. "Come tomorrow and we'll talk more."

Jace handed Papia the cup, then as he had been taught, he quickly moved away from the fire. But even in his haste, the young man moved as silently as a stalking wolf.

"He is genuine," Papia called to the bushes.

Two Hirpinian spearmen stepped out of the long shadows.

"I'm relieved," one of the warriors divulged. "Don't get me wrong, if he was another Latin opportunist, my spear would have been the first in his chest. But I'm glad to find a brother."

"I think we all are," Papia agreed.

Unseen by the wolf-men, Jace Kasia pushed back, then crawled from under the thorn bush. Cretan Archers were trained to be aware of their surroundings. Jace had sensed the two warriors before sitting down with Papia. But the pair hadn't threatened him, so he hadn't killed them.

Once out of ear shot, he jumped to his feet and jogged for the Cretan camp. As he ran, questions of land, spears, and brotherhood turned over in his mind.

***

No answers would be revealed to Jace as the morning brought Captain Zoltar and Lieutenant Gergely to their campfires.

"It seems Legion command has misplaced the Carthaginian army," Zoltar informed Jace and the archers. "The Legions are marching south and abandoning the Anio Valley. If they left it up to us, we'd have found them yesterday."

The archers nodded their agreement.

"While the Minucius Legions trek along the edge of the Apennines," Lieutenant Gergely instructed, "we're sending you ahead to the Liri River. From there, you'll cross the mountains heading east."

"What for, sir?" Eachann questioned.

"To locate the Carthaginian army," Zoltar replied. "Find them, track them, and send runners back to me. Lieutenant Gergely and I are sick of marching to nowhere."

"Any questions?" Gergely asked.

"When do we leave, sir?" Hali inquired.

"As soon as you collect extra arrows and provisions from supply."

"That'll be pleasant," Hali uttered.

"Is there a problem?" Zoltar remarked. "If you don't want the job, I can assign another File."

"No, Captain. You can count on us," Jace assured him.

"Gergely said if there was a difficult job," Zoltar mentioned before walking away, "your File was my best choice. Don't let your Lieutenant or me down."

"The Carthaginians are as good as found, sir," Jace remarked. Then to his archers, he instructed. "Make your long packs secure. We'll be moving fast. Anyone have a problem, you're on your own."

The threat jolted each bowman. But it helped reinforce the importance of the assignment.

"Now, let's go visit Lieutenant Stavros," Hali said with apprehension in his voice.

***

Before the sun touched the midpoint of the morning, the File jogged southward.

"You're setting a good pace," Eachann observed.

"We're searching for a slow-moving army being chased by a slow-moving army," Jace replied over his shoulder. With his arms and legs churning, he moved rapidly over the rough ground. "The only way to accomplish the mission is to move faster than both."

"I'd say we're doing that," Hali commented. "How far to the river?"

"The Legion maps showed forty-five road miles," Jace told him.

"Oh good," Eachann commented, "we'll get there before dark."

Chapter 11 – No Business

The Cretan Archers moved faster than any unit of the Legions. Long before dark, Jace stepped between trees and halted on the bank of a ribbon of water.

"That's a long way across," Hali observed.

The Liri River spanned seventy-five feet to the far bank and its water flowed clear.

"It's not deep. I can see rocks on the riverbed," Eachann pointed out.

"Two words for you, archer, swift and cold," Hali mentioned. "It's a good thing we're following it into the mountains and not crossing over."

"We'll camp here tonight and head east in the morning," Jace instructed. "Be sure we have sentries posted all night."

"But there's no one around," Eachann pointed out.

"We're chasing a lost army," Jace said. "Do you want them to find us before we find them?"

"I can't sleep with that on my mind," the bowman volunteered. "I'll take first watch."

***

Traveling through the mountains in summer brought exhaustion, but not danger. The selection of trails was limited, forcing Jace and his archers to move eastward using detours north and south before connecting to a new eastern route.

Twenty-six miles into the Apennines, the path descended towards a narrow river valley. From a Samnite herder they learned the river was named Sangro and a nearby village, Barrea. Jace guided the File to a spot far from the huts of the mountain people.

"What was that you asked the shepherd?" Hali inquired. "He seemed confused."

"I asked if he was a brother," Jace explained.

"That's not what it sounded like," his second in command argued.

"It's what I meant," Jace insisted. He didn't explain his use of *fratru'm* but added. "Wrong tribe anyway."

"Wrong what?" the Cretan questioned.

"Make sure the bowmen are taking care of their feet," Jace ordered. "I'll be around shortly to make sure they're eating."

"Yes, File Leader Kasia."

***

111

In the dark, Jace had the archers up and packing. By first light, they hiked down the Sangro following the river as it angled off to the southeast. After a series of small steep falls, the river flowed into another valley. On the gentle grade, the File hit a crisp pace and the day passed without incident.

Thirty miles to the east, they reached Lago di Bomba on the Sangro and unpacked for the night. As he did the previous evening, File Leader Kasia had them camp away from the local residents.

"Easy duty," Eachann declared. He sat on a rock, bathing his feet in the lake. "I could get accustomed to this."

"Where's the profit?" another archer inquired. "Will you become a herder of mountain goats?"

"You can't herd mountain goats," Eachann challenged. "They climb to places a man can't reach. Besides, I'm an archer."

"Good to hear," the bowman granted. "Because for a moment, I thought you'd gone shepherd on us."

Jace walked into the four-man camp and squatted near the fire.

"We made progress today but I'm worried."

"About too much distance or is something else bothering you?" Hali asked.

"Seventeen of us are stumbling around in the mountains looking for an army of thousands," Jace clarified. "Tomorrow, we're sending a pair of scouts out front and to the flanks. I don't want to get surprised."

"Or dead," Eachann offered from the riverbank.

"Or dead," Jace agreed.

***

The seventeen ate, and other than the guards, they curled up in blankets and went to sleep. As the night deepened, the flames died, and the hot embers became buried under layers of ash. Darkness as black as the surrounding night soon cloaked the archers' camps.

"Jace. Jace," Hali nudged him. "The lake has company."

In a smooth motion, Jace rolled to his knees with one hand on his bow case and his hatchet in the other.

"Where?" he whispered.

"At the village. I saw movement but discounted it as branches in the breeze. But when fires in the village flared up, I recognized armed men."

"Get our archers out of the valley," Jace instructed as he put away the hatchet and pulled the war bow from its case. "Take them to the top of the ridge and move east until you find enough growth to hide for the day."

"Where are you going?"

"I want to get a look at them," Jace answered. "If they're Samnite warriors, we'll circle them and keep going."

"And if their Carthaginian mercenaries?"

"Then we've located the army," Jace answered. "Which presents unique problems of its own."

Hali Adras took Jace's long pack then herded the archers out of the camp and up the steep slope. For most units, the climb in the middle of the night would have elicited curses and complaints. The most grumbling the Cretan archers could work up included a gnashing of their teeth for being

113

awakened and visualizing more sleep. For the bowmen, the scramble up hurt no more than a day at the Cretan agōgē.

Once the archers were safely away, Jace strolled towards the village. During his training, Zarek Mikolas coached that sneaking took huge pieces of a day.

"If you want to see something or get close enough to hunt meat, walk to your spot then take cover. And if spotted, put an arrow in the game so the beast doesn't run. If spotted by a sentry, put an arrow in the man, then you run. But don't waste your life sneaking around."

The Master Archer said all that while teaching the skills of the silent stalk. Under cover of darkness with a lake shore for a guide, Jace understood the contradiction.

Moving steadily to the rhythm of tree branches in the night breeze, he approached the village unnoticed. In daylight, it was a social distance. At night, the distance provided a screen of invisibility. Jace dropped to his hands and knees and crawled closer to the huts. Finally, he slinked forward and moved to a bush just outside the village square.

Screams and the voices of rough men. let him know the nocturnal visitors weren't a Samnite hunting party.

"Latians, I want Latians," the leader bellowed. From his meager dress, Jace assumed he was an NCO, not an officer. "General Barca is offering a reward for every Latian head. Point to where they're hiding. And I'll share the coins."

Ten Samnite villagers huddled next to a fire in front of the Sergeant and six soldiers.

"We don't need or want your coins," an old man stated.

"I knew it. You are hiding Latians," the Sergeant roared. With a swift kick, he launched the old body out of the firelight. Then realizing he's booted the elder out of view, he instructed. "Bring him back."

The old man hit the ground in an explosion of dirt. Air forced from his lungs created an involuntary grunt. He tumbled, coming to rest beside Jace's bush. At that moment, Archer Kasia needed to go and join his File. He did not have any business untying the top to his quiver, reaching in with his fingers, and blindly selecting five arrows.

A moment later, two of the six soldiers, following the NCOs instructions, moved to retrieve the abused old man.

***

"This is a bad idea," Jace whispered to himself.

The bow came up and while kneeling, Jace drew the bowstring to the side of his jaw.

Zip-Thwack!

The soldier leaning over to grab the old Samnite rolled away. His fingers that intended to clamp onto a thin arm, instead gripped the shaft of an arrow. He rolled into the darkness.

Zip-Thwack!

The second of the pair jerked upright, balanced on his heels, then dramatically toppled over backwards. His face and the stub of an arrow landed in the circle of light.

"What in the…"

Zip-Thwack!

Being first usually had benefits. But being first to notice a fallen comrade, drew the attention of Archer Jace Kasia. The arrowhead of the well-aimed shaft clipped the man's femoral artery. Dropping to the ground, he gripped the inside of his thigh, trying to stem the flow of blood. In the light of the bonfire, the black liquid spread rapidly. And as intended, his yelling captured the attention of the other soldiers.

Except for one, who took a step towards the villagers.

Zip-Thwack!

Whether he planned to run and escape, or to take a Samnite and use the villager as a shield, didn't matter. The shaft through his side entered his liver, and the waves of intense pain drove him to his knees. For a heartbeat, he grabbed the shaft as if a child latching onto an adult's hand for comfort. Then, another wave of agony took his mind and he collapsed into a weeping pile of flesh.

His cries mixed with the whimpers of the last soldier.

"Shields, get your shields and form…"

Zip-Thwack!

Part of Jace's training included target analysis and selection.

"First stop them, then fix them, and finally, locate the commander and nullify him."

A feathered shaft appeared to be emerging from the center of the Sergeant's face. But it was a momentary illusion. For the arrowhead had cut the columella, and after piercing the skin between the nostrils, the iron tip tunneled into the nasal passages. Farther in, the thin bones of the septum shattered before the shaft spiked the NCO's brain.

116

The fifth arrow ended the archer's normal rotation. Having no selected arrows in hand but two enemies remaining, Jace reached under his war hatchet and slammed the bottom of the handle. As if sliding on greased rails, the weapon glided up the holding ring and popped into the air.

In midflight, Jace caught the handle near the end. Slipping his left foot back, he positioned his forward foot, right arm, and shoulder in the direction of one soldier.

The hatchet flipped twice before embedding in the man's chest. He screamed, wrapped both hands around the handle, and started to pull it out. But the soft cartilage of the sternum gripped the steel head. His ribs responded to the pull by flexing. And a rib cage yanked out of shape was an unpleasant experience.

After the throw, Jace reached to the quiver, pulled an arrow, and swung it up and over. The shaft touched his left thumb, the bowstring came back, and the arrow broke the collarbone of the last soldier.

Three of the seven moaned, showing they were alive. The high survival rate made the operation a disappointment.

"Master Mikolas. I know, sloppy work," Jace admitted to the memory of his teacher.

***

Skinning knife in hand, Jace prepared to perform the grizzly act of finishing off the men. Before he could act, one of the village women jumped to her feet. She ran to the first injured man, pulled a knife from under her skirt, and drew the blade across his throat. Then in quick, sure strokes, she cut the throats of five more.

"A little over kill," Jace remarked while putting away his knife. "But I guess, it's better safe than sorry."

Just in case the village vixen decided to cut him after she finished with the soldiers, Jace tugged an arrow from his quiver. When she came out of the light, heading for the soldier in the dark, Jace notched the arrow and backed away from the bush and the old man.

"Don't shoot my granddaughter," the elder ordered.

Then he coughed, pushed to a sitting position, and groaned.

At the sound, the woman wiped her blade clean on the last soldier's woolen trousers, put the knife away, and hopped to her grandfather's side.

"Are you injured?" she pleaded.

"From recent experience, I suggest you answer no," Jace offered. "Or she's liable to cut your throat."

"Stop making jokes," the woman instructed. "Help me get him to the fire so I can check."

"Come *fratru'm*," the old man declared, calling Jace brother, "lend me an arm."

"You speak Oscan," Jace gushed.

"When I was a boy, many old men spoke the ancient tongue," he assured Jace. "Now, I'm the old one. But how do you know the language of the Samnite forebearers?"

"I've recently met my mother's people," Jace answered. With one arm, he lifted the slight man from the ground and carried him to the bonfire. "She was a Hirpini Princess, and after a conversation with a War Chief, he called me *fratru'm*."

118

"High praise from a wolf-man. They are…"

In the light, Jace's Latin features became apparent. The old man, his granddaughter, and the other villagers stared at him with open mouths.

"My father was Latian," Jace rushed out. "I was orphaned on Crete where I became a Cretan Archer."

Carefully, he rested the elder on the ground and stepped back.

"When the soldiers came, I prayed for a Carricini hunting party to come to our rescue. But my prayers went on deaf ears," the woman disclosed while probing her grandfather for broken bones and lacerations. "Or so I thought. No one but Diana, the Goddess of the Hunt, knew we needed a bowman."

Jace felt inside the quiver until he located a specific arrow.

"In Greek culture, we know Diana as Artemis, the Goddess of the Hunt," he stated. "For calling me, brother, I want to gift you an arrow blessed by the Goddess."

"And for saving an old man," the woman offered while sliding an armlet from her bicep, "take this token of a chief's respect, and his granddaughter's gratitude."

Chapter 12 – An Act of Resignation

Tribune Cornelius Scipio dismounted when the Legions and auxiliary troops stopped for the day. He bent and began running his hands down the left foreleg of his horse. Gently squeezing, he checked for tender or hot spots. Then he examined the other leg for comparison.

Although the Via Appia provided a uniformed surface, one hundred and forty miles of hard travel took a toll on the men and the animals. While crouching, Cornelius peered to the south at the town of Benevento.

"Trouble, sir?" Optio Caeso inquired. When he noted the staff officer peering at the town, he offered. "It was a major Samnite city before Latin settlers and the Legions took it over."

"Good to know," Cornelius said. He stood and began to walk away. "But that wasn't what I was thinking about. Have someone rub down my mount."

"And we'll set up your tent. But in case you're needed, sir," the NCO questioned. "Where are you going?"

"To discuss horses with the Master of Horse," Cornelius replied.

***

Unlike the marching Legionaries, supply transports, and allied troops, Director Fabius and Master of Horse Minucius traveled ahead of the Legions to Benevento. Using their positions, they commandeered villas for a brief stay.

At the villa chosen by the Master of Horse for himself and his command staff, Cornelius informed the sentry, "Tribune Scipio to see the Deputy Dictator."

From the raised porch, he saw pastures and orchards. Not far away, hills rose from the river valley and beyond high peaks reached into the sky. In another direction, the cultivated property ended, and a thick forest took over the landscape. His sightseeing ended when an NCO came from the house.

"You're the commander of the right screen, aren't you, sir?" inquired the Optio of the Legion's First Century.

"I am," Cornelius admitted.

"Then you're here for Senior Tribune Opiter," the NCO suggested.

"I can start with him," Cornelius said.

He accompanied the Sergeant into a great chamber of a space.

"If you'll wait here, sir," the Optio instructed. "I'll announce you to the Tribune."

The Sergeant reached a side door and shoved it wide open. Leaving it ajar, he marched into the room. Cornelius couldn't see into the space, but from the sounds of dishes rattling, glasses clinking, and voices conversing, he understood a dinner party was in progress.

When the NCO reappeared, he looked uncomfortable.

"Sir, if it's a small problem you have the authority to handle it," the veteran NCO remarked. Obviously relaying a message, the man shifted uneasily. "If it's a major issue, come back in the morning. I'm sorry Tribune, that's the response."

A burst of laughter floated from the party. Having been dismissed by proxy irrigated Cornelius. He stepped around the Optio and marched to the doorway.

"He should run off to Iberia with his daddy," a staff officer sneered.

Laughter followed the comment.

"You should keep your mouth shut," Cornelius advised as he stepped into the room. "Or do you require a lesson in civility?"

"Tribune Scipio, this is a private dinner," Timeus Opiter scolded.

Cornelius noted the three staff officers to the right side, Senior Tribune Opiter, and a host of junior staff officers. Truthfully, the only staff officer missing was the commander of the right screen, Cornelius Scipio.

"I can see that," he stated.

Turning, Cornelius walked slowly from the banquet room, maintained control through the great chamber, and exited the villa in a dignified manner. Once he left the grounds of the estate, he strutted to burn off emotion.

Still angry when he reached his command area, he noticed but didn't react to four badly beaten Cretan archers. They stood sipping water and dabbing at their bruises.

"Whatever the fight was about, have Captain Zoltar dish out the punishment," Cornelius tossed out while ducking into his tent.

He was two steps in when he stopped, about-faced, and stuck his head back outside.

"Aren't you one of Jace Kasia's archers?"

"Yes, sir," Hali Adras replied.

A wound on the Cretan's cheek leaked blood and the flesh around it was just starting to turn black and blue. But it went untouched while the archer dabbed at a split lip.

122

"Your File was sent to locate the Punic army," Cornelius pointed out. "Why are you here?"

"We found them, sir," Hali replied. It came out slurred from the swelling of his lip.

"And you stopped to fight before reporting in?" Cornelius questioned. "Or did you fight your way out of an ambush?"

"In a way, yes, sir we did. But not on the other side of the Apennines. There we built a wall of brush on top of a ridge and watched their army march by," Hali told him. "File Leader Kasia sent us with the news once we had a count."

"And you saw?" Cornelius urged when the archer stopped to press the cloth on the split lip.

"At fifty thousand soldiers and horsemen, Jace sent us to report to you, Tribune."

"Let's go see Senior Tribune Opiter," Cornelius offered. "He'll have to speak to me now."

"Sir, I'd rather not deal with Legion staff officers," Hali stated while taking a step back.

"That was not a request," Cornelius blurted out. Then he noticed the man's red rimmed eyes, and the gnashing of his jaw. Both signs of a man holding back his temper. "What happened?"

"The exact words were, the Senior Tribune said the Legion doesn't need archers or a daddy's boy in command of the flank," Hali described. "There were ten of them and we were exhausted from running for three days. We'll be fresh and ready for them the next time."

"Someone, locate Junior Tribune Manius and send him to me," Cornelius shouted. "Come inside Cali and show me on a map where you spotted the enemy."

***

At the villa where Master of Horse Minucius was encamped, the NCO came out to greet Cornelius.

"Sir, is there something else?"

"I have the location of the Punic army," he replied while pointing at a rolled map. "But I'll only show it to First Tribune Silvius."

"Yes, sir, I understand," the NCO acknowledged. "I'll see if he's available."

"And Sergeant, if the First Tribune isn't available for me, I'm taking the information to the staff of Dictator Fabius."

The veteran Optio didn't say anything. But he flashed a smile before guiding Cornelius into the great chamber. After the clicks of his hobnailed boots faded, the muffled noises of celebration escaped from the banquet room.

Moments later, the NCO called from the far end of the hallway, "Tribune Scipio, please come this way."

***

The First Tribune of Minucius Legion North was not drinking with his staff. Rather, the top staff officer for the Legion sweated over stacks of scrolls and sheets of papyrus.

"Scipio, things get confused when passed from person to person," Caius Silvius said while tossing a scroll onto a pile. "Suppose you tell me why you're in my office and not in Tribune Opiter's?"

"Two reasons, sir. My Cretan Archers have located the Punic army," Cornelius told him. Whatever game of military courtesy or protocol might have been on his mind, Silvius forgot about it. With the senior officer's urging, Scipio continued. "I have Hannibal's route on the map. And a rough count, or as many as my Cretan Archers cared to count before realizing it was the army."

"Come with me," Silvius instructed.

He stepped from behind his desk and the piles of documents. They marched through a side door and into a hallway. On the other side, Caius Silvius knocked once before pushing the door open.

"General, we have Hannibal," Silvius announced.

"Bellona, bless us," Marcus Minucius prayed to the Goddess of War. "How? Where?"

"Tribune Scipio's archers found him," Silvius said while hooking Cornelius' waist and thrusting him deeper into the room.

"Out with it, Scipio," Minucius ordered.

"I sent one of my Cretan Files across the mountains as a precaution to Barca angling west and ambushing us. And to look for his army," Cornelius informed the General. He unrolled the leather map and placed it on the Deputy Dictator's desk. "They're making their way south along the east coast. And nowhere near Rome."

"But he could swing around, dodge us, and attack the Capital," Silvius countered.

"No, sir. As I was checking my mount, I noticed the deterioration of our men and livestock from the forced march. And we've only been traveling for a few days on the Via Appia," Cornelius described. "General Barca has taken his people over the Alps and fought three battles without a rest. His army has to be exhausted and in need of convalescence. In my opinion, he couldn't attack Rome if he wanted to."

"Excellent work, Tribune," Marcus Minucius declared. "You are a young man with promise."

"Yes, sir. Now if you'll excuse me."

"Yes. Yes, go, we have much to discuss," Minucius said absentmindedly. His focus was on the map.

Just as Cornelius reached the doorway, Caius Silvius called to him, "When I asked why you were seeing me instead of Senior Tribune Opiter, you said two reasons. What did you mean?"

"The information needed to go to someone serious," Cornelius responded. "And I thought it was a good second to last act as a Tribune of Minucius Legion North."

"Second to last act?" Minucius questioned. "What is the last?"

"I'm taking the underappreciated Cretan Archers to Iberia," Cornelius informed the General and the senior staff officer.

"You're what?" Silvius questioned.

"Let's not be rash," Minucius suggested. "I'm sure there's a way of settling this without you taking five hundred warriors from my Legion."

"Oh, I forgot one thing," Cornelius admitted. "General, I resign my commission. As a private citizen of the Republic, I wish you all the blessings of Averruncus."

After invoking the God who Averts Calamity, Cornelius Scipio left the office.

***

He marched with purpose to the great chamber, saluted the NCO, and stopped.

"Sir, is there anything you need?" The veteran Optio inquired.

"You know, Sergeant, there is."

Cornelius faced left, marched to the banquet room, and flung open the door.

"See here, Scipio," Senior Tribune Opiter exclaimed, "if we wanted you here, you would have been invited."

The blunt, cruel statement provoked laughter from the other staff officers.

"I wasn't planning on staying," Cornelius stated as he crossed the room.

Timeus Opiter stood, puffed up his chest, and sneered.

"Then what are you…"

Cornelius brought his fist from waist level, just as his boxing instructors trained. The upper cut tagged Opiter square on his chin. In boxing matches, the opponents were guarded. Caught unaware, Senior Tribune Timeus Opiter rose to the tips of his toes before falling to the tile floor. Stepping over the fallen staff officer, Cornelius punched him again.

"The archers you had beaten were returning from a dangerous mission," he growled before striking Opiter a third time.

"They found the Punic army and without food, rest, or sleep, they ran a hundred miles to deliver the news."

Cornelius didn't remember if the Cretans had traveled one hundred miles, but it sounded good. And the fist to the side of Timeus' head felt just as good.

"Instead of a hero's welcome, the four exhausted men were ambushed on your orders, by ten Legionaries."

Just to change things up and to help Opiter focus, Cornelius slapped him, hard.

"The next time you want to punish me," Cornelius roared, "come for me like a man. Not a whimpering excuse for a Legion officer."

Pulling him up by the neck of his tunic, Cornelius pummeled Opiter's nose a couple of times. Then he dropped the semiconscious Senior Tribune, stood, and faced the other staff officers.

"Anyone here want to step up and defend this wharf rat's honor?"

When no one moved or protested, Cornelius marched to the doorway. He paused long enough to pull the door closed behind him, before stepping into the great chamber.

"Comment, Sergeant?" Cornelius asked.

"No sir, other then the party seems to be getting out of hand," the veteran NCO responded.

Cornelius left the villa with a plan. He would buy out the Cretan's contract, then rehire the archers, and take them to

Iberia with him. An expensive proposition, but not beyond the means of a Scipio.

***

"Junior Tribune Manius, not that it'll do much good, but I'm leaving a letter recommending you as the Legion commander of the Thracians," Cornelius told him.

"Sir, I want to go with you," Pluto pleaded.

"Trust me, your family will be overjoyed you didn't," Cornelius assured him.

Horses arriving, saddle leather creaking, and loud voices created a disturbance outside the tent. Shortly after the noise started, Pedar Zoltar poked his head into the tent.

"You have visitors, sir," the archer Captain informed Cornelius. "We can put them down, but it's not advisable. Still, it's your decision."

Cornelius assumed it was a committee of staff officers come to demand that he surrender himself to stand trial. It wasn't going to happen. If necessary, he would use the archers to fight his way to freedom.

But just to get his mind around how much trouble he was in, Cornelius inquired, "And just whom, Captain, are we putting down?"

"Sir, General Minucius and Colonel Pantera."

"That much trouble," Cornelius commented. "Maybe, I should hear them out."

"Yes, sir," Zoltar allowed.

The flap closed, and all was silent for a moment, then, "For the shield wall."

Twenty voices followed the command with, "Rah."

Almost at the same time, another voice called out, "One. Select a shaft…"

The command to the archers was joined by fifty voices chanting, "And-a-two notch your arrow. And-a-three…"

Cornelius burst from the tent to find the Deputy Dictator of the Republic, and a Battle Commander penned in by a defensive ring of shields. Around the defensive formation, fifty archers targeted the Legionaries.

Spying the young staff officer, Marcus Minucius inquired, "Tribune Scipio. Can't we talk this over like civilized men?"

"Sir, it would please me very much," Cornelius admitted. "Captain Zoltar, stand down the archers."

Fifty arrowheads elevated as the archers relaxed the tension on their bows.

"Centurion, the crisis has been averted," Minucius assured the veteran officer of his bodyguard. "Make a hole. The Colonel and I are going into the tent."

"Sir, I am not comfortable with that," the Centurion protested. "This could be a trick to get you alone and assassinate you."

"Tribune Scipio, are you harboring any murderers in your quarters?" Marcus Minucius inquired.

Just then Junior Tribune Manius stuck his head out of the tent. A five Legionaries stepped forward doubling the number of shields in front of the Master of Horse.

"Sir, there is no one in here but me," Pluto commented.

"Then, I believe I'm safe," Minucius declared while pushing through the bodyguards. "Come gentlemen, let's get this thing settled."

Colonel Pantera and Cornelius followed the Master of Horse into the tent.

Act 5

Chapter 13 – Like Having Two Faces

Junior Tribune Manius poured cups of wine for the visitors while Cornelius paced back and forth.

"Tell me Tribune Scipio, after fighting for the position," Pantera inquired, "why do you want to leave?"

"Is it because you were excluded from the party by Senior Tribune Opiter?" Minucius offered.

The comment brought Cornelius to a standstill.

"Sir, being excluded by a less than average officer has nothing to do with my decision."

"If it's not about your feelings, what is it?" Pantera asked.

"I was present when General Barca, and yes, I will call the invader by his proper title. He's earned it," Cornelius insisted. "He routed our cavalry. Beat two Legions after completing a hazardous journey. And destroyed two more with an army wide ambush. Do you have any idea what that means?"

"The Senate elected a Dictator to enforce emergency measures. And, I humbly submit, they selected me, an experienced General as the Master of Horse," Minucius boasted. "But that's not what you meant. Why don't you tell us?"

"The Republic has lost experienced Legionaries, and the NCOs who teach and maintain discipline," Cornelius listed. "And we have even fewer skilled line officers. Without the Centurions to hold the Maniples, the inexperienced infantrymen burdened with unproven NCOs are more likely to fail. Now, add unserious staff officers to the Legion and you have a recipe for disaster. When a Senior Tribune thinks this is a lark and an easy place to earn a reputation before going into politics, it influences the men under him."

"You reached those conclusions from watching Senior Tribune Opiter," Colonel Pantera challenged. "All that from one weak officer?"

"No, sir. My reasoning formed when I watched a Third Maniple vanish under Punic spears and shields," Cornelius replied. "Nine hundred and sixty veteran infantrymen, their tough NCOs, twelve battle hardened Centurions, and two brave Tribunes, butchered by Carthaginian mercenaries. Watch that over and over again in your sleep, and you'll awaken with a purpose."

"I don't know the value of Cretan archers," Minucius admitted. "I have Legion bowmen. But I do know the value of a good officer. What do you want in order to stay?"

With a disgusted look on his face, Pantera suggested, "Senior Tribune Opiter is being sent back to Rome. Do you want his position?"

"I didn't beat him that badly," Cornelius protested.

"He's been relieved of duty for not doing his job," Minucius clarified. "He should have been the officer bringing me the enemy's route of travel. Plus, his game of revenge delayed the arrival of the news. For those reasons, I had the Colonel dismiss him. Do you want Opiter's job?"

"No, sir, I like the job I have."

"Then why leave?" Pantera questioned.

"The make up of the Legion is changing," Cornelius replied. "I want to go where I can experiment with the new elements."

"What new elements?" Pantera demanded.

"Hold on Colonel," Minucius said. "Tell me Tribune Scipio, what do you want in order to stay with my North Legion?"

"I need Junior Tribune Manius promoted so he has the authority to go directly to you, Colonel, or the First Tribune, with any news," Cornelius answered. "And I want twenty infantrymen. They will guard my headquarters while I'm away."

"Where will you be?" Pantera asked.

"I'll be with the forward elements looking for General Barca. If the Punics are moving, the reports I send back will be useful for a short period. I want to know the information will be passed onto you directly, sir."

"When your archers report to Tribune Manius, he'll relay the information to me," General Minucius assured him. "But what will Manius do between messages?"

"He'll experiment with tactics using Legion heavy infantrymen, foreign archers, and allied light infantrymen."

"Those are the new elements," Pantera proposed.

"Until the menace of Hannibal Barca is eliminated," Cornelius stated, "the Republic will depend more and more on allied troops and mercenaries. As commanders, we need to learn how to win with what we have."

"It's done," Minucius proclaimed. "All of it. Congratulations Tribune Manius."

"Thank you, sir," Pluto exclaimed.

"What's next, Tribune Scipio?" Pantera inquired.

"Before first light, I'm taking an advance force of archers and light infantrymen ahead," Cornelius answered him. "When we locate the Punic army, I'll send back their troop strength and location."

"And we'll march forward and defeat him," Minucius declared.

He ducked out of the tent. Colonel Pantera presented a blank face to Cornelius before he followed the Master of Horse.

***

Once outside, the Colonel rushed to catch up with Minucius. They met where a stablemen waited, holding the reins of their horses.

"I can't believe you went along with that rubbish," Pantera complained.

Marcus Minucius took his reins, waved the stablemen away, and leaned against his horse's shoulder. In his haste to retreat, the stableman who kept his head down out of respect, tripped over a pile of blankets. Both the Battle Commander and the Master of Horse laughed at the clumsy man. After he scrambled out of hearing distance, Minucius addressed the Colonel's concerns.

"Be sure to give a letter of commendation to Opiter before he leaves," General Minucius directed. "We don't want to make an enemy of his family. As for the young upstart, keep sending him and his barbarians on dangerous assignments. Sooner or later, Scipio will die a glorious death. Then, we can mourn the Tribune's passing before welcoming his replacement."

"Yes, sir," Pantera acknowledged with a smile. "I hadn't thought of that. I suppose, sir, it's why you're the Master of Horse."

Marcus Minucius pulled himself into the saddle, then looked down on the Colonel.

"The Republic's Legionaries are the finest fighting man in the world," he declared. "I want our people to live it and believe it. Push the infantrymen and keep our men away from the barbarians. Fraternization with a potential enemy is dangerous for morale. Understand?"

"Yes, sir."

Minucius trotted away with most of the bodyguards jogging around him. The remainder of First Century waited for Colonel Pantera to mount. Moments after leaving the tent, the two senior commanders had cleared the area.

The pile of blankets shook before rising and falling over. An archer named Egidio rolled from under the stack of woolen material.

"It got hot under there," he mentioned. "But you were right, they talked freely after you fell over me."

The stableman stepped forward and licked his cut lip.

"Let's go report to Tribune Scipio," Hali proposed. "I think he'll be interested in the conversation."

***

Later that afternoon, Cornelius Scipio and Alick Ignatius strolled down a lane. On either side of them, tents belonging to the Peltastes sat in relatively straight lines.

"I never thought to see Thracians in an organized camp," Captain Ignatius admitted.

"I've sacrificed to the Two-Faced Janus for this," Cornelius told him. "One of the God's faces looks backward where we started, and one peers at our future."

"Your God didn't do this," Ignatius scoffed. The Captain waved at two sentries standing at different campfires. "We conformed to your Legion ways after you pointed out that guards with overlapping views provided better security."

"Almost like having two faces?" Cornelius pointed out. "Who is the commander you're sending with me in the morning?"

"Lieutenant Kolya Adad. You'll like him, Tribune," Ignatius offered, "he's crazy like you."

"Like me, how?"

"When we first met, you trampled my First Sergeant and rode your horse into my home," Ignatius replied. "Now we hear you kicked down a door to an officer's party. Then pounded the Senior Tribune into the tiles as revenge for him sending Legionaries after some archers."

"That wasn't exactly how it went," Cornelius protested.

"Maybe not to you," the Thracian Captain informed him. "But to my Peltastes, any commander who will fight a superior to defend his flock is a man to follow."

"Will I have to fight Lieutenant Adad?" Cornelius asked.

"Not unless you show cowardness when you face the enemy."

"That's never been my problem," Cornelius assured him. Alick Ignatius raised an inquiring eyebrow. In reply, Tribune Scipio confessed. "It's keeping my mouth shut and my temper in check."

"You might be part Thracian," the Captain suggested.

"Me? I'm all Latin. You must have me confused with the man of many pasts, Jace Kasia."

"Where is the archer? I haven't seen him since Tivoli. Is he alive?"

"Somewhere northeast of here," Cornelius told him. The two faced in that direction out of respect. "Last I heard, File Leader Kasia was very much alive."

***

The four archers crawled from the gully, scurried over a rise, and rolled downhill to reach a row of bushes. One spit out a mouthful of sandy soil.

"I didn't see the bare spot," he complained. "You three got mountain grass, and I ate dirt."

"You'll be eating Punic steel if you talk any louder," Jace warned.

Only five feet from where they lay, a team of oxen pulled a wagon up to the top of the rise. As the wagon passed along a short flat, the four Cretan bowmen drew their blades. Ahead of the wagon, the rest of the caravan followed the dirt road down the far side of the ridge. Behind the nearest wagon, the last transport trailed the others as its team crawled up the steep grade.

Horse's hoofs trampled the grass on the other side of the bushes.

"Pick up your pace," a mounted guard demanded. "Or we'll leave you for bandits."

"If you think you can do better," the teamster shouted up the slope, "come take my whip and do it yourself."

The guard squawked a wordless reply. It could have been a curse or a dismissal. In any case, he reined his horse around, rode by the closest wagon, and moved off the ridge.

"Get ready," Jace alerted his archers.

"This might be the sketchiest plan I've ever heard of," archer Narkis whispered.

"You had an opportunity to question it when we started following the wagon train," Jace reminded him.

"It's too late now," the fourth archer pointed out.

As the wagon rolled away, a silence fell over the ridge. Jace crawled to the far side of the bushes, lifted a branch, and watched the tailgate begin to drop away. In the other direction, the heads of the last team appeared.

"Let's take the wagon," Jace ordered.

He pushed through the branches and sprinted to the approaching wagon.

"Drop your lines and run down the hill," Jace shouted at the teamster. "Do it now or die."

Seeing a bandit waving a hatchet at him, the man threw the reins into the air. With his hands held over his head, he turned, and ran downhill.

Jace sprinted to the back of the wagon, located the wheel stop in the wagon bed, and placed it behind a back wheel. He stood holding the rope of the chock. While he waited, Jace gazed over the load, watching the top of the hill to see if the guard would return.

At the front of the transport, Narkis halted the oxen.

"Whoa my pretties," the archer said while pushing the team back.

As the beasts took a step to the rear, the wagon rolled, and the wheel came to rest against the block. With the tension between the hitch and the wagon relieved, the last two archers freed the team. Then they pulled the harness pieces back and tied them to the sides of the wagons.

"The front wheels are as stable as we can get them," one announced.

"Go," Jace instructed.

He waited for the three bowmen to jump the gully and scramble up the hill. Once they were near the forest, Jace pulled the chock from behind the wheel. For good measure, he pitched the wheel stop into the transport. As he ran for the gully, the wagon rolled backwards.

***

At first, the wheels dug into the dust, keeping the speed down. But the farther the transport rolled, the faster it traveled. Gaining momentum, the wagon began to bounce. Bucking and leaping in bounds, the violence broke the harness straps, freeing the front wheels. Now, wobbling as it flew downhill, the out-of-control transport passed the teamster.

Jace reached the tree line and ducked in beside his three bowmen.

"Sketchy," Narkis remarked.

They watched the transport as it reached the bottom of the hill, careened off the road, and tore across a meadow. Then it bounced over a mound, before the wagon crashed into a ravine.

Far below, eight men raced from the trees and began pulling cargo from the wreckage. At the top of the ridge, two mounted soldiers rode to a stop. After a few moments of watching the far-off thieves, they turned and followed the caravan down the other side.

"Still sketchy," Narkis admitted to Jace while lowering his bow. "But, not bad."

"We've got a long hike to reach camp," Jace announced. "We should get going."

***

A pair of wagons full of captured goods sat in the center of the mountain trail. Not far away, teams of horses grazed. For their entire lives, the draft animals had rested when the sun sank low in the sky.

"Harness them up," Jace instructed. "We're going to find the Legions."

"It's about time," Narkis offered. "The Carthaginian patrols are getting closer every day."

"But they haven't found us," another archer noted.

"Not yet," Narkis said while walking a pair of confused horses to the first wagon.

"And they won't," Jace assured them. "Although, I hate leaving the shelter of this valley."

Trees covered the slopes that rose steeply on either side. From the mouth of the narrow gorge, the sides appeared too close for the passage of a wagon. But that was an illusion. Cretan Archers, as they had been taught, put fresh cut brushes at the entrance and erased any sign of their passage in or out of the valley. Watchers reported the passing of patrols several times a day. Not once had the mounted soldiers stopped to examine the entrance.

When the archers' long packs were hoisted onto backs, drivers installed on the wagons, and pairs of scouts sent ahead, Jace called to the File.

"While making a profit is nice," he announced, "the wagons are not as important as even a single Cretan Archer. If we get attacked, scatter and head south."

"May Erebus cloak our journey," a bowman said invoking the God of Darkness and Shadow."

"Erebus," the other archer acknowledged.

The horses swung their heads looking for a man to unharness them. It was twilight and time to rest. But it wasn't.

Narkis made clicking sounds at the team with his mouth before snapping the reins and saying, "Go."

Archers assigned as scouts removed the camouflage from the entrance and the bowmen and wagons left the valley. At the rear, four Cretans replaced the bushes and erased the marks of the wagon wheel, the hoofprints, and footprints. As Jace Kasia insisted, no one should ever know where the archers came from or how many were traveling in the convoy.

Chapter 14 – Foolhardy Splash

Flames blazed above the horizon. Almost as if fires in the sky, they marked a line the Cretans did not want to cross.

"Carthaginians on the hills ahead," the scout mentioned to Jace.

"Looks like a substantial camp," Jace agreed. "What do you think? Close or far?"

For the last four nights, the File Leader had fast walked between the scouts ahead, the bowmen around the wagons, and the archers walking and dragging branches at the rear. Beyond common sense and talent, the other requirement to be a leader of archers was stamina. Since they left the hidden valley, Jace Kasia had earned his position by staying in contact with every archer during the nights of marching.

"We should bivouac far away," the scout answered. "If that's their main camp, in the morning, this road could get really crowded, really fast."

"Find us a turn off," Jace said. "I'll tell the rest."

He started with the scout on the other side of the road. After explaining the plan, he drifted back and conversed with each of the bowmen until he encountered the sweepers in the back.

"There's a Carthaginian camp on the hills ahead," Jace told them.

"Those lights?" one asked.

By the time Jace reached the rearguard, the caravan had moved far enough ahead, the ones in the back could see the elevated campfires.

"We should be turning off shortly," he told the four archers.

During training, the student archers lived and worked in Herds and later in Troops. As such, they bonded, allowing them to blend a highly individualized skill, like archery, into tightly choreographed maneuvers. One strength of their group attraction mirrored the power of their distant cousins, the Spartans. Like the men of Sparta, Cretan Archers would rather die in battle than break formation and put their File mates in jeopardy.

A drawback to the bonding forced their Captains, Tail-Leader Lieutenants, and File Leaders to provide an illusion of being connected. When Files operated in widespread formations, like Jace's unit, the archers were comforted by frequent contact with their leaders.

"Kasia," one of the archers called to Jace.

Following the whisking of branches erasing their passage, he arrived at the bowmen.

"Yes?" he inquired.

"When they appointed you File Leader," Archer Marsyas declared, "I wasn't sure about the selection. But after patrolling with you for a couple of weeks, I'm almost ready to back you."

"Thank you," Jace said. Then he asked. "What's holding you back? What can I do better?"

Marsyas lowered his voice to relate the seriousness of his reply, "I'm tired. If you would take this branch and sweep for a distance, I'd sure be one happy bowman."

Jace reached out and placed a hand on the bark. Before he could wrap his fingers around the branch, another of the rearguard archers bumped him with his shoulder.

"He was teasing you, File Leader," the archer informed Jace. "Get up front where you belong and find us a good spot for the day."

Marsyas leaned to the side and said, "A camp where we can sleep. Not an exposed area, forcing us to sit up most of the day with our bows out, watching the road."

"I'll do my best," Jace assured them.

"Of that, File Leader Kasia, we have no doubt," both archers said displaying their support.

***

Sunrise found the archers high on a tree covered slope. By tying ropes to limbs already hanging low, they pulled down the branches and created barriers with the trees. Behind the screens of leaves, the two wagons, the teams of horses, and the archers relaxed in the shade. In the other direction, the top of the hill hid them from view of the massive camp of the Carthaginian army.

"One of our best sites yet," an archer complimented Jace.

145

"Considering the few campfires, we could see in the dark, the day could have turned out differently," he responded. "I only wish we were closer to the stream."

Farther downhill and beyond the edge of the trees, a mountain stream bubbled over rocks. Cold and clear, the water represented more than a place to fill their waterskins. It offered a charming spot to bathe with a patch of green grass for lounging and napping. But the meadow and the stream were in view of any patrols traveling on the nearby road.

"That would put us in danger of being discovered," the archer pointed out.

Jace yawned. Then putting his arms over his head, he stretched and announced, "I'm going to sleep. Let me know if anything happens."

"Sure will, File Leader Kasia," an archer replied.

Jace felt as if he'd just closed his eyes when feet kicking dirt and rocks alerted him to someone coming from higher on the hill. Then, whispering woke him.

"What's going on?" he asked.

"The entire Carthaginian army has formed battlelines," a watcher reported. Seeing his File Leader leap to his feet, ready to issue orders, the archer said. "They're marching south, at least most of them. We can see it all from the top of the hill. Cavalry and light infantry on the flanks. Skirmishers and javelin men out front, elephants and phalanxes with heavy infantry in the center. And archers in the back."

"Can you see the Legions?" Jace asked.

"Nope. Not a sign of them."

"Then who are the Carthaginians going to war with?" Jace questioned. "Wait, you said most. I assume they left a light force to guard their camp?"

"Oh no, File Leader, they're keeping well over half of their cavalry and several hundred spearmen in reserve," the lookout described. "That's what Narkis and the other watcher figured. And I agree."

"That's a disappointment," Jace whined.

"What's wrong?" the watcher inquired.

"I was hoping for a view of the Legions," Jace explained. "It would give us an idea of how far we have to go to see a friendly face."

Several archers had gotten off their blankets to listen to the report.

"There is some good coming from this," one of them projected. "The Carthaginians will be exhausted after fighting all day. It'll make it easier for us to slip by them in the dark."

"How far to the Legions?" another asked.

"There are hills in the way," the lookout replied. "Captain Zoltar and the company could be over the next set of ridges, or twenty miles from here. There's no way to know."

"It's not twenty miles," Jace assured them. "If it was that far, the Carthaginians wouldn't have formed their battle…"

Several archers laughing and pointing downhill interrupted Jace. He walked to an opening in the canopy and peered through the leaves.

Narkis and another archer splashed in the creek. Their clothing, scabbards, and blades rested in the grass. Those were universal weapons and could belong to anyone. What sent shivers down Jace's back, they had taken their war bow cases and quivers. For all their reckless behavior, the bows identifying them as archers proved to be the most careless.

Already exhausted, Jace's head throbbed. He pushed aside the branches with the intention of stomping downhill and beating on the two bathers. Before he stepped through the barrier, another archer gripped his shoulder and pulled him back.

"Get off me."

"You're too late, File Leader."

Jace blinked to clear the anger at being stopped and stared at the creek, then the road.

"Thank you," Jace offered.

A mounted patrol of heavy cavalry trotted from around the foot of the ridge. They reined in and a cavalry NCO indicated the two bathers. Four horsemen broke from the columns and rode down to Narkis and the other archer.

Jace pulled his eyes from the plight of his bowmen and focused on the cavalry officer.

The man sat on his horse ignoring the naked men. Instead, he carefully scanned the hillside.

"Bows, File Leader?" an archer asked.

"No. There's nothing we can do that won't get us killed."

The younger archers of the File bristled at the stand down order. Older, seasoned archers nodded in agreement with the File Leader.

Ropes were dropped over the bowmen, and they were led to the road. Two other cavalrymen scooped up the scabbards and quivers. Then one examined a bow case, lifted it into the air, and shouted. The NCO nudged his horse closer to the cavalry officer.

"Secure your long packs," Jace instructed. "If they head up here, run for the heights."

"Can't we fight?" a recent graduate from the agōgē questioned.

An older archer dropped his arm over the young man's shoulders.

"Those are heavy cavalry. The riders have armored chests, as do their horses. Now, if you don't understand the wisdom of our File Leader, there are forty of them. And how many of us?"

"Ten, not counting Narkis and Gyes," the youth answered. "Oh, I see. We can't win a fight."

"But we can die," the experienced archer told him. "Go fix your long pack."

Jace squatted and watched as four horsemen separated from the patrol. Two took the rope ends and pulled Narkis and Gyes down the road. Apparently satisfied the pair of bathers were alone and the hillside empty, the cavalry officer signaled for the columns to move off.

Once the officer couldn't see them, the four horsemen kicked their mounts. The ropes went taut. Narkis and Gyes sprinted until first one then the other tripped. At the end of the lines, they kicked and tried to regain their footing. But the rough ground, the pace of the horses, and the rocks knocking them from side to side, prevented the captured bowmen from standing and running behind the horses.

"They know their Cretan Archers," someone swore.

"How can you tell? By the refreshments offered, or the gestures of kindness from their hosts," another sneered.

Jace spun on the File.

"Everyone not on watch, sleep," he exclaimed. "Tonight, we'll locate the Company and end this patrol. No more tearing of the flesh. Save your sarcasm for a lighter subject and another day."

While the archers unpacked their blankets, Jace climbed to the top of the hill.

"Help me watch where they're taking Narkis and Gyes," he requested of the lookouts. "Point out landmarks and camp features."

Four pairs of eyes noted the horsemen when they stopped and allowed the archers to stand. Then, the riders walked their horses and the staggering prisoners slowly into the Carthaginian camp.

"Why allow them to stand?" a young watcher inquired.

"They want them alive for questioning," Archer Marsyas answered.

"Neither Narkis nor Gyes gave our position away," the newer archer commented.

"It's what we expect of every Cretan Archer," Jace stated. "I see a big tent with flags out front. That's a recognizable marker. Help me find more."

***

Long past sundown, when sentries grew sleepy and campfires ebbed, Jace ordered the convoy off the hill. The two wagons and ten archers moved unchallenged around the Carthaginian camp. Not until they headed south did a guard on the road question them.

"Who are you and where are you going?" the soldier demanded.

"Greek mercenaries who are suffering the vengeance of our Captain," Marsyas, the driver of the first wagon, replied.

Unlike the other nights, the Cretan File remained near the transports. Considering the amount of traffic during the day, erasing their footprints served no purpose. And attempting to dodge the sentry posts was a fruitless endeavor.

"Destination?" the sentry insisted.

"We're javelin throwers and our Captain is positioning up at the vanguard," Archer Marsyas told the sentry. "He's dooming us to the front of the battle formation. Can you believe that? Most of us won't make it to midday, so wish us luck."

The sentry spit and laughed at the projection.

"The Latians won't come out of their fort and off the hill to fight," he informed the archers. "You'll be as safe up front as you would be back at camp."

"From your lips to Soteria's ears," Marsyas said.

He snapped the reins and the wagons and Cretans moved beyond the checkpoint.

"You don't need the Goddess of Preservation from Harm," the sentry announced as the convoy moved by his post. "You'll need games to keep you from being bored."

Farther along the dirt road, they encountered spearmen at the front of the Carthaginian army.

"Brave souls," the soldiers teased. "Come back when we face a worthy enemy."

"Set your camps up out there and let us know when or if the Legions come out to play."

None of the archers replied. They shuffled ahead like condemned men, just as Jace coached.

The spearmen lost track of the convoy in the dark. It would be much later when the lack of campfires caused the spearmen to send a patrol forward to investigate. They wouldn't find the camp of the Greek mercenaries or any sign of the men or the wagons.

***

Barriers on the road leading up to the Legion stockade forced the convoy to stop.

"You with the wagons," a voice challenged from the other side of the barrier, "we have arrowheads aimed at you. Turn around and leave."

For several tense moments, the Cretan Archers stood motionless on the road while the bowmen in the dark held tension on their bows.

Then the driver of the first wagon called out, "Lasion. You couldn't beat me at the academy. What makes you think being a File Leader has changed anything."

After a short delay, a reply came from over the barricade.

"Marsyas?" File Leader Lasion asked. "What are you doing out there?"

"Trying to find a friendly face," the archer replied. "Maybe we should head home to Crete, seeing as we're not wanted here."

"Relax your bows and open the barrier," Lasion instructed his bowmen. "Kasia's File has been recovered."

The convoy rolled up the hill but was stopped again at the gates to the fort.

"Who are you?" a Legionary inquired from the top of the log wall.

"Kasia File, returning from patrol," Marsyas answered.

Voices from the other side of the stockade called out for the officer and the NCO on duty.

"Maybe we should camp here," an archer suggested.

"We've come this far," Marsyas barked. "I want to sleep in safety and beside a road is not what I had in mind."

Not long after they spoke, a familiar voice bellowed from inside the fort.

"Open this gate, right now. Or I'll make it my mission to find a way to put every one of you on the punishment post."

The archer beside the wagon chuckled, "Tribune Scipio does not sound happy."

"Perhaps our late arrival disturbed a pleasant dream," Marsyas suggested.

The gates opened to reveal Tribune Scipio, Centurion Restrictus, Captain Zoltar, and Lieutenant Gergely. Worried lines creased their faces and they counted as the wagons and archers entered the fort.

Without knowing where the Cretan campsites were, Marsyas pulled his team up to an open area in front of a large tent. He turned his head and watched the second wagon roll to a stop. Behind it, his officers marched from the gate. Oddly enough, Lieutenant Gergely waved his arms signaling for the convoy to move. But Marsyas didn't know where he should take the wagons.

Armored Legionaries rushed from around the tent and formed a double line of shields. Then servants, carrying torches, poured from the tent. A distinguished, older man in a toga strolled from the entrance.

"Who are you to disturb my sleep with a shipment from Rome?" he asked. Then spying the piles of goods on the overloaded wagons, he added. "What have you brought us?"

"Sir, this isn't from Rome," Marsyas explained. "While on patrol, we attacked Carthaginian caravans and captured these supplies."

"You denied Hannibal provisions," the elder statesman exclaimed. "And killed his soldiers, I hope."

"Yes, sir. Quite a few," Marsyas assured him.

Tribune Scipio circled the wagon and placed himself between the archer and the older man.

"Dictator Fabius. I apologize for the disturbance," he said. "The fault is all mine and I'll accept any punishment you deem sufficient."

"Who are these warriors?" Quintus Fabius inquired.

"Sir, they're Cretan Archers from Jace Kasia's File," Cornelius replied. "This is the patrol that located the route of General Barca's army."

"And then disrupted his supply lines," Fabius announced. "Many of our Legionaries are young and inexperienced. They wouldn't stand a chance against the Punics in battle. But maybe we can formulate a strategy of intercepting Hannibal's supplies and harassing his forces. At least until we're ready to fight him."

"Yes, sir, an excellent idea," Cornelius agreed.

How could he not? As the Dictator of Rome, Quintus Fabius was the most powerful man in the Republic.

"I'd like to meet this Jace Kasia," Fabius remarked.

Cornelius glanced back at the ten Cretan faces glowing in the torch light. After scanning the archers and not seeing the File Leader, he asked, "Where's Jace?"

"Sir, two of our men were captured," Marsyas explained. "Earlier, File Leader Kasia changed into the clothing of a teamster, then left us."

"Where did he go?" General Fabius questioned.

"Sir, I believe File Leader Kasia has gone to the Carthaginian camp," Cornelius told the Dictator, "to get his archers back."

Chapter 15 – Another Sketchy Plan

Itthoba dipped the cloth and brought it out with a dab of wine on the material.

"Don't spare the old wine," a cavalryman called out as he passed the corral.

"Yes, sir," the stableman replied.

With a splash, Itthoba sank the rag into the bowl of red wine and brought it out, soaking wet. Slinging streams of red on the ground, he sloshed it over the back of a calvary mount. While he approached the work in a slipshod manner, before the linen touched a patch of raw skin, he slowed and gently patted the saddle wound.

"In Thessaly, we drink wine, not bathe our livestock with it," said a stranger standing at the rail of the corral.

Itthoba stopped applying the wine and looked at a young man. Barefooted, he wore a loose linen shirt and a pair of baggy woolen pants held up by a rope belt. Both garments were old and well used. A wide brimmed straw petasos, dipping forward, hid the upper part of his face. The hat carried sweat stains from long days under the sun.

"We drink wine," Itthoba told him. "But the livestock and men have abrasions from the trip over the...Say, who are you?"

The stranger ducked under the rail and entered the corral.

"Name's Kasia," Jace introduced himself. "I wasn't being smart. We don't use wine on wounds in Thessaly. Mostly, we just allow the injured mount to roam with the herd until the saddle wounds heals."

"We do the same back home in Libya," Itthoba said. "But the squadrons are a long way from home."

156

"Aren't we all," Jace added. He approached the bowl and the stableman. "You say the treatment heals wounds."

"It's not like an act of God," Itthoba explained. "But the wine wash seems to speed up healing. And because we've captured so much, there's no reason not to use it on abrasions and raw spots."

"What about the rot?" Jace asked while squatting and studying the bowl of red wine.

"There's been very little after the wine baths," the Libyan reported.

"Do you mind if I try?" Jace inquired.

"Sure. But be gentle when you apply the wine," Itthoba cautioned. He tossed a rope over the neck of another horse and walked it to Jace. "This one is a favorite of Captain Shama'. Unfortunately, he rode the horse even after the skin rubbed off, making it worse."

Jace put a hand on the muscular neck. The horse moved away, apparently nervous at the touch of a human.

"Whoa there, big fellow," Jace said in a soothing voice. He dipped a spare rag in the bowl and dabbed at one of the two lines across the horse's back. The red and inflamed marks mirrored the front and back of a saddle. While the stallion might be favored by the cavalry officer, Shama' didn't spare the mount from hard riding. Perhaps too hard. As he washed the wounds, Jace whispered. "We should be friends. Maybe later, I can find a treat for you."

After bathing the back, Jace washed down the horse's legs.

"You know horses," Itthoba remarked.

"I'm a handler for the Thessalian cavalry," Jace lied.

A deep voice challenged from outside the railings, "There are no Thessalians in the army, cavalry or otherwise."

Jace relaxed a little when informed that there were no Thessalian Greeks in Hannibal's army. And while Itthoba stiffened in the presence of a cavalry officer, Jace continued to wash and feel the legs of the stallion.

"Not yet," Jace answered. "My Captain is at the battle line with an advanced force."

"If that's true," the officer inquired, "what are you doing here?"

"Waiting for our supply wagons," Jace told him. "I've got a few days before they arrive from the coast."

"Captain Shama' this is Kasia," Itthoba stated. "He's helping out with the wine treatments."

"How is my boy?" the Captain asked while gesturing to the stallion.

"He needs to be walked and bathed at least twice a day, sir," Jace responded. "And I fear his diet isn't good for healing. Do you have any beets?"

"I'll have the cook send over a bag of them," Captain Shama' replied. He examined Jace for a moment before declaring. "As long as you work, Kasia, you can stay with us until your squadrons arrive."

"Thank you, sir," Jace said accepting the offer. Shama' strutted away and Jace pointed to a storage tent. It sat just over the rails of the corral and an armed soldier circled it. He inquired. "Is that where you sleep?"

"That's the grain tent and it was mine for sleeping," Itthoba confirmed. "Before they brought in the Cretan Archers. Now, I have to sleep under the stars."

"Cretan bowmen?" Jace gasped. He glanced around, peering at the camp as if afraid. "Where did they come from?"

"There's only two of them," Itthoba replied. "They were scouting for the Roman Legions and stopped, in the middle of the day, to take a bath. Imagine that? Captain Shama' and a combat patrol came along and took them into custody."

"Have they taken their hands, yet?" Jace questioned.

"No. I think the Captain is waiting for the other half of our riders to return."

"Before he moves this reserve force to the front?" Jace guessed.

Itthoba bit his lip and admitted, "What you see is the half of our cavalrymen who don't have healthy horses. We're lucky to field the half we sent to the battleline. And our patrols are limited."

"That rough a trip?"

"If you think our cavalry mounts are bad," Itthoba suggested, "you should see the heavy infantrymen. Their backs are shredded from the weight of their packs and armor."

Armed with that news, Jace thought about leaving and sneaking away. Tribune Scipio and the Legion commanders should know about the poor condition of the Carthaginian army. But he came to rescue his archers, not to spy for the Republic.

"If the tent is in use, where do we bed down?" Jace asked as he pulled the rope from over the horse's head. After setting the mount free, he walked across the corral to rope another wounded and exhausted horse.

***

Late in the afternoon, Jace strolled the perimeter of the corral. Walking behind him, the Captain's stallion followed, nibbling pieces of beet from Jace's open hand.

"He's a fine animal," Jace remarked to the tent guard when their circuits overlapped.

"He's as mean as Captain Shama' is strict," the soldier noted.

They separated going in opposite directions. Jace sped up, so they met again.

"You've got Cretan Archers in there," Jace rushed out as if nervous. "Are the bowmen as dangerous as they say?"

"As dangerous as any pair of tied up, naked men," the soldier told him, "no more, no less."

"Have they bitten anyone?" Jace asked as they parted ways.

This time, the guard slowed to allow Jace to complete his circle of the corral.

"What did you mean, did they bite anyone?"

"There's a rumor in Thessaly that as children, Cretan Archers are fed the spines of stonefish. The venom permanently poisons their mouths," Jace replied. "If they bite you, the limb will rot off. If you're lucky."

On the next loop, they easily met across the corral fence.

160

"All it takes is a bite?" the soldier questioned.

"Not just a bite. Sometimes their spit can blind a man," Jace warned.

As the guard quick stepped to where he could call to an NCO, Jace strolled to Itthoba. "The stallion is doing well. I'll walk another one."

"I've been so busy washing wounds, I haven't had a chance to evaluate any of the horses," the Libyan stableman commented. "I'm glad you're here."

"As am I," Jace assured him.

***

The cavalrymen, all Libyan nobles, enjoyed privileges far in excess of the support staff. One being long communal dinners. In order to prepare for the nightly feasts, the cooks fed the guards, supply men, assorted servants, and the stablemen early.

"Looks delicious," Jace remarked.

His bowl was filled with grain and vegetables in a broth with a large piece of beef. Flat bread covered the surface of the food.

"We do eat good, now," Itthoba admitted. "But going through the mountain passes, we starved. Froze during the day. And spent restless nights on hard ground. I butchered ten fine horses when they went lame. It was the only time we ate for days."

Jace and the stableman sat with their backs against the rail fence. Both had beer in their mugs. They agreed, the idea of smelling or drinking red wine turned their stomachs.

"That was a daring journey," Jace ventured. "But your pantries are full, and the animals are on the mend."

"As are the infantrymen…"

A pair of boots stepped in front of them, interrupting Itthoba.

"Are you the Thessalian?" a Libyan soldier inquired.

"I am," Jace admitted. "Why do you ask?"

"My guard said you know about Cretans and their tricks," he explained. "I want you to feed them."

"Hold on," Jace protested. "I don't want anything to do with those bowmen. No, sir, they're creatures of the shadows. You should kill them and be done with it."

"That's my thought," the Sergeant admitted. "But the Captain wants them kept alive. He thinks skinning the archers will show the men that they are only human."

Jace shifted his eyes as if looking for an escape route. What he did during the scan was check the position of the sun. He needed darkness before chancing a get away with Narkis and Gyes.

"Tell you what," he offered, "let me finish my meal and my beer. Then I'll come over and feed the prisoners. Itthoba will be sure I don't run off."

"The camp is big, but not that big," the NCO threatened. "If you skip out on me, I will find you. And you'll be naked and in the tent with the Cretans."

"Think of this as my last meal," Jace requested. "You know, for a condemned man."

"You Greeks are really dramatic," the Sergeant commented. "When you're done eating, come to the tent's entrance. The guard will have the food there."

Jace touched the brim of his hat in acknowledgement. Not daring to look up for fear of divulging his Latin heritage, he focused on the bowl of food. Eating slowly, he savored it while waiting for the sun to touch the horizon.

***

Later, when the shadows stretched long across the ground, Jace approached the supply tent.

"I'm here to feed the Cretans," he informed the guard.

"Their food is on the stool," the soldier told him.

He started to do another lap around the tent.

"Do you expect me to go in there alone?" Jace asked.

"I'm not going in there with you," the soldier informed Jace. "Their bite is poison, and they can blind you with spit."

"That's not good," Jace said with a shiver of fear. "Tell you what. I'll go in, but please stand by the entrance in case you need to pull me out."

"I'm not going in."

"I understand," Jace assured him. He picked up a slab of wood with two mugs of wine. Beside the mugs sat two bowls of broth with a few kernels of grain and a whisps of vegetables, but no meat or flat bread. "Just be here in case I need you."

The sentry planted the butt end of his spear beside the tent flap and rested against the shaft. Jace picked up the rustic tray, bowed to the guard, ducked lower, and pushed aside the tent flap.

***

The interior of the tent stunk. Ironically, Narkis and Gyes had been caught washing themselves. But after a day and a half of laying in their own filth, they were far from clean.

"I guess the Cretan poison isn't from your mouth," Jace said loudly enough for the guard to hear.

Chuckling came from outside and both captured archers rolled to sitting positions.

"I've brought food, but don't try anything," Jace told the prisoners. He set the tray to the side and lit a candle. Then he pulled four large beets free before taking off the loose shirt. His war hatchet hung from a leather shoulder strap and two dark tunics were wrapped around his waist. "Spit once or try and bite me, and I'll leave and take your food."

"We'll behave," Narkis whispered through a dry, parched throat.

"You better," Jace said as he cut the ties and freed Narkis' hands. "Because I've heard Cretan archers were great bowmen, but not too bright. Rumor has it some are downright stupid."

The sentry laughed at the remark. After freeing Gyes' hands, Jace gave them the beets and moved to the rear of the tent. In moments, he had sacks of grain stacked on the sides, forming a passageway to the back of the tent.

"I don't care if they haven't given you anything to drink," Jace scolded. "You drink slow and keep your hands down."

While he talked, Jace sliced an opening in the tent. As their File Leader worked, Narkis and Gyes sucked down the wine and devoured the food. After eating, they slowly and painfully slipped the tunics over their heads.

"Don't rush it," Jace warned. He ran his hands over their arms and legs. Once satisfied nothing was broken and neither had a debilitating injury, he added. "Slow down, you'll make yourself sick. I don't need your puke on me."

He waited for a few moments before whispering, "Head northwest to the spot where you were caught."

Then he shoved the archers to the back of the tent and pulled his linen shirt over his head.

"Snap at me again," Jace growled to the empty tent, "and I'll kick your teeth out."

From outside the tent flap, the sentry giggled at the threat. Jace moved to the back and restacked the sacks to close the passageway.

"Tomorrow or the next day, Captain Shama' is going to skin you," Jace announced to the sacks of grain. "This could be your last meal. Slow down and enjoy it. But you don't spit at me."

***

Jace emerged from the tent with the tray and the empty bowls and mugs.

"Without their bows and arrows, they aren't so tough," he remarked to the guard.

"Because they're tied up," the soldier reminded Jace. "A stableman like you wouldn't stand a chance against them if they were free."

165

"Then, it's a good thing there are soldiers like you around," Jace complimented the guard while walking away from the empty tent.

Once out of sight from the guard and the tent, he stuffed the tray and containers behind a bale of straw. In a few swift sprints from shadow to shadow, File Leader Jace Kasia reached the edge of the Carthaginian camp. And as he'd been taught, he dropped to his belly and moved unseen through the weeds.

Somewhere ahead of him, Narkis and Gyes also snaked through the wild grass.

"I couldn't believe it when File Leader Kasia came into the tent," Gyes whispered. "And he brought food. It was the best sight of my life."

"It's hard to argue with his results," Narkis allowed. "But you have to admit, it was another sketchy plan."

"I suspect we'll hear about the creek thing," Gyes offered, "when he catches up with us."

"Of that bowmen, I have no doubt."

Act 6

Chapter 16 – Fabian Strategy

Cretan scouts had reported the movement of the Carthaginian army to the Master of Horse two days earlier. By dawn, the Legionaries dismantled the hilltop fort and prepared to march. As the Legions broke camp, Cornelius Scipio's auxiliaries raced ahead searching for the Punics.

A Legion infantryman in the advance force, shifted his shield to a more comfortable place on his back. After settling the scutum, he moved the javelins to his other hand. Now with the throwing weapons on the same shoulder as his spear, he lifted a waterskin, pulled the stopper free with his teeth then dropped the cork. It dangled at the end of a short lanyard while he took a stream of water.

"I can't figure out if we're cursed or blessed," he pondered.

"That would depend," his squad mate noted.

"On what?" the Legionary asked.

A horse and rider overtook the ten infantrymen.

"It's a personal choice," Kolya Adad mentioned.

The Thracian officer reined in and paced beside the Legion squad.

"Why's that, Lieutenant Adad?" the Legionary asked.

"The Legions are four miles behind us and under orders not to fight the Carthaginians," Kolya explained. "We're out front with our javelins at the ready."

"Because we're hunting their supply wagons," another infantryman offered.

"Which proves my point," Kolya Adad stated before kicking his mount. "The supply wagons will be protected by cavalry and spearmen. Therefore, we will have to fight, making the blessing or the curse a personal choice."

"He's pretty smart for a Thracian," another infantryman suggested as Adad rode away.

"I was referring to not having to carry provisions like the other Centuries. Look at us, we're traveling light," the first Legionary described. "So, is working for Tribune Scipio a blessing or a curse?"

"We're marching in our armor because we're out front with the forward element," the squad leader told him. "And we may have to form a defensive screen at any moment."

"What I was asking, Decanus…" the Legionary insisted.

But the voices of his squad mates drowned him out by yelling, "It's a personal choice."

***

Lieutenant Adad allowed his mount to slow and fall in beside three other horses.

"The left flank is positioned like a cocked fist," the Thracian officer notified Captain Ignatius.

"This is a good plan, Tribune, if it works," Alick Ignatius declared to Cornelius. "If not, we'll all die a glorious death."

"No one except Carthaginian cavalry and spearmen are going to die today," Captain Zoltar assured the commanders of the vanguard. "Besides, we haven't located the wagon train. It could take us a week to catch them."

"Do you feel you're cursed to be working with a staff officer who is given the most dangerous assignments?" Cornelius questioned.

"If I might answer, sir," Kolya Adad requested. Nods from the three senior officers relayed permission. "Thracian javelin men get bored easily. Not one of us would switch with the units marching behind us. We are proud to be singled out. And we are honored to be your hunters, Tribune Scipio."

While Cornelius formulated a reply worthy of the short speech, Lieutenant Hylas Inigo trotted up. He reined in his mount on the other side of the group and saluted.

"Captain Zoltar, our right flank is positioned like a war hatchet," Hylas reported.

"What about you, Lieutenant Inigo?" Alick Ignatius asked hoping to catch the Cretan junior officer off guard. "Is being attached to Tribune Scipio a blessing or otherwise?"

"Well, sirs," Hylas stated, "Cretan Archers are trained killers. Back there, in the Legion's ranks, they move with the swiftness of an oxen. We're out front like the head of an arrow. It's where we should be to deliver death with the swiftness of a straight shaft from the string of a war bow. Without a doubt, the Gods gave us Tribune Scipio so we could apply our craft, unobstructed."

169

"I guess that answers your question, Tribune Scipio," Captain Zoltar summed up the conversation.

***

In silence, the five officers traveled along the foothills towards a mountain valley.

"This might be news," Pedar Zoltar announced. In the distance, a lone rider galloped in their direction.

"It's Lieutenant Gergely," Cornelius noted when the rider drew closer.

Moments later, Acis Gergely pulled his mount up in front of the officers.

"Captain Zoltar, we've located File Leader Kasia," he reported.

"When I heard he went to try and rescue his archers, I knew it was a bad idea," Zoltar remarked. "Is he injured? Where has he been?"

Acis twisted around and pointed north. Far away, a figure moved. At first, they thought it was a mounted rider in the distance. But soon, the officers realized it was a single man running at a steady pace.

"File Leader Kasia and archers Narkis and Gyes met us on this side of the valley," said the junior Cretan officer. "After the escape, they fled to the high ground. Our scouts found them hiking to the Legion camp."

"He could have waited for the supply wagon," Captain Zoltar suggested.

"Jace said, he had to speak with Tribune Scipio straight away," Acis countered. "Something about a weakness."

170

Cornelius wanted to charge ahead and ask Jace about the message. But, a Legion commander of auxiliary troops needed to maintain his dignity. Plus, having all the vanguard officers together would cut out rounds of reporting the same message by File Leader Kasia.

"While we wait, Lieutenant Gergely, what's your status?" Captain Zoltar inquired.

"We're dispersed in a thin arrow formation," he replied. "From all sides, our mixture of archers and Thracians appear to be relaxed and unaware of any danger."

"We have our chin jutting out begging for a punch," Zoltar exclaimed.

"And two fists ready to punch back," Ignatius offered.

"All we need now is a unit of the Punic army to take the bait," Cornelius added.

The six officers followed Jace's progress as he raced across the level ground. Unfortunately, unlike a leather belt, the rope around his waist came loose. He stopped in front of the horses, holding the baggy pants up with his right hand.

"Ah, Tribune Scipio, forgive me if I don't salute," Jace said with only a slight hint of breathlessness. "My attire is in disarray."

"No excuse needed, File Leader Kasia," Cornelius assured him. "We're all curious to hear about the rescue."

"That's not why I wanted to see you, sir," he explained. "The Carthaginian army is weak. Their horses are exhausted and hurt from the long ride. As are their infantrymen. If the Legions attack now, General Hannibal Barca will not be able to defend himself."

"How would you know these things?" Alick Ignatius demanded.

"Well sir, when I was rubbing down the Libyan Captain's horse with red wine…"

"You were what?" the Thracian officer interrupted.

"Most of their horses have saddle and harness burns as well as sore muscles," Jace explained. "I was helping the stableman wash the wounds with wine and he told me. It seems they can only effectively field half their cavalry. And about the same for their infantry. They're treating them with wine but what they need is a long rest."

"With red wine?" Ignatius questioned.

"Yes, sir. They have lots of the stuff," Jace reported.

"Jace, go change into something resembling archer clothing," Cornelius instructed. "Then take three of your archers as bodyguards and get this information back to Tribune Manius. General Minucius needs to know."

"Sir, do you know the location of my File?" he asked while fumbling with the rope belt.

"They're walking security around the supply wagons," Captain Zoltar told him. Then he saluted Jace. "File Leader Kasia you are dismissed. And good job son, on saving your bowmen."

"Thank you, Captain," Jace acknowledged before racing by the officers, heading for the wagons and his File.

"What are you thinking, Tribune Scipio?" Zoltar asked when he noted Cornelius looking at the sky.

"I believe gentlemen, we need to test File Leader Kasia's assertion," he answered. "We're no longer simply searching for a rear element that will fall back on us. I want to plow through their rearguard and attack the tail of the Punic army."

"Lieutenant Gergely. Find us that tail," Captain Zoltar ordered.

As Acis Gergely rode north, Jace Kasia and three of his File ran to the south.

***

Jace's chest ached, his legs burned, and his breath came in short, painful gasps. But the forward elements of the Legion came into view, and Jace dug deep for strength. With no let up, he and his escorts sprinted by the forward line.

"It's good to see you alive, File Leader Kasia," Pluto Manius greeted Jace when he halted by the Tribune's horse. "Give me your report."

"Tribune Manius, the Carthaginian army is spent," Jace uttered.

He quickly went through the information about the raw spots and the wine baths. He ended with a description of the beat-up mounts and spent infantrymen.

"All in all, sir," Jace said finishing his account, "they are ready to fall down."

"Come with me," Pluto instructed.

Wheeling his horse, the Tribune walked back through the ranks of marching Legionaries. As he approached Marcus Minucius, Legionaries of the First Century moved to block him.

All they could see was a Tribune being trailed by four Cretan archers carrying war bows. Although the General was surrounded by political associates and junior staff officers, the Legionaries closed ranks.

"I have important information for the Master of Horse," Pluto told the officer in charge of the veteran bodyguards.

The Centurion turned and said, "Please inform General Minucius that Tribune Manius requests an audience."

Long moments later, a Senator replied, "Tell him to come back tonight after we make camp."

"I have a spy who has been in the Carthaginian camp," Pluto said. "His information grows old by the moment."

Caius Silvius rode his mount from the cluster around the Master of Horse.

"What news?" he asked.

"Senior Tribune Silvius, Hannibal is done," Pluto stated. "One of our Cretan Archers, File Leader Kasia, was in their camp the day before yesterday. They are barely functioning at half strength. This is our opportunity to end this."

***

The Dictator should not have been in the field and on horseback. Only through a dispensation from the Senate of Rome was Dictator Quintus Fabius allowed to ride a horse. In the past, the few times they elected a Dictator to handle emergencies, the Senate limited travel to carriages. A ridiculous restriction, Fabius argued, for chasing down an invading army. Enough Senators agreed and they lifted the restriction. Although a few resisted, because a mounted Dictator appeared as a heroic leader and the Senate feared a General who grew too strong.

"Allow the Master of Horse through," Fabius ordered.

Marcus Minucius eased his horse between the Dictator's bodyguards and rode into enemy territory. Not that the men surrounding Quintus Fabius were necessarily violent. But they all came from the other side of the Senate aisle from Minucius' coalitions. None would hesitate to metaphorically stab him in the back. And some, quite possibly, were prone to actually sinking a blade into his body.

"What news?" Fabius inquired.

"We have an eyewitness who saw firsthand the weaknesses of the Punic army," Marcus Minucius declared. "Dictator. We have Hannibal. He can't withstand a Legion offense. It's time we ended this invasion."

"Our Legions are untested," Quintus Fabius explained. "And the Republic has lost too many sons. No, Master of Horse, we will not attack."

"But sir," Minucius pleaded, "we can end this now."

"The Senate elected me to end the loss of life," Fabius replied. Around them, the sycophants nodded and mumbled their approval. Encouraged by the support, Quintus Fabius pointed at Marcus Minucius and directed. "Until I am relieved by the Senate, you will drawback from confrontations with the Punic army. In fact, stop the march. We will resume following in the morning. From here on out, all of our attacks will be against Hannibal's supplies and foraging parties. I will starve him into submission. Now, Master of Horse, you have your orders. Go execute them."

Embarrassed by the abrupt dismissal in front of his political opponents and the rejection of his ideas, Marcus Minucius rode from the Dictator's party.

Once away, he galloped back to his staff, where he issued orders to carry out the Fabian Strategy. Because his emotions ran hot, the Master of Horse and his staff almost forgot to notify his froward elements.

"Send a runner to Manius and have him pass the word to Scipio to halt his advance," First Tribune Silvius told the nearest junior staff officer.

That teen pointed to a younger noblemen and passed on the responsibility. Because his orders came from another Junior Tribune and it was already midafternoon, the messenger stopped to chat with friends. After a few jokes, he trotted to Manius' location and delivered the instructions.

Immediately, Tribune Pluto Manius realized the inherent danger. The distance between the main body of the Legions and the vanguard, left Tribune Scipio's command beyond the range of reinforcements.

Before he could send runners to warn Scipio, two sweating archers dashed into his camp.

"Sir, compliments of Tribune Scipio," one said between deep breaths. "We have located the rear of the Carthaginian army and have initiated an attack. The Tribune requests reinforcements, sir."

Chapter 17 - Assault on Paradise

Cornelius Scipio kicked his mount and galloped from the right flank to the center of the valley.

"We've almost got another of their transports," he shouted. "Standby for one more push, Legionaries."

In response the ten heavy infantrymen holding the center of the line shouted, "Rah! Standing by Tribune."

"Hold your line," the squad leader reminded his charges as the staff officer raced to the left flank.

Ten shields barely covered any of the thousand feet of flatland in the valley. The Carthaginians to the front of them could hypothetically circle the Legion infantrymen. But Thracian javelin throwers flooding the sides prevented an end around. On the slopes above the fighting, Cretan bowmen targeted any Carthaginian cavalrymen or skirmishers attempting to rush froward and add weight to the assault on the center of the Legion line.

"Orders, Tribune?" Kolya Adad asked as Cornelius pulled up at the left flank.

"How did you get blood on your tunic and arms?" Cornelius inquired.

"Can't let my javelin throwers have all the fun," the Thracian Lieutenant replied.

"Alert your units. We'll be fighting forward when I give the signal."

Kolya glanced back. Three Punic supply wagons sat abandoned in the center of the valley. The only sign that they had been driven and guarded were the bodies on the ground.

"You've been right so far, Tribune," the Thracian officer acknowledged.

Cornelius whipped his horse around and dashed to Captains Ignatius and Zoltar. He pulled his horse between their mounts and raised both arms. Lieutenants Adad, Inigo, and Gergely mimicked the Tribune to show they were aware of the pending assault signal.

"Scipio, you are truly blessed of Ares," Alick Ignatius announced.

"He does have a touch of the God of War about him," Pedar Zoltar agreed.

"Gentlemen, we are about to…" Cornelius clamped his mouth shut and closed his fingers into his fists, signaling hold.

From up the valley, a wave of Iberian shields and spears jogged towards the small battle. Cornelius had successfully orchestrated attacks against a couple of cavalry squadrons and a thousand or so light infantrymen. While his auxiliary forces had managed against the detachments guarding the Punic wagon train, he was under no delusion about their chances against ranks of heavy infantry.

"Gergely, we are about to step back, rapidly," Cornelius told the Cretan Lieutenant. Acis Gergely stood behind the Legionaries with fifty bowmen. He nodded his understanding. Cornelius then addressed the Thracian commander. "Captain Ignatius, please take command of the left flank and organize the retreat."

"I'll command the right," Captain Zoltar volunteered.

"Our rally point is the beginning of the valley," Cornelius directed. "We cannot allow their cavalrymen to get behind us or get caught in a stand-up fight against their infantry. Open land is bad for us. We stop them at the mouth of the valley, or we die. All ready? Signal the retreat!"

After giving the orders to set the operation in motion, Tribune Scipio dismounted. He pulled the horses' head around, then slapped a hindquarter. Frightened by the harsh treatment, the horse bolted down the valley. After a mile, the mount would be stopped by the men guarding the vanguard's supply wagons. They may not know what was happening at the site of the fighting but seeing the riderless mount would alert the rear guard that there was a problem.

"Sir, you should be mounted," the Legion squad leader mentioned.

"None of my Legionaries, Cretans, or Thracians are mounted," Cornelius responded. His neglect at mentioning the mounted Lieutenants and Captains wasn't lost on the infantrymen and bowmen. "Let's get this festival started. Gergely roll your archers back and keep the Punics off our shields. Lance Corporal of the Legion. Maintain order but get us the Hades out of here."

"Advance," the squad leader shouted. Along the line, ten shields smashed froward and as the Legionaries stepped into the gap, they withdrew the shields while driving the blades of their gladii into the narrow space. "Step back, step back, step back."

The move only gutted ten soldiers on the front rank. But the coordinated brutality shocked the rest of the warriors. For several moments, the Carthaginian line stopped fighting and watched men tend to their dead and wounded. Taking advantage, the Thracians moved back like a herd. Only the Legionaries stepped together with their shields locked.

"Excellent work," Cornelius complimented the squad.

Hearing their Tribune, on the ground and right behind them, gave the Legionaries a new sense of obligation. They were trained to fight in a combat line. But none expected to hold the life of their staff officer so close. It was a responsibility each took seriously.

Then behind the Legionaries, and to the rear of Tribune Scipio, a clear, crisp voice sang out.

"Still your breath so your hands are steady. Calm your heart so your eyes are clear. And focus your mind on the task," Lieutenant Gergely exclaimed. "One. Select-a-shaft, and-a-two notch your arrow…"

Before he reached, "And-a-three pick your target," fifty archers were chanting with him.

"And-a-four, draw. And-a-five, release…"

Zip-Thwack, Zip-Thwack, Zip-Thwack, Zip-Thwack…

Ten arrows tore into the Carthaginian forces. Until now, they had experienced the Cretan war bows from a distance. With the arrows coming directly over the shoulders of the Legionaries and the Thracians, the arrowheads on impact jerked shields aside, allowing the following shaft to find flesh. But it wasn't once or twice. Almost immediately ten more, then another ten shafts tore into the Punic lines.

After fifty Zip-Thwack, Zip-Thwacks, the Cretans archers chanted, "and nine. Step up. One, Select-a-shaft…"

They rotated ten fresh archers to the front, and they delivered fifty shafts. While the Cretans performed their maneuvers, the Legionaries and Thracians flowed around the formation.

"Set a new line, and let the bowmen through," Cornelius ordered. Then he alerted the archer officer. "Lieutenant Gergely, pull them out."

In neat files, the archers jogged between the infantrymen. They set a new formation while shields clashed, and gladii and spears dueled holding the new line.

Then from the flanks, Cretan File Leaders roared, "One. Select-a-shaft, and-a-two notch your arrow…"

Well over four hundred arrows delivered to exact targets by men trained to pull powerful war bows proved to be too much. The Carthaginian light infantrymen broke. While they ran from the fighting, coming up behind them were ranks of Iberian heavy infantry.

"There's one good thing," Cornelius declared.

"What's that, Tribune?" a Legionary asked in a shaky voice.

Everyone could see the heavy shields, armor, metal helmets, and steel tipped spears. A few arrows might get through but certainly not enough to stop the ranks of soldiers.

"They aren't cavalry, and we can outrun them," Cornelius answered. "Lance Corporal of the Legion."

"Yes, sir."

"Break your shield wall. And run."

Close to fourteen hundred men strong, the vanguard raced for the mouth of the valley.

"Sir, thank you," the Legion squad leader said as he and Cornelius jogged along with the mass of retreating men.

"What for, Decanus?"

"For showing the squad and me what true leadership looks like."

The compliment boosted Cornelius. Enough so that when Lieutenant Adad offered his horse, it was turned down. Tribune Scipio proudly ran with his men all the way to the position of his rearguard.

***

Shortly after the retreat and while the units of the vanguard settled into a new defensive formation, forty Legion cavalrymen, Centurion Restrictus, and Tribune Pluto Manius rode to the wagons.

"Tribune Scipio," Pluto called out when he couldn't locate Cornelius among the mounted officers. Fearing the worst, he scanned the wounded and inquired again. "Tribune Scipio?"

From beside a wagon, a cluster of Thracian javelin men broke apart to reveal a Legion officer bent forward and pouring water over his head. Shaking off the excess like a beast of prey, Cornelius Scipio stood upright and smiled.

"You missed the fun," he shouted to Pluto. Then to the longhaired wild men from Thrace, he said. "Gentlemen, if you'll excuse me, I need to get back to my duties."

Cheers followed Cornelius as he marched to his horse and mounted.

"Give me a cavalry line," he ordered the mounted Legionaries. "I want to remind the Punics that the Legion only backs up so far. Archers on the flanks and Thracians, guard our edges."

After some shuffling, the Legion riders occupied the center with the Cretans and Thracians bracketing the cavalry. The solid formation had the desired effect. The Iberian heavy infantry stopped at the last abandoned supply

182

wagon. After installing teamsters on the transports, the infantrymen walked back up the valley escorting the recaptured supplies.

"Where are the Legionaries?" Cornelius demanded. "We can cut the tail off the snake, right here, right now."

"Tribune Scipio, per General Minucius, you are to stop all aggressive operations," Pluto explained. "Only isolated foragers, scouts, and supply trains are to be attacked. None of our assets are to engage with the main body of the Carthaginian army."

"What kind of war strategy is that?" Cornelius growled.

"It is the will of Director Fabius," Pluto replied.

***

Five days later, a game had developed along the mountain trail. Punic riders or light infantrymen would backtrack, locate the tip of the vanguard, throw several javelins, back away, and laugh.

"Let me set an ambush," Lieutenant Adad begged. "We'll teach them not to bait the bear."

"Give me leave to take a couple of Files ahead," Lieutenant Inigo offered. "We'll put enough arrows into their behinds that they'll stop this nonsense."

"As much as I want to draw blood," Cornelius replied, "if either of you got in trouble, I couldn't call on the Legion to pull you out. Until we receive orders to the contrary, we'll stay on their tail without contact."

Acis Gergely rode up to the group.

"Kasia's File is back from scouting the ridges ahead," the Cretan officer reported. "Benevento has closed their gates. And the Carthaginian army is marching by the town."

"That's good news," Cornelius told the junior officers. "If Benevento went over to Hannibal Barca, we'd have to dig him out. But now I worry about the direction of his march. If he turns north, he might go against Rome. To the southwest is Capua then Naples. If either city made overtures to the Punic General, he could have a wealthy area for his base of operations. Unless..."

Cornelius rode in silence for several moments.

"Unless what, Tribune?" Hylas Inigo questioned.

"Unless he marches directly west into Ager Falernus," Cornelius replied. Puzzled looks greeted the statement. The young Tribune explained. "It's a lightly defended agricultural valley. With abundance like that, Hannibal can fatten up his troops and livestock. After his men are rested and healthy, he can attack the villas and estates, forcing us to fight to defend the property of Republic citizens."

"The place sounds like paradise," Kolya Adad remarked. "Too bad for the farmers, but at least we'll have a battle."

***

Three days later, Hannibal's vanguard dropped from the mountains, crossed a flat plane, threaded between foothills, and emerged on the Ager Falernus. Across the Volturno River, the military of Capua sent reinforcements to the bridges to harden them against the Punic invaders. While the river created a southern limit to Hannibal's advance, no such barrier prevented General Barca from marching northwest into the heart of the lush valley.

184

Nobles of the Patrician class and their families loaded up wagons and fled towards Rome. The poor had no choice but to sacrifice to their household Gods and pray.

***

Several days later, Tribune Scipio and his auxiliary Captains rode to the top of a hill. From horseback, they gazed at the fields and farms of the Ager Falernus valley.

"We have him," Cornelius declared. He held a leather map in one hand and used the other to point out areas of high ground. "The Legions of Director Fabius have closed the north end with garrisons along the Aurunci Mountains. Capua has the south sealed along the Volturno, and General Minucius has the east escape routes blocked. Gentlemen, this is the end of the Punic invasion."

"If that's so," Captain Ignatius inquired, "why are we digging defensive trenches and building long sections of barriers?"

"Truthfully, I don't know," Cornelius admitted.

"It does appear as if the Dictator will be satisfied just watching," Zoltar remarked.

A Legion courier rode his mount up the slope and halted beside Cornelius.

"Tribune Scipio. Your presence is requested in the Senate of the Republic within the month," the junior staff officer read to him from a scroll. "Signed, Alerio Carvilius Sisera, Citizen of the Republic and Senator of Rome."

"Are you being promoted Scipio?" Alick Ignatius asked.

"That's not likely," Cornelius said. "The Dictator and Master of Horse are more inclined to ship me off to Iberia."

185

"Send word, and the Cretan archers will join you," Zoltar promised.

Cornelius nodded to show his appreciation of the offer. Then, the three officers followed the courier downhill where they parted ways.

***

At the Cretan camp, Jace Kasia saluted his File as they set the final log in the barricade at their area.

"Now that's a pretty sight," Egidio commented.

He looked down the line of weaving poles. For men who could shoot arrows straight, their skills at building an aligned wall lacked the same point to point exactness.

"What's pretty about a drunken line of stumps buried on the side of a hill," Narkis scoffed.

"Because we're done with it," Eachann answered. "File Leader, what's next?"

Jace examined the drifting stockade wall and smiled.

"We've got a patrol in the morning," he told the File. "Until then, you're on your own."

"Gyes and I are going hunting," Marsyas suggested. "Want to come?"

Jace touched the bronze band on his upper arm.

"Thanks, but no," he declined. "I want to go ask the Samnites about this piece of jewelry."

Hali Adras pulled himself up on the wall, climbed to his feet, and balanced on top of the logs.

"What more is there to know?" he offered from the perch. "You got it from a beautiful Samnite Princess."

"How do you know she was beautiful?" Narkis challenged. "It was dark, and we were climbing out of the river valley. You never saw her."

"Didn't have to," Hali exclaimed while holding his arms out. "In every mythology, the Princess is always beautiful and the hero handsome."

"There's the flaw," Marsyas boomed while giving Jace a friendly nudge in the shoulder. "Have you seen our hero?"

Jace collected his quiver and war bow. Then he walked down the defensive line heading for the Hirpini camp and Lieutenant Papia.

Chapter 18 – Character Witnesses

"No man of sound sense goes to war with his neighbors simply for the sake of crushing an adversary," Papia stated from the other side of a campfire. "Just as no one sails on the open sea just for the sake of crossing it. Indeed, no one takes up the study of arts and crafts merely for the sake of knowledge. But men do as they do for pleasure, good, or utility."

"I'm not clear on your meaning," Jace admitted.

The Hirpinian War Chief swirled hot embers with the tip of a stick and continued without addressing the confusion.

"At the dawn of time, the Hirpini people migrated down the Apennine Mountains. We encountered hostilities and had to fight our way through," Papia closed his eyes as he told the tale. "Our weaker brothers and sisters died from slaughter or starvation. Strong but never strong enough, we pushed farther south. Upon reaching the land of the Pentri Tribe, our forefathers were few, but formidable. The Pentri offered the art of iron forging and the craft of club and shield making. But the price was high. In return for the gifts, our tribe left the land of the Pentri and journeyed into the high peaks."

"I think I understand. As the Hirpini moved, they became stronger until the Pentri gave knowledge rather than fight," Jace summed up. "But what was the purpose of the trip? I mean where were they going?"

"To a land, we could call our own with borders we could defend," Papia answered as if he had been with the ancients. "But the steep slopes, the freezing nights, and the snow ate through our supplies. Lost in deep valleys below towering summits, we Hirpini became doomed. Death followed, walking on the bodies of our dead. Livestock, falling to their knees, provided an occasional meal. Then at the River Miscano, the tribe paused. And the elders argued. To stay on the undefendable riverbank meant death. Yet many were too weak to travel onward. A few families were selected to ford the river and seek a new home for the Hirpini."

"And they settled Benevento?" Jace guessed.

"No. Benevento, as the Roman's call it, was built later," Papia corrected. "Five miles downstream, the explorers turned west following a branching creek. After hiking along the creek, they entered a wide valley with rolling hills. Except, the families had traveled so long, they had grown accustomed to looking ahead and missed the beauty and promise around them. Later, they entered a narrow valley with trees and leaves so thick, it resembled a green fog. Lost, they stumbled on until they, like the livestock, fell to their knees."

The War Chief paused in the rendition to toss a split log on the fire. Jace waited, showing patience, although his heart was pounding with anticipation. Finally, Papia placed the stick on the fire and waited for the thin rod to burst into flame.

"You are quiet, when need be," Papia acknowledged Jace's silence. "When hope had fled, a wolf appeared to the families. Figuring it would take them to another stream, they climbed to their feet, and followed like a pack slaved to a lead wolf. For miles, they pushed through the thick forest until, as if a window covering had been lifted, they emerged at the base of a mountain. High up, a rocky fist projected from one side. Anticipating the meaning, several men climbed the steep slopes. Once on the rocky knoll, they saw the land spread out below them. Howling with excitement, they acknowledged that the wolf had guided them to the new home of the Hirpini."

"And they called themselves the wolf-people," Jace offered. "But how is the Goddess Mefitis associated with the Hirpini?"

"You've heard of our deity?" Papia said. "Let me reveal a mystery of the Hirpini. From the top of Monte Tuoro, two spring-fed ponds are visible. Several of the men saw the water and, believing a mountain retreat would be easily defended, they trekked to the springs. Five men approached the watering holes. Four fell to their knees, gasping. Only two of those men managed to crawl away and find fresh air in the trees. The other two died from breathing noxious vapers from the earth."

The War Chief lowered his head as if in prayer. Figuring he was offering thoughts to the deceased, Jace sat with his own head bowed.

"Are you not curious?" Papia questioned after a few moments.

"Four men approached," Jace began. Then he revised his statement. "No, wait. You said five men approached the ponds. What happened to the fifth?"

"With the blessing of the Goddess Mefitis, he took a handful of mud from each of the toxic ponds. Then he stacked them away from the vapors so the pile would act as a warning to other travelers who might happen upon the springs," Papia answered. He stopped but after a breath, the War Chief added. "He became the first Chief of the Hirpini People. Since that day, every chief and war leader must prove that they have the blessing of the Goddess of Noxious Gases before claiming a title."

"You've been to the ponds?" Jace inquired.

"I fasted for three day before climbing to the outcrop," Papia told him. "After resting for a night on the rock, I waited for the sun to reveal the location of Mefitis' garden. Then I climbed down and walked to the ponds. There I found bodies of failed chiefs littering the ground. But I burned with the desire to lead wolf-men in battle. And so, ignoring the warnings, I stepped over the bones. First at one, then at the other pond, I took scoops of mud and added them to the Goddess' garden wall."

Jace studied the middled aged man as the flames reflected off the lines on his face. In Papia's features, he noted the strength and drive of a man who would die for his people and his beliefs.

"As would I," Jace uttered without thinking.

Papia stood and moved around the fire to stand beside Jace. Reaching down, he clasped the metal band on the archer's arm.

"You wear a warrior's armlet of the Carricini Tribe," Papia noted. "Are you pledged to a Carricini War Chief?"

"Not that I know of. I happened to be there when a group of Carthaginian mercenaries attacked a small river village," he explained. "Afterward, an old man's granddaughter gave me this armlet. I didn't know he was a chief."

"How many warriors did you slay in the name of the Carricini Chief and his family?"

"I don't remember. Maybe? Ah, got it. An NCO and six soldiers," Jace informed him.

"That explains it," Papia said as if everything was clear. He pulled an armlet from his arm and positioned it next to the Carricini band on Jace's thick upper arm. "From this day forward, you are a warrior sworn to me and to the Hirpini people."

"I am honored," Jace said accepting the bond to his people. "But what does the other armlet mean?"

"It seems, Jace Otacilia Kasia, you are the adopted son of a Carricini Chief," Papia answered. "It's a rare token of respect. He must have been very impressed with your prowess in battle."

"When I sailed from the Island of Crete, I was an orphan with no title," Jace remarked while caressing the armlets. "I'm still an orphan, but I know of my parents. Plus, I have brothers. Thank you."

"Come tomorrow and I'll tell you more of your people," Papia offered as they gripped wrists.

Jace floated all the way to the camp of his File.

"Did you take any game?" he asked.

"A deer, one arrow through the heart," Marsyas bragged while handing Jace a slice of venison. "And it'll provide a nice length of sinew and hide."

"Did you find out anything about the armlet?" Hali inquired.

"More than I could have ever dreamed of," Jace replied before sitting down to enjoy the meat.

***

Cornelius Scipio accepted a glass of wine from the servant and settled back on the sofa.

"I have sent the documents to your father," Senator Aemilius Paullus told him.

They reclined on the Senator's patio, enjoying a warm fall afternoon.

"I trust he will sign and return them by the fastest ship," Cornelius assured him. He took a sip before changing the subject. "Senator, I've been languishing in the Capital for a month now. The summons from the Senate sounded urgent. But every request for an audience has fallen on deaf ears."

"That's Alerio Sisera's committee and has nothing to do with me," Paullus deflected. "Right now, he's dealing with nominations for next year's group of *Aedilis Curulis*. Seeing as you're too young to run festivals or to oversee city buildings, I can't understand why he wrote you. Unless, the committee is looking for a wild, gladius brandishing, underaged *Aedilis* to keep order."

Aemilius Paullus laughed at his own joke. Young men with political ambitions ran for the office of *Aedilis Curulis*. As the first step in a career, getting the public to know one's name at festivals helped, as did meeting Rome's wealthiest citizens. And while keeping order in the city could be part of the duties, using a blade wasn't in the job description. Plus, at seventeen almost eighteen, Cornelius hadn't reached the age of majority. An *Aedilis Curulis* needed to sign contracts which precluded anyone younger than the age of twenty-five.

"Hopefully, I'll get the appointment soon, straighten out whatever the committee needs, and get back to my men," Cornelius remarked.

"You know, I can easily get you a position in Legion command," Senator Paullus offered. "That'll get you away from those auxiliary barbarians."

"Your generosity is much appreciated, sir," Cornelius replied. "But I'm working through a number of new tactics. The Cretans and Thracians provide a good working sample."

"Legionaries on assault lines, son, are the mightiest formations in the world," Paullus declared. "You'd be well advised to stick to what's tried and true."

"I understand, sir..."

193

A rustle of fabric and a slight girl of sixteen breezed onto the patio. Cornelius stood, but the girl ignored him.

"Father, you have a visitor?" Aemilia Paullus questioned.

Senator Paullus beamed a smile at his daughter.

"As if you weren't aware as soon as Cornelius arrived," he teased. "At least you gave us a chance to discuss the contract before interrupting. You can assure your mother that the documents have been sent to Iberia. Once we have them signed and back, we can hold the betrothal ceremony."

"If you are done, father, you wouldn't mind if Tribune Scipio walks me around the garden?" Aemilia inquired.

"Not at all, I'll leave you two to the business of getting to know one another better," the Senator stated. He stood then faced his future son-in-law. "Really Cornelius, should you change your mind, I will get you a position."

"Thank you, sir," Cornelius replied. After a salute to the departing Senator, he held out an arm. "Miss Paullus. Would you escort me on a tour of the villa's gardens?"

"It would be my pleasure, Tribune Scipio."

***

In a crowded city, rumors and news traveled as fast as aromas from cook fires on the evening breeze. And recently, both were bad, raising passionate opinions among the citizenship. It was no less so on the steps of the government building.

"Thirty estates burned to the ground," a Senator complained, "while our Legions sit, picking their noses, and watching them go up in flames."

"They're blocking Hannibal Barca from marching to Rome," another Senator argued. "If it wasn't for Dictator Fabius, the burning buildings would be in your neighborhood."

"Spare me your watch and wait justification," a third legislator barked. "We misplaced Marcus Minucius. Rather than Master of Horse, he should have been elected Dictator."

"He'd get..."

The three reached the door to the senate building and went inside.

Although the door cut Cornelius off from the discussion, his hands remained clenched into fists. Frustrated at being away from the Ager Falernus valley and having to depend on unreliable third hand information, drove the young officer to act. And so, he stood on the steps of the Senate early in the morning, waiting for Senator Sisera.

"You're out early, Tribune," Hektor Nicanor's voice came from behind Cornelius.

He jumped in surprise before gathering his wits and addressing Alerio Sisera's assistant.

"I've got to get back to the Legions," Cornelius pleaded. "Please. I need to resolve any issue Senator Sisera has with me."

"Oh, it's not with you, Tribune Scipio," Hektor informed him. "It's about Master Romiliia."

"What about him? He's a File Leader for a rank of Cretan Archers," Cornelius described. "I've very little to do with him. But I do have the responsibility for fifteen hundred other men. And they need me."

"If you'll follow me, Tribune," the Greek invited.

They passed through the door the Senators had used. But rather than crossing to the senate chamber, Hektor guided Cornelius down the hallway to a side room.

"Please go in," Hektor encouraged while opening the door.

Six men sat around a table covered with scrolls. But none were reading the rolls of parchment. Rather they were pointing and discussing spots on a map that covered a section of the tabletop.

"Ah, good, you're here," Alerio Sisera greeted Cornelius. He indicated the young officer to five men in togas with the purple stripes of a Senator. "This is Tribune Scipio."

"Sir, why am I here?" Cornelius inquired as he marched into the room.

Before he reached the table, one of the Senators quickly rolled up a leather sheet. Then he stacked a couple of scrolls on top as if to bury the map.

"As a test, I ran Lucius Romiliia's name by a few colleagues," Senator Sisera replied. "I received some odd reactions."

"Sir, Jace is just an archer, no matter who his family was," Cornelius offered. "I'm not sure why anyone would care."

"That's what I thought," Alerio Sisera told him. "But from a few, the reaction fell just short of a threat if I dared mentioned the boy's name and social status."

"Is that what this meeting is about?"

"These are my closest associates," Sisera responded. "We're trying to understand what common thread links the most vehemently anti-Romiliia Senators. So far, we have nothing."

"I don't know what I can add," Cornelius admitted. "You'll need to look from Genoa to Benevento and that's a long way."

The Senator holding down the map, unstacked the scrolls and unrolled the leather sheet.

"Why Benevento?" he asked while examining the map.

"Jace or rather, Lucius' mother was a Hirpini Princess," Cornelius responded. "It would be odd if her people didn't have farms in that region. Will that be all, sirs?"

"We brought you here as a character witness to see if revising the Romiliia name was worth pursuing," Senator Sisera informed him. "But you've dropped an interesting pebble into the pond."

"Lucius Jace Kasia Romiliia is a talented warrior who keeps his head clear when the situation deteriorates into chaos," Cornelius volunteered. "At Lake Trasimene, we worked together to bring out who we could. I have nothing but respect for File Leader Kasia."

"Would he be a worthy addition to the Patrician class?" the Senator holding the map inquired.

"He's frontier rough and has an attitude," Cornelius described. "But Jace is smart and learns quickly. I don't see why not."

"Thank you, Tribune Scipio," Alerio said dismissing him. "You may return to your Legion."

Cornelius saluted, turned about, and marched from the room. Something about the interview screamed for his attention. But the idea was quickly overridden by the excitement of getting back to his men. He would be riding south long before darkness fell, but not soon enough to reach his camp.

Act 7

Chapter 19 – It's a Trick

The Legion sentry squinted into the distance. From his post high on the hill, the only identifiable features were the ordered campfires of the Punic army. Everything else was lost to the night. For more than a month, the bright spots had been in a consistent pattern. Now they weren't.

"Optio of the Guard," he shouted. "We have movement."

The sounds of grumbling accompanied the NCO as he climbed the hill and scaled the ladder to the platform.

"This better be something and not a trick of your eyes," the Sergeant warned as he stood. But after peering into the night and blinking, he too noted the change. "Good call. It seems our Carthaginian friends are breaking camp."

"Are we going after them, this time?" the Legionary asked.

"Sick of training, are you? Want to dip your blade in the blood of your enemy?" the NCO challenged the young infantryman. "Well, before you go charging down onto the plain and singlehandedly taking on the Punic mercenaries, remember they also have thirsty blades."

"Yes, Optio," the Legionary said.

Despite his caution to the inexperienced infantryman, the NCO slid down the ladder, and rushed from the hill. He too wanted to face the army of Hannibal Barca and end the destruction of his homeland.

***

Below the eastern slope of the Volcano of Roccamonfina, at another sentry's post, a Legionary stepped into the firelight and leveled his spear.

"What are you doing on the Via Appia at night?" he shouted.

The yell wasn't so much for the lone horseman. Its intention was to wake the rest of his squad. Before they could gather, the rider pulled up a safe distance from the Legionary.

"If Hannibal Barca is still in Ager Falernus, you're to be commended on your diligence," Cornelius greeted the sentry. "What Legion are you?"

The campfire light reflected off a Tribune's armor and the sentry answered, "Sir, Fabius Legion East. And yes, the Punic army is still on the plain."

"Excellent. I didn't miss the battle," Cornelius Scipio remarked. "Where is your headquarters?"

"Up the side road at Pugliano, Tribune," the Legionary replied. He pointed his spear to the left indicating a flat dusty track. "It's three miles and one hundred and ninety-three paces."

Cornelius chuckled as he turned the horse. He had observed new Legionaries being drilled on keeping track of distance by counting steps. Apparently, the practice was still being taught.

As dark as the night was, the trail, beaten down by footfalls from thousands of hobnailed boots, glowed like a pale colored ribbon against the gray landscape. With the way clearly marked, Cornelius nudged his mount into a fast walk.

Halfway to the headquarters at the town of Pugliano, he met columns of marching Legionaries coming from the other direction. A Legion's Senior Centurion led the infantrymen.

"What news?" Cornelius asked as their horses came abreast.

"The Punic army is breaking camp," the combat officer answered. He reined in next to Cornelius to allow the Centuries to pass and advised. "You should get to your Maniple, Tribune."

"That's what I plan to do," Cornelius assured him. "But I'm the commander of the right flank of Minucius North. A month ago, our headquarters was at Vitulazio. Unless things have changed, that's ten miles through Carthaginian held territory and twenty miles around. I thought I'd rest with the East before pressing on in the morning."

"It's a plan," the Senior Centurion commented. "Now if you'll excuse me."

"Where are you heading?"

"We're moving Legionaries and auxiliaries to the fortifications at Allifae," the combat officer told him. "With four thousand men on hand, we'll be able to stop the Punics if they manage to escape from the upper corner of our kill box."

On a map, the upper section of the Ager Falernus plain didn't have square sides. But the Centurion wasn't referring to a geometrical shape. Rather, he meant that the gladii and shields of the Legions guarded the routes off the plain.

To the east, the coastline of the Tyrrhenian Sea offered no route. In the northernly directions, the roads between the summits amounted to strangulation points for any army fleeing with miles of supply transports. And without a doubt, after months of raiding and savaging the fertile plain, Hannibal Barca's army had hundreds of wagons, thousands of draft animals, and mountains of supplies.

On the other side of the Ager Falernus were three possible ways out. The northeast corner was the most porous with trails though the foothills. Legion East was positioned where they could cover the face of those hills should Hannibal try to snake along those paths. At the center of the eastern boundary, the men of Legion North controlled the entrances to a few high passes. And the final and least likely way out of the Legion kill zone was a slick road running alongside the Volturno River. Although Hannibal Barca has used it to come onto the plain, with so many heavy transports, leaving along the river would prove too slow.

The Senior Centurion kicked his mount and trotted off to retake his place at the head of the columns. Cornelius sat pondering his next step. He could accompany the Centuries of Legion East off the plain but that meant fifteen more miles of riding and his horse was exhausted.

"Come on," he uttered while encouraging the horse forward, "we'll get a good night's sleep and get started early tomorrow morning."

The horse would enjoy hay and a comfortable night in a corral. Tribune Scipio, during that period, would not get the rest he promised the mount.

***

Ten miles, on raven's wings, to the southeast from the town of Pugliano, Jace Kasia slept. Wrapped in a warm blanket, he dreamed of mountain warriors.

Before coming to the Republic, his imagery would have been of slopes climbing from shallow valleys as found on Crete. But since crossing the Apennine range a few times, his idea of heights and of the men who used the features for warfare had changed. Now, he could see the advantage of almost unfathomable heights…

"Kasia, get them up, you're moving," Lieutenant Gergely ordered. "The Senior Tribune wants to harden the pass at Rocchetta. And Tribune Manius thinks it's a good idea to send a File of archers with the extra Century of infantrymen."

Jumping up with his knife in his hand, Eachann asked, "What is it? Are we under attack?"

"That depends, is Gyes alive?" Jace questioned.

He uncurled from the blanket and sat up, rubbing sleep from his eyes.

"I'm alive," Gyes assured him from his guard position away from the sleeping archers. "There's no attack, except for the Lieutenant's assault on your rest."

"It's only six miles to Rocchetta," Jace suggested. "You can sleep there."

"But it's all twisting and climbing roads," Eachann pointed out.

"Are you sure you're from Crete?" Hali inquired.

"Secure your long packs," Jace instructed the archers, before addressing the Cretan officer. "You can tell Tribune Manius, Lieutenant, that we're on the move."

***

Cornelius stood on the crest of a hill, staring across the dark plain. On either side of him, squads of veteran Legionaries blocked a road leading down to the Ager Falernus. Instead of sleeping, staff officer Scipio had been drafted to command and hold back any Centuries that broke with orders and attempted an attack on the Punic army.

Now, in the blackest part of the night, hundreds of torches climbed out of the plain, heading for Allifae. Cornelius remembered the Senior Centurion and cursed at not going with the officer. At least there, he could fight Carthaginian mercenaries, and not stand around, preventing like-minded Legionaries from engaging.

A group of officers walked their horses across the road. As they passed, Cornelius heard familiar voices.

"He has got to listen this time," Marcus Minucius complained. "There is Hannibal, spread out in the dark with no way to signal his army. We can march across the plain in Maniples and slaughter them before they're aware of us."

"General Minucius, the Dictator has said it before. He believes the night maneuvers are a trick to draw us out of our forts and down into traps," a staff officer informed the Master of Horse. "Besides, sir, no successful General ever fought a night battle."

"That's exactly what I'm going to tell Fabius," Minucius declared. "General Barca cannot win a night battle. But we can disrupt his plan."

The riders moved out of hearing range and Cornelius understood why he and the veterans were guarding the road. Most Legionaries, their NCOs, and officers wanted to punish the Punic army. But Dictator Fabius was sticking to the safest possible activity, that of not entering into battle.

"I count six hundred torches," an infantryman said about the lights moving rapidly up the slope at Allifae, "that's about a quarter of them."

"Four thousand warriors," another estimated. "Probably the Iberian heavy infantry. I hope our guys at garrison stay behind their walls."

"Me too," their NCO added. "But they don't have Dictator Fabius there to remind them to stay out of the fight."

"Or us to hold them back," a squad leader ventured. Then he gasped. "God Epiales, spare us."

The prayer to the God of Nightmares came as the flames of torches in the distance scattered into broad attack units. Like stars fallen to earth, the clusters of burning brands raced towards the slopes at Allifae.

"There's the breakout point," the NCO shouted. Although it was impossible for the Legionaries at Allifae to hear, he encouraged. "Don't engage. Don't engage."

But it became clear, by the divisions in the torches, that the Legion Maniples had come out of their stockade and were attacking the Carthaginian army. And although invisible in the dark, the Legion's effect on the torches became immediately apparent, for a moment.

A shield wall held by Legionaries was almost impervious to breaches by infantry or cavalry. Only an elephant or a shaft from a bolt thrower could breach a Legion line. Yet, based on the movement of the torches, the Iberians tore holes in the Maniples as easily as the sheers of a cloth maker cut material for a tunic.

A gang charging Cornelius' blocking force met the shields of the veterans. A shoving match began between men who wanted to fight and men who were ordered to stop them.

"Stand down. In the name of Dictator Fabius, stand down," Tribune Scipio shouted. "Follow orders. Do you want to die in the dark?"

"We want to save out brothers, Tribune," one Legionary replied.

"You are not alone," Cornelius confirmed to a choirs of Rah. "But now is not the battlefield we want."

"When will it be?"

"Next year? When the Dictator's term expires?"

"If that's what the Gods will," Cornelius responded. "And on that day, I will be up front with the First Maniple. Until then, go back to your camps."

By the time the crowd turned and migrated away, the torches across the plain were running chaotically over the slopes of Allifae. There were no zones with dark patches of shield walls, or Legion defensive squares. The Legionaries from the fort seemed to have vanished.

***

Even with their training to pick out specifics, the Cretan Archers couldn't make out any more details than Cornelius and the Legionaries. Jace turned from the hilltop and faced Hali Adras and the town of Rocchetta. Fire pots marked the streets, but the cottages along the twisting roadway were lost in the dark.

"Hali, keep the Centurions happy," Jace told his assistant File Leader.

"And where will you be?"

"Something is wrong with that attack," Jace told him. "Narkis and I are going down there to see what's happening."

"And get caught in the middle of a big battle?" another of his archers asked.

"From what we can see," Narkis offered, "the battle is over."

Jace and Naris slid their war bows from the cases, checked the arrows in their quivers, and secured them to their sides. Then, blending into the night like ghosts, they slipped over the hill and vanished into the lower trees.

Eight hundred feet below and two miles from Rocchetta, the two archers arrived on relatively flat land. Their view of the battle was gone, blocked by the foothills to the northeast.

"Ready?" Jace asked.

"Still my breath, and all that motivational stuff?" Naris answered. "Yes, let's cover some ground."

They jogged into the night as if it was daylight. Both shifting their eyes, so they didn't focus and narrow their vision. With pupils wide and gathering starlight, the bowmen raced for the foothills.

"There's a narrow trail a mile to the north," Naris mentioned after a two-mile jog.

"Good call," Jace agreed. "It'll be faster."

Adjusting, they ran directly for the pass. Counting paces, they were almost to the pass.

Jace threw his arm around Naris' shoulders and pulled the archer to his knees. Being trained in fieldcraft, neither man said anything. They just listened. And what they heard were NCOs calling for soldiers to stay together, the rattle of armor and heavy shields, cavalrymen walking horses, and teamsters swearing at draft animals.

Naris hooked Jace's head and pulled it down beside his.

"If this is the Carthaginian army," he whispered. "Who attacked the slopes at Allifae?"

"I'm sick of jogging," Jace responded. "Let's join General Barca's parade."

The Cretan Archers stood and strolled to the marching army. Then, as if they belonged, the two fell in beside an overloaded transport.

"Who are you?" the animal handler asked.

He peered into the dark at two shapes beside his wagon but couldn't see them clearly.

"The Sergeant wanted to be sure you had extra hands nearby if this tower starts to topple," Jace told him.

"Glad you're here," the man said. "The no stopping for anything order makes me nervous."

"Not to worry," Naris assured him. "We'll get you over the pass."

Jace and Naris put a hand on the transport and walked it up and over the narrow pass. On the far side of the foothill, the handler looked back to thank the light infantrymen. But they were gone.

Probably to scout ahead, he thought as the army turned south on a heading for the pass at Samnium and the Apennine Mountains beyond.

***

With dawn touching the horizon, the Centurions pulled their Legionaries out of their tents and ordered them to get into formations. The passion of the night had faded, and the officers were taking back control. As the ranks formed, Tribune Scipio galloped out of Pugliano.

In the distance, the infantry at Allifae occupied the slope in scattered groups. Between the clusters of Legionaries were unidentifiable dark spots dotting the hill. Cornelius lost sight of the garrison as he rode down onto the flatland. There, he allowed the mount to settle into a trot as they crossed the Via Appia and headed for the exit to the Ager Falernus.

Sixteen miles later, he arrived at the base of the slope at Allifae. At the top, the logs of the Legion stockade appeared small against the backdrop of the lower mountain. On the hill leading down from the fort, dead oxen, Punic pikemen, and Legionaries littered the ground. Standing at the bottom, he spotted two Cretan Archers.

"What happened here?" Cornelius questioned. "Where is the Carthaginian army?

Jace Kasia turned and pointed at the dead and then to a meandering herd of oxen munching on grass farther down.

"Narkis, show the Tribune," he instructed.

The second archer walked to a dead oxen and straddled the creature's neck. Lifting the massive head by the horns, he turned the face towards Cornelius.

"Look at the horns," Jace advised. "They tied dry branches to their horns, lit them on fire, then drove about two thousand of the animals up the slope. In the dark, the Legionaries thought it was the Carthaginian army."

"They came out to fight men. But were trampled by raging and frightened oxen," Archer Narkis explained.

Cornelius scanned the slopes. Groups of Legionaries were either carrying dead and wounded to the fort or were collecting Punic pikemen and herders into holding areas.

"But what happened to Hannibal and his army?" he inquired.

"Come with us," Jace encouraged.

He and Narkis jogged away from the slope. Cornelius followed.

***

They crossed to the foothills that created the eastern edge of the fertile plain. At the west side of those hills, the archers turned left. Two miles later, the three arrived at a narrow pass.

Cornelius didn't need to be told what happened. From the trail of fresh animal droppings, hoof marks and footprints from thousands of beasts and men, and deep ruts from heavily loaded wagons, he knew.

In the dark, while the Legionaries from Allifae battled enraged beasts, three miles away, Hannibal Barca squeezed his army and supplies through the narrow pass. Then, the crafty General moved them south, retracing the route he took to reach the plain of Ager Falernus.

"Tribune Scipio," Jace said pulling Cornelius out of his thoughts.

"Yes?"

"We need to go," Jace directed.

"I need to get back to Allifae to see if I can help," Cornelius protested.

Narkis had climbed to higher ground. From the top of the hill, he waved signals at his File Leader.

"You'll never make it to the fort, sir," Jace informed Cornelius. "There are Iberian heavy infantrymen marching to the stockade and light cavalrymen heading this way. We need to go, now, sir."

Jace raced up the roadway and Narkis ran to meet him. They stopped high in the pass and glanced back. Cornelius jerked his reins and kicked the mount. As he rode to the two archers, he fumed.

Hannibal had tricked the Legion again. Cornelius cursed as he and the Cretans sped through the pass, heading for Legion lines and safety.

Chapter 20 – Aleph! Aleph!"

Dictator Quintus Fabius mounted his horse. With bared teeth, he silently expressed a challenge to his second in command.

"Marcus, I expect the camp to be intact when I get back from Rome," he instructed. "While I'm away, the only thing you're to disrupt are Hannibal Barca's supply lines."

"As we've been doing, per your plan, for most of the year," Marcus Minucius responded.

Fabius missed the dissatisfied undertone of the comment. Or maybe he just ignored it. After the tragedy at Lake Trasimene, the Senate appointed Fabius as Dictator of Rome. With the power of the Senate vested in one man, Rome intended to see Carthaginian General Barca crushed. But Fabius surprised the Senate. Not only had he not forged a plan to bring Hannibal to battle, but the entirety of his strategy called for doggedly following the Punic army. Attacking small detachments where possible and disrupting the enemy's supply lines constituted the bulk of Fabius' approach.

Another wonder, rather than selecting his second in command from his own party of supporters, Fabius picked Marcus Minucius as his Master of Horse. A vocal opponent and a man holding distain for the Dictator's guerrilla tactics, Marcus had opposed the restraints ever since the plan was revealed.

Swinging his horse towards the gate, Quintus Fabius and one hundred Legion cavalrymen trotted from the marching camp. Once the Dictator vanished down the hill and around the first bend, Marcus Minucius waved a young staff officer to the steps of the headquarters tent.

"Tribune Scipio, what can you tell me about the enemy camp?" he inquired.

"Sir, I have Cretan Archers ferrying reports twice a day," Cornelius informed him. "As of this morning, the Punics remain behind the trenches and palisades around Geronium."

"If anything changes, I want to know right away," Marcus responded. Disregarding the fact that a young Tribune stood in front of him, the Master of Horse swore. "This Fabian Doctrine is causing unrest. Not only in the Legions, but with the people of Rome and the Senate. Do you know what they're calling our illustrious Dictator?"

"No, sir," Cornelius replied, before cautioning. "Are you sure you want to say it publicly?"

"No. Yet I have an urge to live dangerously, unlike our leader," Marcus sneered. "They call him a paedagogus for Hannibal."

At a time when the Senate had consolidated power in one man, disparaging the Dictator could get the offender exiled or crucified. And, referring to Quintus Fabius as a slave who walked behind a Roman child carrying his books to school, qualified Minucius for corporal punishment.

Despite the seriousness of the slander, Cornelius chuckled.

"See, even my staff officers understand it," Marcus Minucius observed. Before turning to go back to his tent, he reiterated. "Any change at all in the Carthaginian deployment, I want to hear about it. In short Tribune Scipio, find me a reason."

"A reason for what, sir?"

But the Master of Horse, the second most powerful man in the Republic, had already gone into the headquarters tent.

**

Fifteen miles northeast of Larinum, four frustrated horsemen held back their mounts. It wasn't the trail in the narrow valley forcing them to bridle the high-strung horses or causing the energetic riders to fidget. Behind them, a slow, stolen mule plodded along, pulling a wagon of confiscated grain. To the rear and completing the mini caravan, four Iberian light infantrymen easily kept pace with the wagon. With their round shields on their backs and their spears on their shoulders, they had no complaints about the lack of haste.

"Jugurtha, I think we should patrol ahead," one of the riders suggested to the Numidian NCO.

"We're still miles from Geronium," Jugurtha scolded. "The grain is more important than you joyriding around the countryside."

"It's more like mountainside," another complained. He scanned the trees and high hills surrounding the valley and announced. "I hate this land."

"Miss the warm climate of home?" the fourth teased. "Well, join the party. We all miss the plains, rolling hills, and the warmth of Numidia."

"What's that?" one asked.

"Where did he come from?" another questioned.

Jugurtha studied the trail ahead. In the middle of the path and strolling directly at them was a Latian teen in a tunic with a crate balanced on his head. A standing order

214

from General Barca flashed across his mind. Every man in the Carthaginian army was encouraged to slay any military aged Latian they encountered.

The cavalry NCO's next command gave a nod to their duty to the General while providing a distraction for his light cavalrymen.

"Kill him," Jugurtha shouted.

Hearing the command and seeing four horsemen surge forward, the young Latian tossed the crate, spun around, and ran.

***

Jace Kasia pitched the package into the path of the cavalrymen, pivoted, and sprinted back down the trail. The sounds of hoofs on the hard packed dirt let him know the crate did nothing to slow the riders. However, their presence just behind him confirmed the success of the File Leader's plan. Considering the thunder coming closer and closer, maybe too successfully. Glancing over his shoulder would slow him, so he bent forward, pumped his arms and legs, and raced ahead of the horses.

The voices of the riders grew louder and more excited. They shouted, "Aleph! Aleph!"

Jace's shoulders tightened, imagining a javelin burying itself in his back.

"Aleph! Aleph!"

Just as the hot breath of the horses seemed to claw at the back of his neck, Jace pivoted to the left, planted a foot, and vaulted over a row of thorn bushes.

The call of "Aleph! Aleph!" followed him into the greenery.

***

The four riders reined in and turned to face the thorns.

"Anybody want to go in there and flush him out?" Jugurtha inquired.

Getting negatives from his three men, the NCO wheeled his horse and…

Zip-Thwack!

Jugurtha tumbled from his horse with an arrow shaft in his chest.

Zip-Thwack, Zip-Thwack, Zip-Thwack… The other three horsemen followed him to the ground in quick order.

***

Jace dashed around the bushes. His small shield already strapped on his left arm and the war hatchet gripped in his right hand. At the bodies, he nudged each with the toe of his foot. None of the cavalrymen moved.

"Good clean shots," he declared to the three archers who scrambled from the tree line. "Search the bodies for coins. You've earned the profit."

"Where are you going, File Leader?" one asked.

"To be sure the mule, wagon, and grain are secured," he replied.

"Take a horse," one of the archers suggested. "You've got four."

Cretan Archers trained in the peaks and valleys of the Island of Crete. Years of speeding up and down slopes made

216

them fleet of foot and gave them stamina beyond most light infantrymen.

"The beasts take too long to gain momentum," Jace said before sprinting away.

***

The sun rested just above the horizon when the sentries at the gate called for the duty Optio.

"Sergeant of the Guard, they look suspicious," one Legionary warned.

The NCO took a moment to examine the wagon, the mule, and the four riderless horses. Six men walked in a procession around the wagon. None of them were mounted.

"Cretan Archers," he explained. "I don't think any of them can ride a horse."

"Barbarians," one infantryman commented.

"Thieving barbarians," the second sentry added.

Despite their opinions of the archers, the Legionaries stepped aside. And the Cretans, horses, and the wagon entered the Legion marching camp unmolested.

With day-to-day operations confined to drills and little else, word passed quickly about a wagon full of grain and the horses. Cornelius rushed to the Cretan area.

"Tribune Scipio, one of these horses is your profit," Jace said while handing him the reins.

"It's not common to distribute spoils from raids," Cornelius offered.

"Maybe not in the Republic. But on Crete, it is."

Before the Tribune could voice an opinion about the traditions of Cretan Archers, Marcus Minucius boomed from the end of the street, "On Crete, it is what?"

"Customary for everyone involved to make a profit, General," Jace replied. To reinforce the idea, he handed Marcus the reins of a second horse. "The last two mounts are for Lieutenant Gergely and Captain Zoltar."

"No movement by the Punics?" Marcus questioned.

"No, sir," Jace answered. "They're still hold up in the hill town."

Noises from the back of the wagon drew their attention. Four round shields crashed to the ground. An archer yanked at the rear of the transport and several spears and javelins fell from the bed, landing in a racket on top of the shields.

"How many Carthaginians were there?" Cornelius inquired after counting the weapons.

"Only nine," Jace commented. "None got away, if that's your worry."

"I was thinking six archers against nine soldiers is not good odds," Cornelius observed.

"Nine mercenaries from the Punic camp," Marcus stated. "Is that rare?"

"Oh, no sir," Jace assured him. "They have hundreds of foraging parties out searching for food."

"There it is, my reason," Marcus exclaimed. "Our mission is to cut off their supplies. Is it not, Tribune Scipio?"

"Yes, sir," Cornelius agreed. "But General, reason for what?"

"To move our camp closer and end their scavenging," the Master of Horse said. "And maybe, to bring Hannibal out from behind his stockade."

He strutted away quickly with the horse prancing happily at the end of the reins.

"Tell me, Tribune Scipio," Jace inquired, "what does the expression aleph-aleph mean?"

"In Punic, Aleph means ox," Cornelius replied. "I would assume Aleph-Aleph would be a call used to herd oxen. Why?"

"Just something I heard recently," Jace said, dismissing the comment. "It's nothing important."

***

In the morning, a cold rain fell on the town of Larinum. But the Master of Horse had given his orders, and although damp, chilled, and miserable, the Legionaries began dismantling the stockade walls and tents. As the stockade lumber and watch towers came down, the sections were placed in wagons.

Engineers and surveyors raced north, circling the Carthaginian captured hill town of Geronium and the lower city of Casacalenda. On the far side of enemy held territory, they located the requirements for a Legion camp.

Lago di Guardialfiera fed a stream providing a source of freshwater. Open ground would let the Legionaries construct the walls and defensive trenches without a need for additional landscaping. And the openness of the surrounding land would provide good visibility from the guard towers.

Plus, the new site had a benefit requested by General Marcus Minucius. From a portion of their palisade wall, Hannibal Barca and his men could gaze by a tall hill and see down into the Legion camp. It was a not too subtle reminder that four Legions and auxiliary forces of the Republic held the flatland to his north.

***

"Should we wave to the Carthaginian mercenaries?" a Thracian asked.

One hill over and higher in elevation, Punic soldiers stood behind a log wall peering down. It was too far for voices to carry. But the Thracian javelin man stopped to wave at the heights.

"Come down here and I'll shove my knife down your throat," he shouted.

"I don't care what you do," Lieutenant Kolya Adad scolded him. "As long as you don't hold up my march. Get moving."

He wasn't the only one to find the enemy-on-high position unnerving. Most of the Legionaries felt as if they were being watched. Mainly, because they were. But one person in the camp held a completely different view.

***

As proscribed by Legions of the past, defensive trenches were dug. The walls of the stockade went up as did guard towers. Before sundown, tents were erected, and livestock corralled. While the Legionaries prepared dinner and dried out undergarments, Master of Horse Minucius appeared on the boulevard outside his tents. He faced the Punic encampment with his fists defiantly placed on his hips.

"That's right, Hannibal Barca, I'm here watching you," he shouted. "If you don't like it, come down and taste some Republic steel. If you have the nerve."

While the camp settled in and men with sentry duty went to their posts, he stood on the street staring at the hills. Finally, as night fell, General Minucius pointed at the heights, growled, then marched into his compound of tents.

***

In the middle of the night, selected Centuries of Legionaries and light infantrymen left their tents and formed up on the streets. Without light, they easily followed the roads to the back gate where they left the marching camp. Once away, they divided into squads and circled the walls of the Legion camp.

Before dawn, the Legionaries were hidden in ambush spots along most of the trails leaving the Carthaginian position.

At sunrise, Hannibal and his staff watched as the Legion camp came awake. Legionaries marched in formations and drilled with shields and spears. But no one left the Legion camp except for water porters and a few mounted messengers.

"Nothing has changed with those Republic cowards," a Punic nobleman offered. "They'll sit on their behinds just like they've been doing all year."

"We should send out our foragers," another stated. "You've collected a large and formidable army, General. If we don't supplement our provisions, we'll soon run through our food supplies."

Hannibal peered down at the peaceful camp for several heartbeats.

"Send out the scavenging parties," he instructed without looking away from the Legion camp. "And double the guards on our walls."

A third of his army collected empty sacks, slung the straps of waterskins over their shoulders, and strolled from their campsites. Once through the gates of the Punic stronghold, they spread out on well-worn trails, heading for farms and orchards where they could collect food.

Chapter 21 – The Thirteenth Lictor

Almost as if a prelude to a festival, cookfires spewed the aroma of roasting meat into the air. Widely spaced pavilions with tables holding parchment and ink bottles sat beside the fires. Adjacent to the tents, officers in clusters talked. During their conversations, first one then another would look away and glance south along the empty road.

In the opposite direction, the stockade wall of the Legion camp stood tall behind the defensive trench. "Left, stomp, left stomp," came from inside the camp. Responding to the sound of marching feet, the sentries charged with guarding the gates, parted. First through the opening was a mounted Senior Tribune followed by two more staff officers. Close behind, Legionaries in three ranks marched from the camp.

"Do you think it'll work?" Pluto Manius asked.

At other groups of officers, his question was repeated in different forms.

"That, Tribune Manius, will depend on the success of this morning's operation," Pedar Zoltar suggested.

"However, if our ambushes failed," Alick Ignatius submitted, "sending twelve Centuries will do nothing."

"On the plain of Ager Falernus, the Punic General challenged us to come out of our forts and fight," Cornelius Scipio offered to his command staff. "Success of the ambushes aside, sending a Maniple of heavy infantrymen to stomp back and forth in front of Hannibal Barca will be a nice reversal."

When the last of the nine hundred and sixty Legionaries passed by, a momentarily silence fell over the campfires, tents, and clusters of officers.

"We didn't come out and fight, then," Pluto Manius mentioned, breaking the tranquility. "Why would the Punics surrender their advantage now?"

No one had a response. Down the road, a mixture of armored heavy infantrymen, light infantrymen, and auxiliary troops appeared. More came from the woods and joined those on the avenue heading to the camp.

"We'll soon know about the Master of Horse's tactic," Captain Ignatius stated.

Captain Zoltar smiled and projected, "From the bounty my archers are carrying, I'd guess some of the ambushes were successful."

"But if they don't make the Punics desperate enough to fight," Pluto commented, "it'll be for nothing."

"Not for nothing," Cornelius corrected. "Any victory over Hannibal, even from small traps, is good for morale. Both here and in Rome."

The clusters broke apart as officers went to gather and identify the returning units. Every man sent out the night before needed to be vouched for before he was allowed in the Legion camp. And before they entered, all the Centuries and Companies had to be accounted for to eliminate any Carthaginian spies. Hot food and beverages would soften the waiting period.

Far down the road, a single rider came, not from the woods, but from the distance. Wrapped in a dark gray robe, he and his horse walked slowly. Although the stallion displayed muscles capable of much more, as did the legs of the rider, they moved so the returning Legionaries and allied troops could get out of his way. Few of those returning from the operation paid attention to the man on the horse or the thick bundle tied to the back of his saddle.

Greeting each other and talking excitedly, everyone wanted a chance to tell their story about their ambush. One consensus came from the chatter. The morning's operations of stopping the Carthaginians from seizing food and disrupting the lives of local farmers were a success.

***

After days of having his scavengers attacked and the movement of his patrols restricted, Hannibal Barca tested General Marcus Minucius' resolve.

"There's movement on the hill between us and the Carthaginian camp," Hali mentioned to Jace.

Following his assistant's gaze, File Leader Kasia watched as shields of pikemen jogged around the hilltop until they ringed the summit.

"Stow your gear," Jace announced, "and fill your quivers."

"Why?" Marsyas asked. "I haven't had a chance to eat."

He had a pot of cold water suspended over a cookfire and a small sack of grain beside the fire ring.

"I've worked for Tribune Scipio long enough to know what grips his soul," Jace told the hungry archer. "And on that hill, bowman, is a sight to fire his passion."

"Do you think we're going up there?" Eachann inquired. "Maybe he hasn't seen them."

From the officers' tents, hobnailed boots pounding on the street drew their attention. They just caught a glimpse of Tribune Scipio's back as he sprinted around the corner, heading in the direction of the Battle Commander's complex.

"He's seen them," Marsyas remarked while removing the copper pot from the flames.

***

Marcus Minucius strutted from his compound. Following the General were a collection of Senators, forty Legion bodyguards, three priests, and thirteen Lictors in red coats. The scarlet attire symbolized their authority and duty to the Master of Horse. In the Capital they wore white, it was only outside of Rome the Lictors put on the red.

Marcus crossed the camp with the entourage in his wake. At the northern gate, he found nine hundred Thracian javelin men and four hundred Cretan archers. Cornelius Scipio stood at the front of the auxiliary formations.

"Tribune Scipio, I'm surprised to find you here," Minucius admitted. "I've spoken with Colonel Pantera about his issue with you. He's supposed to have stopped sending you, your archers, and skirmishers on dangerous missions."

Cornelius saluted then pointed over the stockade wall to the slope and the shields of the pikemen at the top.

"General Minucius, I've faced Hannibal Barca three times," Cornelius informed the Master of Horse. "In all three battles, I didn't have the fighters or the authority to control the situation. Now I command some of the best light infantry in the world. With your permission sir, we'll remove the Punic scum from the heights."

"I was going to take sixteen Centuries of Veles up there," Minucius said. "But I'll cut that down and use the Legion light infantry as a reserve force. Tribune Scipio, the field of combat is yours."

Cornelius saluted again, then spun to face Captain Zoltar, Centurion Restrictus, and Captain Ignatius.

"I want two ranks of shields out front of the archers," he directed in a loud, booming voice. "Protect the Cretans while they soften the pikemen up with arrows. Then Thracians, take their heads."

Zoltar, Restrictus, and Ignatius replied but their response when unheard. Cheering from the auxiliary Companies drowned out the voices of their officers.

"Open the gates," Marcus Minucius ordered when the shouting ended.

226

After his head Lictor unwrapped a large fasces to show the power of the Republic, the General and his staff marched through the opening in a ceremonial display. With the need for the records to show that the Master of Horse led the assault, Minucius and his group stepped aside.

"Forward," Cornelius ordered.

He marched from the Legion camp with his Cretans and Thracians.

"Who are the guys in the red?" Narkis asked as they passed the General's party. "They're dressed pretty."

"I've seen them around the Dictator's and Master of Horse's compounds before," Hali replied. "Some kind of Priests, I'd guess."

Jace hadn't really looked at the men in the scarlet coats. Then, he did, taking particular note of the one holding the large double-bladed ax with the handle wrapped in birch branches and bound in red leather strips.

"Those are Republic enforcers called Lictors. I saw them when I was in Rome," he told the File. "A Dictator has twenty-four assigned to him."

"How many Lictors does a Master of Horse get?" Egidio questioned.

"A Consul gets twelve," Jace recalled. "I imagine a Master of Horse will also have twelve."

"So why does General Minucius have thirteen Lictors?" Egidio asked.

Before Jace could admit his ignorance on the subject, Lieutenants Gergely and Inigo issued commands.

"File Leaders form your ranks," they instruct as the archers spread across the slope. A few steps later and higher on the hill, the two officers started the Cretan war chant. "One. Select a shaft…"

***

"And-a-six, release…"

The Carthaginian pikemen held formation, for the most part. But arrows slamming into their light shields jerked the barriers around allowing an occasional arrow to slip through.

Jace and the other File Leaders walked a circuit from the back where they inspected the supply of arrows. Then along the shuffling file of archers, giving words of encouragement, and up to the front where the war bows sang.

"The tall one," Jace pointed uphill at a huge pikeman.

Archer Gyes, second from the front, nodded his understanding.

Jace turned to the File beside his and addressed their second archer. "The tall pikeman."

After a signal of understanding, Jace faced to the front with his arms by his side.

"…and-a-nine, step-up…"

Jace allowed the archer from the adjacent file to come off the line and go to the back before he moved forward with Gyes and the other File's bowmen. He addressed Gyes, "You take the big man's shield." Then turning to the other archer, he instructed. "And you take his soul."

"One. Select a shaft, and-a-two, Notch arrow. And-a-three, Pick target. And-a-four, Draw. And-a-five, Release…"

Gyes' arrow came off the bow a little high. The other bowman's shaft zipped up the slope as if suspended on a string. The high shaft slammed into the upper corner of the big pikeman's shield. Despite his enormous strength, the impact hammered the top back and lifted the bottom, exposing the pikeman's belly to the second arrow.

Until he bristled with shafts and toppled over dead, the two archers used the huge pikeman as their private targets.

Jace hurried to the rear and waited to congratulate both bowmen on their fine archery.

"…and-a-nine, step-up…"

A roar from the Thracians announced the next phase of the assault. Rushing between the Files of the archers' formation, they screamed a bowel loosening war cry while running uphill.

"Gyes. Nicely done," Jace said handing a waterskin to his bowman. Turning to face the rear of the other File, he bowed in respect as he offered a second waterskin to that archer. "Nicely…"

The sharp burning in Jace's upper back came as a shock. The source of the pain, as he had been taught, was less important than the cause. Training took over, and he gripped his war hatchet high on the handle. Pulling it free, Jace twisted at the knees, lowering his stance, and savagely swung around.

The long handle parried an arm and a hand holding a knife. Then the razor-sharp edge of the hatchet easily parted the flesh on the neck of Jace's attacker. With little drag, the weapon opened the man's throat. Tendons, muscles, and cartilage parted, creating a gaping second mouth. Bile and blood bubbled up and spilled down the man's chest.

Gyes kicked the dying assailant. The body collapsed and fell to the ground.

"Who is that?" Jace asked while trying to feel the wound between his shoulder blades.

"Let me see, File Leader," the other bowmen offered while turning Jace around. "It's a good thing you were humble and bowed to my great ability with the war bow. Or the knife would have taken your spine."

"Humility is a virtue," Jace advised. "And a lifesaving one, it seems."

"He's a stout one. Look at the muscles in his legs. Ah, he's only got a few coins and a non-descript dagger," Gyes said as he searched the body. "But nothing else. You want the coins or the dagger, File Leader."

"Give one to the great archer, here," Jace said turning down the profit. "I'm going to see how the battle progresses."

He jogged to the front of his File in time to see the Thracians roar through the last of the pikemen. Staged for the records, General Minucius and his staff charged up the hill.

"File Leader Kasia, you're bleeding," Eachann pointed out.

"It's just a scratch," Jace guessed.

"You know," Egidio ventured, "I was wrong."

"That's not news," Narkis teased. "You're wrong about a lot of things. But what specifically?"

230

"About the Lictors," Egidio explained. "I thought there were thirteen. But I just counted, and there are only twelve of them."

"What's one more Republic enforcer, more or less," Hali commented. "We need to get to the top and see if the Thracians need our help."

"Let's move," Jace announced.

The Cretan Files raced to the top to find most of the pikemen dead and the rest running down the backside of the hill.

"Send to the marching camp," the Master of Horse demanded. "Hannibal wanted my attention. Well, he has it. We'll build a fortification here and every day, I'll watch him eat breakfast."

"General. I've got wounded," Cornelius informed the Master of Horse. "Permission to withdraw, sir?"

"Granted and thank you. Tribune Scipio," Marcus Minucius replied.

While they had come up the slope in tight formations, the Cretans and Thracians strolled downhill in a loose manner, taking their wounded with them.

***

With the second most powerful man in the Republic in residence, information needed to travel between the Legions and Rome. To facilitate the transportation of the messages, Legion couriers rode into and out of the marching camp several times a day.

The afternoon of the assault, a messenger galloped from the gates with Marcus Minucius' report to the Senate on the

231

battle for the hilltop. A mile from the stockade wall, the messenger met another mounted courier racing towards the camp. They exchanged waves of acknowledgement but neither slowed.

The courier galloped through the gates of the camp but didn't ride to the compound of the Master of Horse. Instead, he asked for and was directed to the camp of the Cretan Archers.

"This is an odd delivery, sir," the courier said as he handed a letter to Cornelius. "From a Greek named Hektor's description, I wouldn't have known you were a staff officer."

Tribune Scipio didn't engage in a conversation. He handed a few coins to the courier and took the letter to his tent.

Commander, I hope this letter finds you in good health.

If you recall the subject of your last visit with me.

At first Cornelius was confused by the lack of his rank and the obscure wording. Then, he remembered who employed a Greek name Hektor.

He is in bad health and requires a change of scenery.

Please see to his transportation as soon as you can.

It's very important for his wellbeing.

All the best, Hektor

Was the letter about the health of Alerio Sisera? If so, why would Hektor ask him to transport the Senator. Then he recalled the main topic of their discussion, Jace Kasia.

Cornelius held the short letter over a brazier until the parchment caught fire. Then with it burning, he walked out of his tent. Once the letter was no more than a small corner, he dropped it into the dirt and went to find Jace.

***

The next morning, Jace and his File had Legion orders to report to the garrison at Rimini as couriers and scouts.

"I didn't think the Legion used foot messengers," Marsyas remarked as he settled his long pack on the wagon bed and untied the reins.

"What are you worried about?" Hali asked. "You're being paid, and we're out of the war with Hannibal Barca."

"Just when the Republic is winning," Eachann complained. "Just when…"

"Be quiet," Egidio scolded. "Getting paid for not fighting and dying is the best job."

Away from the File and the wagon, Cornelius gripped wrists with Jace.

"When I get to Rome, I'll ask Senator Sisera for more specifics," he told the archer. "But the bandage on your back is a plain enough warning, even if Sisera's message was less than clear."

"A stone tossed in a pond splashes in all directions," Jace advised. "You be careful not to get wet from whatever has me targeted."

When Captain Pedar Zoltar, Lieutenants Ladon Stavros, and Acis Gergely arrived to see them off, the archer and the nobleman released grips and parted ways.

Act 8

Chapter 22 – Engagement Arrangements

Cornelius Scipio located a still corner. With the move, he avoided the inadvertent shoulder brushes from most people and the sharp elbows from the self-important visitors. Yet, being out of the flow of people did nothing to block the chatter of the crowd.

To their credit, the servants in Villa Paullus kept the wine and snack stations in the public rooms replenished. Timing his passage, Cornelius ducked into the press of bodies and emerged next to a refreshment table. He poured a glass, skipped the honey cakes, and escaped the villa through a door to the garden.

"I tell you, if the Senate had made me co-dictator," a youth declared, "I would have marched my Legions right into Hannibal's camp and slapped the mucus out of the Punic upstart's nose."

A group of young men puffed up their chests and made grunts of agreement.

"I would sit Fabius down in his tent," another boasted, "and tell the frightened old man that I was taking over."

More coos from the inexperienced boys greeted his statement.

The hairs on Cornelius' neck bristled. He reminded himself that they were unbloodied youths. He was half turned to go back in and face the mob, when a third thumped his chest.

"What we need is to push aside the old men," he announced, "and let youth take the field of battle. We'd show them how to stop the invasion."

Beads of sweat appeared on Cornelius' forehead and the vino in the glass sloshed over the rim from the shaking if his hand.

Spinning to face the youths, he shouted, "You weren't there. Not at Lake Trasimene, the Ager Falernus plain, or at Geronium."

The force of his voice, developed from months of drilling Cretans and Thracians, rocked the youths. And, as the volume carried, it pummeled the ears of other guests strolling in the garden. Turning, they faced young Tribune Scipio, frowned, and many commented on his rudeness. Ignoring them, Cornelius advanced on the youths.

"That old man you referred to as frightened, dressed and marched two full Legions forward in less time than it takes you to bathe," Cornelius spit out. "And he personally, at his own peril, led them to save Master of Horse Minucius. You stupid boys weren't in the battle. General Minucius had marched us into an ambush by the Punic General. Did Marcus Minucius have to resign the Co-dictatorship after the battle and step back into the role of Master of Horse? No. The Senate awarded him the tile for his aggression. He could have clung to it. But General Minucius realized that Dictator Fabius understood one thing. The hills of Geronium were not ideal for his Legionaries or his cavalry. And lastly,

Marcus Minucius accepted the fact that there can only be one commander in charge, and it must be the Dictator of Rome."

Slightly out of breath, Cornelius hesitated. Prepared to challenge the first youth to speak, the battle-hardened staff officer stood with fire in his eyes.

"A very impassioned rendition of the battle," a voice offered as a muscular arm dropped over Cornelius' shoulders. He started to shake off the restraining arm when the familiarity of the voice stopped him. "Truthfully, it made for a livelier oratory than simply reading the official reports."

Cornelius ducked out from under the arm and looked at the eyebrows of Appius Pulcher. A year ago, the young Scipio had to look up at the officer who had been his father's First Centurion and, afterward, Cornelius' mentor. Now, he was taller than the man.

"Tribune Pulcher," Cornelius said in greeting before stopping and ogling the insignia of a senior staff officer. "Senior Tribune, I apologize."

"Nothing to be sorry for," Appius Pulcher responded as he took Cornelius' elbow and walked him away from the youths. "You were pretty hard on those sons of Rome."

"They were making ridiculous statements," Cornelius said, defending his outburst. "Stupid boys."

Appius laughed.

"What's so funny, sir?" Cornelius inquired.

"Those boys, as you call them," Senior Tribune Pulcher explained, "are the same age as you."

***

In the great room, with the doors opened to the garden for the overflow, Aemilius Paullus strolled to a desk. For the ceremony, servants had moved the desk from his office earlier in the day. The Senator ran his hands fondly over the oak top as people faced him.

"Friends and colleagues," he began. The voice of their host ended the last of the individual conversations. "Today is a special day for any father. My sweet daughter, and my name's sake, Aemilia, is about to become engaged."

To the applause of the crowd, he waved two stacks of parchment in the air.

"We've hammered out the dowry and the specifics of property despite the distance," Paullus stated. He spread the documents on the desktop and picked up an ink pen. "As I sign these agreements, I do more than permit my daughter to marry. I gain a son. Aemilia. Cornelius. Come forward and witness the signatures of your future fathers-in-law."

At the bottom of the parchments, the heads of the families had signed in bold strokes. Clearly and legally, the commitment of Proconsul Publius Scipio in Iberia, and Senator Aemilius Paullus in Rome were on display.

"Now, everyone come froward, witness the documents," Paullus urged, "and give your blessings to the couple."

Cornelius and Aemilia withstood words of praise, the invocation of Gods and Goddesses, diatribes about marriage, and overly long hugs from matrons. Near the end of the ceremony, as servants removed the desk, the youths from the garden filed up.

"We're sorry, Tribune Scipio," one said. "Had we known you were close by, we would have asked you about being in battle."

"In battles," another corrected. "Cornelius Scipio has been in more battles than anyone in Rome."

Aemilia was hustled away by a cluster of giggling girls, leaving Cornelius alone with the young men.

"I don't think that's right," he pleaded. "I'm sure there are Legionaries who survived the…"

Very few men had lived through the massacre on the banks of Lake Trasimene. And none of them had been at Geronium. Before the weight of the circumstances became too much for the young officer, Appius Pulcher pushed through the line of boys. He dropped a hand on Cornelius' shoulder.

"You're not wrong," he informed the youths. "But right now, Scipio, is not available to spin war stories for you. He is needed for a consultation with me and Battle Commander Lucan."

They left the youths behind. And while they walked from the room, Cornelius asked, "Who is Colonel Lucan?"

"Virgil Lucan," Appius replied. "He and your future father-in-law are waiting in the Senator's study."

The pair approached a household guard, standing at a hallway.

"Senior Tribune," the guard acknowledged Appius.

He stepped back and opened a door, then the sentry resumed his position blocking the hall.

"What's he guarding?" Cornelius asked.

He had been to the Paullus villa, and the Senators study many times. But never had there been a sentry posted in the hallway.

"A secret," Appius answered as they entered the office.

**

Back in its original location, the desktop held no documents. However, a Senior Tribune's helmet rested on the oak surface.

"Appius. Cornelius. Come in and have a seat," Aemilius Paullus invited. He indicated a man standing across the room. "This is Virgil Lucan. He's just arrived from Iberia."

"You've seen my father?" Cornelius asked.

"Your father and uncle send their regards," Lucan told him.

"Virgil has spent the last half a year as Battle Commander for Scipio Legion North," Paullus said. "Any idea why he's in Rome?"

"My father is coming home?"

"I'm afraid not," Paullus replied. "Virgil Lucan is an answer to my question about how to defeat Hannibal Barca. Or, maybe I should say, Publius Scipio's reply to my question about how to deal with the Punic General."

Virgil Lucan began pacing, his eyes shifting as if recalling memories.

"In Iberia, we found a wedge driven through the heart of the Carthaginian forces works best," Lucan explained. "Take out their center, and their command becomes disjointed. Then the Punic mercenaries stumble around falling on our blades. I'm here to train a new Legion to defeat Hannibal."

Aemilius Paullus and Appius Pulcher held their faces as if they were wise old men and had just heard a truth. Both gave slight nods to show they agreed with the concept.

"Hannibal has never beaten us in the center," Cornelius pointed out. "He's always come at us from outside in surprising numbers. No offense to your experience, Colonel. But I've been against him in five separate instances. We've never lost the middle until he collapsed our flanks."

"I'm sure as a junior officer, and a commander of auxiliary forces, you've had experience with small segments of the battles," Lucan offered. "While I've had the benefit of a wider overview of Carthaginian tactics as a Battle Commander."

"As you will, sir," Cornelius said folding his argument. "Senator Paullus, if you'll excuse me, I need to get back to my command."

He stood and politely waited to be dismissed.

"You'll not be returning to Minucius Legion North and your barbarian playmates," Paullus advised.

"I'm going to Iberia, sir?"

"No, you're staying here as part of Paullus Legion West," Aemilius Paullus instructed.

"But Senators don't get Legions, sir," Cornelius remarked. "And you haven't been a Consul so you can't be elected a Proconsul or a Praetor."

"Haven't been a Consul," Paullus repeated then added, "yet. On March Fifteenth, I will be elected a Consul of the Republic. Before then however, I'm building my Consul Legions. And training them to defeat Hannibal."

"Which flank will I be commanding, Senator?"

"You're going to be my son-in-law," Aemilius Paullus reminded him. "Colonel Lucan."

Virgil Lucan approached the desk, picked up the senior staff officer's helmet, and faced Cornelius.

"You should expect obedience from your Legionaries and their officers," the Battle Commander intoned. "As I expect obedience from my staff officers. Can you follow my orders without delay?"

"Yes, sir."

"With that provision, Cornelius Scipio, take this helmet and wear it with pride as the left side Senior Tribune of Paullus Legion West."

"I've sworn to see Hannibal defeated," Cornelius said while taking the helmet from Colonel Lucan. "With this position, I come one step closer."

The helmet, although hefty, didn't weight as heavily as the responsibility. When they assembled and trained the Legion, he would have the lives of twenty-two hundred men in his young hands. Every Legion heavy and light infantryman, all the left side auxiliary forces, plus NCOs, and their officers would look to him for directions.

"There is one condition," Aemilius Paullus informed him. "You can't tell anybody until after the election."

"That's the secret?" Cornelius asked Appius Pulcher.

"That is the secret," his right-side counterpart confirmed.

***

After spending the afternoon with Aemilia greeting well-wishers, Cornelius said goodbye. He was almost to the stables when he noted Hektor Nicanor stepping away from a corral.

"Master Scipio, the Senator would like to see you?" the Greek informed him.

"Ever since I got back from Geronium, I've sent notes requesting an audience. A few to his office in the Senate and more to Villa Sisera," Cornelius complained. "And I received no reply. Now you show up and I'm supposed to follow you?"

"Follow me? No sir, I'm not comfortable there," Hektor replied. "But if you want to speak with Senator Sisera, he will be at the Temple of Nenia until just before sundown."

The Greek went behind the building and reappeared driving a donkey cart.

"Sundown," he repeated as the donkey passed Cornelius.

***

Located on the outskirts of Rome, the temple dedicated to the Goddess of Death lacked the grandeur of other temples. By the nature of their duties, the Priests who sang to the dying failed to attract big donors to pay for stately columns.

"Wealthy patrons seek out and pay for the blessings of useful deities," Alerio Sisera suggested when Cornelius approached him. Dim and solemn, the temple seemed to offer no hope for the living. "The only time she is called upon is when the elderly, injured, or the infirmed are in pain. Then people donate for a temple choir to sing for the Goddess. Not a happy experience, I'll grant you."

"You have to admit Senator, it's a sad place," Cornelius said while looking at the multi columns of the interior. Coming from the rear of the temple, a choir chanted, calling for Nenia Dea. "And really, who wants to voluntarily deal with death?"

"You do, Senior Tribune Scipio," Alerio Sisera remarked. Scipio did a head twist of surprise which brought a smile to the Senator's lips. "Don't look so shocked. I was a Legionary. A distributor of death, and I was good at it. You've just begun to honor the Goddess."

"I, I…How did you know about the position?" Cornelius stammered.

He missed the ramification of being identified as a vessel for the Goddess of Death.

"Your future father-in-law is hinting at bribes for votes," Alerio responded. "It makes sense he'd put his son-in-law in a staff job to insure his future."

"I'd like to keep Senator Paullus out of this," Cornelius requested. "Who tried to murder Jace Romiliia?"

"Twenty years ago, the Republic made a treaty with the Hirpini tribe," Senator Sisera reported. "It locked the land up so tribe members could not sell their land to a Latin or anyone not a Hirpini."

"Jace's mother was Hirpini."

"That's right and she was a Princess," Alerio clarified. "The last of her bloodline. And the sole owner of a fertile valley south of Benevento."

"So what? As you said, sir, the land is blocked from sale," Cornelius concluded.

"If the owner is absent, but the land is perpetually owned by the ghosts of royalty, what happens to the land?"

"I imagine it sits idle," Cornelius said. Then he raised his eyes and commented. "Unless adjacent farmers use the land to grow crops. It's easily done by paying community leaders in the area to look the other way."

"And what do you suppose the yield is from good bottom land?"

"It would be like harvesting gold," Cornelius responded by tapping his mouth with his fingers as he thought. "The person who tried to kill Jace is connected to the land near his mother's property."

"Persons, Senior Tribune, we're talking several powerful men," Sisera told him. "Remember, there is also the estate at Genoa. The land scam, the criminal charges, and the trial took more than two men to orchestrate."

"And we don't know who they are?"

"My inquiries touched a nerve, and an informant warned us about the attempt on Jace," Alerio told him. "Our problem is we don't know who actually ordered the assassination. Fortunately for us, he kept it in house and used a Lictor."

"I don't understand. Did they have another option?"

"Hopefully, you'll never learn the answer to that question," Senator Sisera told him. "Keep Jace hidden until we know more."

"Can I escort you to your horse, Senator?" Cornelius inquired.

"No. You go ahead," Alerio said refusing the offer. "I'm going to stay and listen to the chanting. There's one part of the song I could never get right."

Chapter 23 – Traces of Larceny

After attending the fourth feast to celebrate the Ides of March, Cornelius returned to the Scipio Villa. Restless despite the long day, he walked into his father's study and smiled. Memories flooded his mind. He could almost hear his father's voice describing the tactics of old battles and see the man's arms sweeping back and forth over a parchment map as he described the fighting. Carried by the recollections, young Scipio crossed to a bank of shelves. For a moment, he touched an old map with the intention of recalling a lecture. But his hand drifted and landed on the Scipio/Paullus engagement agreement.

On his father's desk, he unrolled the parchment and touched his father's signature out of respect. Then he read the agreement. As a plan for a young couple's future, it read just as it was, a legal contract. Once through the promises, he skimmed the property Aemilia would bring to the marriage. Not only was his betrothed intelligent and from a noble household, but she came with farms, orchards, and stone quarries. All of it would add to the substantial holdings of the Scipio family.

He put his fingers on an edge and began to roll the document when a page flipped, and his eyes caught the word inheritance. On a separate sheet, almost scribbled as if to hide them, was a list of properties that Aemilia and her husband would receive in the event of Aemilius Paullus' death.

In the center of the catalogued properties, a description brought him to a stop.

One quarter of the farm located five miles southwest

from the city of Benevento and bordered two miles

to the east by uncultivated lands of the Hirpini Tribe.

And to the south by...

Why would four men own one medium sized farm? Surely, after so many years, one of the original owners would have bought out the shares of the others. It could mean nothing. Cornelius hoped it was while writing a message to Senator Alerio Sisera, noting the odd ownership of the farm.

In the morning before mounting his horse, he passed the message to a servant with instructions to deliver it to the Sisera Villa. Then Senior Tribune Cornelius Scipio rode from his father's estate. In a day, he would join up with the Legions of the newly elected Consul, Aemilius Paullus.

***

Almost three hundred miles northeast of Rome, Jace Kasia soaked his feet in the Adriatic Sea. A voice hailed him from the direction of the port of Rimini.

"File Leader Kasia," Hali Adras shouted, "we're leaving."

Jace lifted his feet from the salt water and picked up his bow case and sandals. Then he hobbled to the assistant File Leader.

"I don't know what the Company or Lieutenant Gergely are doing," he said with a smile, "but I bet it's not bathing their feet in the sea."

"You can play innocent all you want Jace," Hali scolded. "But you and I know if you didn't play head scout for most of the Legion patrols, your feet wouldn't need soaking."

"I like the salt water," Jace protested.

"We'll be back in a week," Hali warned him. "Then we'll talk about your inability to delegate authority."

Hali Adras walked to where three archers waited. They shouldered their long packs, waved at Jace, then jogged into the Legion post.

"Be safe," Jace offered.

He was standing in the same spot when Hali and the archers marched from the fort. Moments later, eighty heavy infantrymen and a mounted Centurion emerged and followed his bowmen up the road.

"Be safe," Jace repeated as the patrol left the outskirts of the harbor city.

That night, the remaining Cretan Archers at Rimini ate together before turning in. The next day, Jace ordered them to the range outside the Legion fort.

"Let's have a contest," he declared. "Distance shooting. Eachann, walk off fifty paces."

At the starting distance, none of the twelve bowmen would miss. And there would be a lot of ribbing and questioning of manhood and skill should an arrow not strike the center of the target.

After a round, they moved the shooting line back another hundred feet. A crowd of Legionaries gathered to watch the competition. Laughter greeted one bad release.

"What was that, Archer Egidio?" Jace asked when the bowman's arrow tumbled half the distance to the target before flopping to the ground like a wounded bird.

"Jace, my bowstring broke," he replied. "I didn't notice the frayed section."

"In combat, that error will earn your family a bonus," Jace told him. "And get you a small piece of burial ground in the Republic."

"File Leader Kasia," Eachann pointed out, "we're not in the Republic. Rimini is in Cisalpine Gaul. It's home to Gallic tribes. The western end, where we are belongs to the…"

A shout from a guard tower ended the lecture.

"Ready squad, we have wounded coming in," a sentry called down from the platform.

Jace sprinted back until he could see around the corner of the walls. He watched ten Legionaries jog from the fort in response to the alert.

In the distance, the Centurion of Hali's patrol wobbled on his horse almost falling off. Behind him, only about forty of the original eighty infantrymen limped along the road. Jace raced to the wounded officer.

"Where are my archers?" he demanded.

"Keep a civil tongue and speak to me with respect, Cretan traitor," the Centurion warned, "or I'll cut it out."

"I'm sorry, sir," Jace apologized. "I don't see my archers. What happened?"

"A war party of the Boii," the officer answered, "hundreds strong, were waiting for us at dawn. Your scouts had already gone ahead. I didn't see them later. So, they either ran away, joined the tribe, or are still out there hiding."

"You forgot the most obvious," Jace said. "They're dead."

The post's Senior Centurion rode up.

"Boii tribe," he guessed, before asking. "Are they gathering to attack the city?"

"I don't think so," the patrol's Centurion replied. "After jumping us, the warriors moved south."

"Probably on their way to join Hannibal," the Legion's top combat officer ventured.

Jace didn't hear the last part as he was racing for his File.

"We have four missing archers," he exclaimed. "We're going out to locate them. Alive or dead, we will bring our brothers back."

***

The government building buzzed with excitement. As a matter of fact, most of Rome pulsed with anticipation. Newly elected Consuls Aemilius Paullus and Gaius Varro had already appointed Atilius Regulus and Servillius Geminus, last years Consuls, as Proconsuls of Legions.

"We will field eight Legions with auxiliary troops," Aemilius proclaimed. He looked around the chamber, collecting nods of support, before continuing. "With a force

249

of that size, we will sweep Hannibal Barca into the sea. But, to the north, the Boii tribe have broken treaties and may have sent warriors to Hannibal Barca. This outrage must be addressed. To accomplish the task, I am calling Lucius Albinus out of retirement. I ask for a vote to elect Lucius as a third Proconsul of Legions."

Grumbling came from the Senators. Praetors and Proconsuls were normally assigned to regions as governors with only Proconsuls authorized to mobilize a Legion for emergencies. To have three former Consuls commanding pairs of marching Legions stunk of Generalship. Ever fearful of a revolt by too strong a commander, a few balked at the idea. But on the final tally, the Senate of Rome elected Albinus as the commander of two Legions.

"If there's no other business," Consul Paullus announced, "I will end…"

"Consul, I have a small proclamation," Alerio Sisera said from his seat.

"The chamber recognizes Senator Sisera. Please state your issue."

"Thank you, Consul," Alerio answered while pushing slowly to his feet. "Please excuse the delay. My knees suffered much abuse when I was with the Legions."

Most Senators had served a year or two with the army of Rome. It made for a good public image to be seen as an armed defender of the Republic. But they served as staff officers with few actually seeing combat. Senator Sisera was the rare exception. He had been an infantryman, NCO, Centurion, Tribune, and a Battle Commander before going into politics.

"I think in light of your past service to Rome," Paullus assured him, "we will be patient."

"Thank you, Consul," Alerio replied while straightening his back and allowing a slight moan to escape his lips. Then he glanced around as if confused before stating. "Now, where was I?"

"You had a small proclamation," Aemilius Paullus reminded the senior Senator.

Although the Consul promised patience, it was clear, his was fast running out.

"That's right. There's a rumor going around that I felt needed to be addressed. It...," Alerio stopped talking and glanced around.

"Senator Sierra, you were saying?" Paullus coached when the old Senator paused for too long.

"Yes, yes. A few years ago. When you reach my age, the years tend to bleed together," Alerio Sisera remarked. "The Senate convicted Lucius Romiliia of treason. The state confiscated his land, and he and his family were exiled. Now, I hear a rumor that his son has returned to the Republic."

A coughing fit took the Senator's breath. He covered his mouth with an arm and bent forward to clear his throat. His assistant Hektor Nicanor moved to his side with a glass of water.

"Any reactions to my announcement?" he whispered to Hektor.

"The three you suspected flinched at the mention of the boy," the Greek told him.

"Good. I have their attention," Alerio said. "Now, let's see if we can save Jace's life."

He stood, gulped a mouthful of water, and handed the glass to Hektor.

"Again, I apologize for holding up the Senate," Alerio stated. "When you're my age, you have bad days and not so good ones."

Chuckles rippled through the chamber. Some responding to the joke and others because they understood the aches and pains of aging.

"I propose we stop any petition for citizenship by the son of Lucius Romiliia before it gets started," Alerio informed the Senate. "I request a vote to preemptively deny Roman citizenship to Lucius Jace Romiliia."

In a rare unanimous vote, the Senate of Rome decreed that Jace Romiliia was not a citizen of Rome. Senator Sisera sat as if exhausted.

"Do you think it's enough, Senator?" Hektor asked.

"Without the promise of citizenship, Jace is no longer a threat to the conspirators. I think it's enough for them to call off any more assassination attempts," Alerio replied. All hints of reduced capacity from aging vanished as he spoke. "And no one thinks he can claim his Hirpini heritage. He'd need to be a chief of the tribe first."

"Then, we're done with the affair," Hektor presumed.

"Oh, there is one more thing," Senator Sisera told his assistant. "Jace needs to get an anonymous letter with the names of the conspirators."

***

Two weeks later, Proconsul Lucius Albinus arrived at Rimini. Armed with two Legions and a decree from the Senate of Rome, the General planned to march north and punish the Boii tribe. But first, he wanted to enjoy the social activities of the wealthy port city.

Couriers hauling hundreds of letters accompanied the General. Most were for shipping agents, merchants, transport captains, and sailors. As they were distributed, one letter, simply addressed to Cretan Archer at Rimini, landed on Jace's bunk.

After removing the twine, he spread the small piece of parchment across his knees and read.

Lucius Jace Kasia Otacilia Romiliia

We trust this missive finds you in good health. For our safety, we must remain unnamed. And for yours, you are advised to keep the contents herein confidential. Do as you will in the future but resist any rash actions at the present. Your father was wrongly convicted by a gang of greedy and unscrupulous men. Despite their crude actions, they have advanced to powerful positions. Proceed with caution when dealing with Consul Aemilius Paullus, Proconsul Servillius Geminus, and Proconsul Lucius Albinus. The fourth conspirator is deceased. We will not sully the name of the dead. Again, be wary.

Jace rolled the letter before burning the parchment. Then he fell back on his blanket and dreamed of revenge.

Chapter 24 – That's All I Ask

A few thousand marching men, divided into two Legions under the command of one General, created a logistical nightmare. The army of the Republic was forty thousand men strong, and under the command of four Generals when it left Rome. A troop movement of that magnitude could have been a disaster, except the Senate had built supply depots around the Republic. One of the largest occupied a small but defendable hilltop near the town of Cannae.

Located three quarters of a mile from the Ofanto river, the garrison had access to fresh water. Although only sixteen feet above the plain, the elevation offered an advantage for the protectors of the stockpiles. And being eight miles west of the Gulf of Manfredonia, the site was too far inland for pirates. Yet, close enough to the port city of Barlett to provide reinforcements should a band of renegades dare to attack the depot.

For years, the geography and two Centuries of heavy infantrymen from the Legion of the Eastern region kept the supplies secure. However, on a morning in late summer in the year of Consuls Paullus and Varro, they were not enough.

"Centurion, we have riders coming from the west," a Legionary called down. "Hold on, sir…"

The officer had half risen from his desk in response to the young infantrymen's alert. Settling back at the 'hold on' remark, he hoped the Optio would arrive and clarify the definition of riders.

"Squadrons of riders, sir, coming down the river," the guard said after a few moments.

"Can you identify their Legion?" the Centurion asked. "Eastern or another?"

"No, sir. They aren't Legion," the guard shouted from the wall of the citadel. "Sir, you need to call the alarm."

Hearing the fear in the young man's voice, the officer ran from his office, raced up a set of stairs, and quickly reached the top of the wall.

"Where?" he demanded.

The Legionary lifted an arm and pointed upstream. From the bank of the Ofanto river and stretching to a line of hills, Carthaginian horsemen filled the plain.

"Gear up. Man, the walls," the Legion officer bellowed. "Optios, we have an enemy force coming at us. Get them armed and on the walls."

Often, life can hang in the measurements of efficiency. On one hand, an apprentice potter could finish a project in a much shorter span than a master metalworker. The Legionaries were proficient at infantry tactics and as solid with their steel as a metalworker was with hot iron.

The flaw rested in the dissimilar skills. Like the potter verses the metalworker, the Numidian light cavalry flowed around the citadel throwing javelins as other riders drove their horses directly up the slopes. And like the fluid movements of a potter at his wheel, the rider leaped from horseback to the top of the walls.

Unfortunately, as a metalworker must first fire up his forge, the Legionaries first needed to strap on their armor. In measuring their efficiencies, the Numidians stormed over the walls and raged through the supply depot murdering half-dressed Legionaries.

By noon, Hannibal Barca rode through the open gates and claimed the grain and the stored equipment for his Punic army.

Two months later, forty thousand Legionaries and auxiliary troops hiked over the Apennine mountains, heading for the plains around Cannae. Hannibal, rather than moving on from the supply depot, remained, waiting with his army for the Legions to arrive.

***

"It's not a good location," Cornelius Scipio noted to his riding companion.

With a quizzical look, Appius Pulcher shot the young Tribune an expression of amusement.

"What happened to the youth who asked questions," the right side Senior Tribune teased, "and listened for the answers."

"I don't need to ask if the landscape favors cavalry over infantry," Cornelius offered. "Look at the flat cleared areas. It's made for horses."

"We have cavalry," Appius reminded Cornelius.

"Legion horsemen are excellent utilitarian cavalry. But they aren't specialized like the Numidian light horsemen or Hannibal's Libyan heavy cavalry."

They rode in silence for a mile when a messenger galloped to them.

"Senior staff meeting at General Paullus' headquarters," the Junior Tribune instructed, "at dusk."

This time it was Cornelius offering the puzzled expression to Appius.

"It's one of the drawbacks to being the last Legion over the mountain," Appius informed Cornelius. "Those thirty-five thousand Legionaries ahead of us have already begun setting up their camps."

Cornelius glanced back, peering over the heads of the infantrymen trying to locate their baggage train.

He couldn't, but he did observe, "They'll eat and rest, while ours are still on the march."

"We have dried meat and barley cakes for nourishment while on the trail," Colonel Lucan stated. The Battle Commander rode up beside his Senior Tribunes and immediately, the Legion's First Century surrounded the three officers. After his bodyguards settled, he inquired. "Did you get the word?"

"About the meeting at Consul Paullus' headquarters, Colonel?" Appius asked.

"Not that. There was a skirmish between Velites from Varro Legion South and a unit of Punic light infantry," Lucan reported. "Varro's lads held their ground until some Punic cavalry showed up. The Legion skirmishers were pushed back. Then a couple of Centuries of Legionaries joined in the fun. The Carthaginians turned tail and ran for their lives."

"Excellent news, Colonel," Appius offered.

"I tell you I can't wait to get to the front, and get a victory for our Legionaries," Virgil Lucan declared. "But seeing as the enemy is running horsemen in behind their light infantry, I want to be sure our Velites don't get too far out."

"Let me draft the Cretan archers into our Legion, sir," Cornelius requested. "They'll keep the cavalry off our skirmishers."

"They're better off with the other auxiliary Companies," Lucan sneered. "I'll not have Greeks in amongst my Maniples."

During the months of training the Legion, Cornelius had offered suggestions and every time, he was slapped down by the Battle Commander. Biting his tongue, he let go of the idea of working with the archers or of helping Lucan.

***

With darkness closing in, the three senior officers for Paullus Legion West left during the construction of their marching camp. A mile away, they entered the stockade for Legion East and walked their mounts to General Paullus' compound.

"That's a big crowd," Appius Pulcher ventured.

Horses, handlers, and Junior Tribunes stood in clusters on either side of General Paullus' tents. Beyond the staff officers, three separate heavy infantry Centuries lined the camp road. Colonel Lucan's bodyguard fell in with the other veteran infantrymen.

"What's with the mob?" Cornelius asked one group of staff officers.

"All four Generals are here," a Junior Tribune answered. Mistaking young Scipio for a Maniple Tribune, he held up a wineskin and added. "Nobody goes in except Battle Commanders and his Senior Tribunes. You can stay with us if you want."

Cornelius ignored the invitations, but Colonel Lucan laughed.

"Maybe you should stay out here, Scipio," he said, "with the other young folks."

"I would, Colonel," Cornelius responded with an edge to his voice. "But I wouldn't want you to have to explain to my father-in-law where you left me."

"Good point," Lucan admitted. He slid off his mount. "Come on, let's go see who wants a fight and who would rather be at the baths in Rome."

***

Gaius Varro stomped back and forth. The Consul's nervous energy gained him one end of the huge tent, but not control of the rest.

"General Varro, you had command today and did yourself proud," Aemilius Paullus acknowledged. "However, let me remind you that tomorrow is my turn as commander of the expedition."

"Then you should press our advantage," Varro practically shouted the statement.

"Your advanced Centuries engaged forward units of the Punic army," Paullus corrected. "While noteworthy, the skirmish wasn't a decisive victory. Tomorrow, we'll move closer to Cannae and set up our camps where they can provide support to our Legions."

"Then the day after, I'll lead us to victory over the Carthaginians," Varro promised.

"I can't prevent you," Paullus admitted. "All I can do is advise caution."

To the timid sounding remark, Colonel Virgil Lucan sneered, "bath water."

Cornelius twitched, preparing to round on his Battle Commander. A hand grabbed the back of his arm, holding the young officer in check.

In a hiss, Appius Pulcher questioned, "Do you want to be in this fight? Or get dismissed and spend your days in the Consul's entourage?"

A sudden silence filled the tent. Appius and Cornelius found themselves the focus of four Generals, four Battle Commanders, and six Senior Tribunes.

"Do you have something to add, Senior Tribune Pulcher?" Paullus inquired.

Pulcher swallowed, opened his mouth, but no words came to his tongue.

"He was correcting me, sir," Cornelius blurted out. "I'm worried about the terrain. This is cavalry country. And our Legions are primarily infantry."

"And what did the Senior Tribune have to say on the matter?" General Paullus asked.

"He reminded me that, according to reports, our eleven thousand Legionaries outnumber the heavy infantry of the Punic army," Cornelius replied.

"And, right he is," General Varro exclaimed. "That is the specific reason to attack in the morning."

"No, Consul Varro," Paullus said using the political title to enforce his right as the other Consul. "It's a reason to wait. We need to give our infantrymen a few days to recover from the march."

***

Aemilius Paullus ordered two camps to be constructed. The smaller, he placed on the north side of the Ofanto. The larger camp went up on the opposite bank. Strategically located next to a shallow section suitable for fording the river, the stockade forts provided mutual support against either being overrun. Then, true to his words, the General declared a holiday.

In the smoke of hundreds of cookfires, Appius Pulcher and Cornelius Scipio gazed at the sky to the east.

"That's the lazy smoke of our enemy," Colonel Lucan informed them. "They shouldn't be comfortably eating their dinner. We should have used today to rout the mercenaries."

"Well-fed and rested Legionaries fight harder and longer, sir," Cornelius suggested.

"If I wanted words of wisdom from an inexperienced child, I would go to a temple," Lucan said disclosing his feelings towards Cornelius. "Just follow orders, Scipio. That's all I ask of you."

"Yes, sir," Cornelius assured him.

After Lucan had gone to speak with his Senior Centurion and First Tribune, Pulcher pointed to the thick smoke from the distant Carthaginian camp.

"Unless General Varro changes his mind, we'll be advancing tomorrow," Pulcher announced. "I'm going to check on the Maniples."

"As always, Senior Tribune, excellent advice."

"Now you're listening to me?" Appius Pulcher inquired.

"Someone in this Legion should be listening," Cornelius replied, frustration dripping from every word. "Because, despite the Colonel's confidence, victory is not assured."

"Nor is survival," Appius added. "Go check on your Legionaries."

They parted. One going to the right side and the other to the left. For the rest of the day, the Senior Tribunes would cross paths three times, one for every half Maniple.

***

Just as Consul Paullus enforced his will the day before, in the morning, Consul Varro got his way. Before dawn, Varro's staff officers raced to the other seven Legions ordering them to face the gathering Carthaginians.

"We'll punch through Hannibal's center. Like one of your Cretan arrows, Scipio," Lucan boasted. "Get your Maniples in line."

Then the Colonel splashed into the river and raced to the head of his Legion.

"Yes, sir," Appius and Cornelius said as they nudged their mounts into the water.

Coming up on the far side, Cornelius yelped.

"Something wrong?" Appius inquired.

"Our Legions are facing the rising sun," Cornelius replied while squinting.

"And the wind is blowing grit and sand into our eyes. So what?" Appius asked.

"I hope General Varro notices the irritants," Cornelius stated.

As if an anthill had been kicked, over eleven thousand Legionaries marched across the plain with the sun and wind in their eyes. From thirty-two columns, the eight Legions spread into their Maniples. Each of three lines extended nineteen thousand feet, stretching much wider than the front ranks of the Punic army.

"This might be good," Appius decided. "We've got them flanked by our formation. All we'll need to do is close around them. It'll be like hugging them to death."

A mile later, Virgil Lucan trotted up with his staff trailing behind.

"Why is the center of their line all armored in Legion equipment?" Cornelius asked.

"The Punic army certainly collected enough gear off our dead Legionaries at Trebia and Trasimene," Appius offered.

"And they just captured more equipment from the supply depot at Cannae," Lucan informed him. "It's not a difficult question to answer."

"Yes, sir, I understand that," Cornelius allowed. "But Hannibal has his own infantry. I've seen their armor and shields. Especially the Iberians and their African Corps. They're recognizable on any battlefield. But I don't see them."

"It's obvious, General Barca is replacing used armor, shields, and helmets with newer gear," Appius guessed.

"It doesn't matter how they're armored," Colonel Lucan declared. "Hannibal's heavy infantry is right there in front of us. As we've drilled them, our Maniples are going to push through. Then we'll curl our Legionaries around them and destroy the Carthaginians."

"And what if they get into our ranks?" Cornelius asked. "How do our Legionaries know who they're fighting?"

Before either Colonel Lucan or Appius Pulcher could form a response, the First Tribune galloped up.

"General Varro said we're spread too wide, sir," he reported. "He wants every Maniple to close in and bunch up. Form a spearhead and run it straight through the heart of the Punic army."

"You heard the order," Lucan told Cornelius and Appius, "pull them in and stack up the Maniples."

"But where are the rest of Hannibal's heavy infantry?" Cornelius demanded.

"Senior Tribune Scipio," Lucan scolded while facing his horse towards the center of his Legion, "either follow orders or resign. But stop with the incessant questioning."

The Colonel rode off with his staff to inspect the Legion.

"Watch yourself today," Appius Pulcher urged. "Do well and I'm sure the Battle Commander will back off."

"You've faced Hannibal on almost as many occasions as I have," Cornelius pleaded. "Do you think the sun, the wind, and his center resembling Legionaries are accidents? Hannibal is doing it again. Can't anybody see it?"

"I can see that you're getting worked up about normal events," Appius said. "Stop seeing everything as a trick. Go take charge of your half of the Legion."

Appius Pulcher saluted, then kicked his horse, and rode to his position on the right side of the Battle Commander.

Act 9

Chapter 25 – At Cannae to End Hannibal

Stacked up as if they were phalanxes, the Legionaries could only shuffle forward.

"They can't move laterally," Cornelius observed as he shouldered his way between individual infantrymen. The clash of shields, gladii, spears, and swords carried through the densely packed bodies. "Centurions, back them up. Put space between the Maniples."

"Senior Tribune, what are you doing down here?" a combat officer asked.

"We trained in triple lines," Cornelius told him after putting his head near the officer's ear. "This isn't the correct formation, and I can't get a horse through it. I need to see the front."

The Centurion grabbed three big infantrymen.

After placing them in a triangle formation with Cornelius in the center, the Centurion instructed, "Get the Senior Tribune to the fighting. Then get him back to his horse. Move it."

Arms heavy with muscles began parting armored Legionaries. Walking as if strolling through the Forum,

Cornelius moved from rank to rank. Just before the sounds of battle became deafening, his escorts stopped.

"Three ranks forward, sir," one told him.

A bleeding Legionary fell back and bounced off the chest of an infantrymen on the fourth rank. Then he collapsed between the legs of his comrades.

"Create space," Cornelius instructed while pushing men back from the three lines that were engaged. "Back off and open a space for the wounded."

"Thank you, sir," an Optio acknowledged. "Our Centurion was killed in the first assault. I've been trying to reestablish order."

Cornelius pushed the NCO in beside his escorts, and the four quickly created a patch of open ground. Unfortunately, the cleared zone soon filled with wounded Legionaries.

"Make it wider," Cornelius shouted.

In the press of combat, when men lose sight of their officers and NCOs, the highly skilled infantrymen can fall into a herd mentality. A disaster in the making if any of them turn and run. It could cause an unauthorized retreat. The surprise presence of Senior Tribune Scipio near the fighting gave the Legionaries a sense that someone was in command.

When he could see from one side of the Legion to the other, Cornelius instructed the Centurions and Optios, "Standby to rotate your Maniples."

Unlike the shifting of a second line forward to fight at the front, Senior Tribune Scipio's order called for a full rotation. In a few heartbeats, the Legion would replace the three ranks at the assault line.

"Standing by, Senior Tribune," the Legionaries roared back.

For the men on the attack lines, the raised voices, and the mention of the rank of a senior staff officer, gave them energy. With renewed vigor, they beat on the Punic shields.

"Front rank, advance, advance, step back, step back, step back," Cornelius bellowed. And his words were passed forward to the men on the attack line. They responded by smashing forward with their shields then stepping into the gap. Using the pace to add speed to the thrust of their gladii, they butchered the Carthaginian front rank. Then, they did it again. Before the enemy regained their composure, Scipio ordered. "Rotate your Maniples."

As the exhausted infantrymen folded backward, nine hundred and sixty rested Legionaries took their place. With the infusion of fresh arms, legs, and sharp steel into the front, the assault line rolled forward.

"We got that sorted out," Cornelius told his escorts. "Get me back...hold up."

The high pale colored horsehair comb on his helmet identified him as a Senior Tribune. In response, the Carthaginian line attempted to surge forward to kill him. Ignoring the danger, Cornelius pushed his head between two infantrymen on the third line.

"Who are you fighting?" he demanded.

"They're dressed like us but using long swords," one answered. "I'd say they're Gauls."

Cursing, Cornelius pulled back from the assault Maniple. He gathered his three bodyguards.

"Things aren't what they seem," he told them. "Get me to my horse, fast."

Just as they plowed a path to the front for him, the infantrymen parted the ranks to get the Senior Tribune to his mount. Once in the saddle, Cornelius kicked his horse and raced for the Battle Commander.

***

Virgil Lucan's head pivoted, looking for an advantage. But there was no place to go or anyway to maneuver his Legionaries in their tight ranks.

"Sir, up front," Cornelius told the Colonel, "we're fighting Gauls."

"So what?" Lucan shot back.

"There's no sign of Hannibal's Iberian heavy infantry or his African Corps," Cornelius warned. "The Punics have yet to commit their heavy infantry."

"If they're not up front," the Battle Commander asked, "where are they?"

A roar rolled from the forward lines and the entire Legion surged ahead. Cornelius pried his eyes from the shuffling infantrymen and scanned the Legion on the left flank.

His stomach tightened. All he could see were Numidian light cavalrymen dashing in, throwing spears, and riding away. There was no sign of any Legion cavalry.

"The other Legion has riders attacking their flanks," he reported to the Battle Commander.

"Soon it won't matter," Lucan boasted. "Their center is breaking. We've done it. Broken the back of Hannibal Barca. We came to Cannae to end Hannibal. And, we are doing it."

Since the first clash, the Legion had moved very little. But, as the Punic center gave way, the eight Legions came to a blunt point, and pressed deep into the middle of the Carthaginian lines.

"Colonel Lucan, we need to withdraw the Legion and create an escape route for survivors," Cornelius told the Battle Commander.

"And why would I do that?" Virgil Lucan asked.

"Because I've located Hannibal's African Corps," Cornelius informed him. Lifting an arm, he pointed at the far away flank. "They were waiting for us to get sucked into their center. But now, their infantry is moving forward to attack our flank."

"What?" Lucan questioned. He glanced to the left and back quickly. "I don't see any infantry. Besides, we're too deep in to retreat."

"Please Colonel, allow me to pull my Maniples and create an escape corridor," Cornelius begged.

"I don't care what you do," Lucan growled. "I'm sick of your whining. I'm going forward and claim my victory."

Virgil Lucan kicked his horse and raced for a gap in the Punic line. Close behind, his veteran bodyguards sprinted to keep up. Following the Colonel, his staff chased after him, including ten, Junior Tribunes.

In other Legions, the same number of young sons from noble households followed their Colonels and Generals into the dusty center of the battle. While most of the commanders rode forward, Cornelius galloped across the field to his veteran Centurions.

"Pull back and create a corridor," he instructed.

"We're running, Senior Tribune Scipio?" one asked.

"No. We're pulling back and regrouping," Cornelius lied. "Up front is too bunched up. I want to give our wounded a way out."

"Very good, sir," the combat officer acknowledged.

In a few moments, his half of the Third Maniple had formed a double fence line of shields.

Appius Pulcher rode up and noted the corridor.

"What are you thinking?" he asked.

Cornelius pointed to the left.

"The Legions have tripped another of Hannibal's traps," he said with sadness in his voice. "We need to begin an orderly retreat before our sides completely collapse."

"I'll handle defending the gathering area," Pulcher told him. "You keep the gate open for as long as you can. And Cornelius."

"Yes?"

"Don't wait too long before coming through yourself."

After delivering the advice, Senior Tribune Pulcher galloped down the row of shields.

***

Resembling a vessel after being sucked dry through a straw, the center orb of the battlefield lay dormant. Around the edges, combatants fought in groups of concentric circles. In each, Legionaries, standing back-to-back, fought off Carthaginian mercenaries. And as the battle went on, the rings of Punic warriors tightened as Republic infantrymen died. Cornelius scanned the plain searching for anyone who escaped from those circles of death.

"Sir, we need to move," a veteran Centurion suggested. "There's no one else coming."

Cornelius bristled and started to scold the combat officer for his defeatist attitude. Then, he examined the scene and realized, it was his hopes that endangered the survivors.

"Maybe, we…" Cornelius started to agree when a group of riders appeared between clusters of fighting. "Stand by, we may need to retreat behind a shield wall."

Thinking the riders were Punic cavalry, Cornelius walked his horse between the shields. Just before he ordered the defensive formation, he recognized the horsemen.

"Hold," he instructed.

Consul Gaius Varro and twenty-five Junior Tribunes galloped up and reigned in at the start of the corridor. Behind them, seventy beaten and bloody Legion cavalrymen brought their mounts to a stop.

"Who are you?" the Consul/General demanded.

"Senior Tribune Cornelius Scipio, sir, of Paullus Legion West."

"Yes, yes, the one worried about cavalry," the Consul noted. Then he asked. "How many of us got out of this level of Hades?"

"Sir, I don't know," Cornelius admitted. He studied the faces of the junior staff officers accompanying the General. All from noble families, the boys had blank stares on their faces. They had seen too much blood and experienced too much violence for ones so young. "Senior Tribune Pulcher is on the other end, sir, organizing the retreat."

"We've lost Paullus, Geminus, and Regulus," Varro told him. "I'm assuming command. And my first order is to roll back your men and join the retreat."

After delivering the order, the General, the young noblemen, and the cavalry trotted down the rows of shields.

"Centurion, withdraw your Legionaries before we draw too much attention."

"Yes, sir," the combat officer replied.

***

Ten thousand strong, the survivors of the battle limped home to Rome. News of the disaster spread through the city and the citizens panicked. Not spared from the emotions, the Senate was in an uproar. Consul Gaius Varro marched into the chaos, flanked by two Senior Tribunes. One appeared to be too young for the position.

"Senators of the Republic," Varro announced, "I've just arrived from the plain at Cannae."

"Come to beg forgiveness for your incompetence?" a Senator asked from behind a hand.

Unable to isolate the offender, Varro ignored the remark and continued, "Although a great battle, we fell short of victory."

"How short?" another challenged. He also hid his mouth behind a hand to remain anonymous.

Not shying away from the truth, Gaius Varro lifted his chin and declared, "Twenty-one thousand sons of Rome and fourteen thousand allied troops short."

Rumors always held a hint of truth. And while the gossip carried news of huge losses, to hear the number of dead from one of the commanding generals shocked the Senate.

"My grandson was with Regulus Legions, what news of him?"

No longer worried about political ramifications, the Senators called out for their sons, grandsons, uncles, brothers, and other Senators.

Varro signaled to the door and twenty-five lads marched into the chamber. The Junior Tribunes came down different aisles and went to their family members. Amid crying from men with their arms folded around loved ones, and others openly crying because their arms were empty, the Consul called for order.

"As difficult as it is, we must elect a replacement Consul," Varro informed the body. "I nominate Lucius Albinus."

"He's not in the city," a Senator informed Varro. "He's with the Legions at Rimini. We sent him there to punish the Boii."

"Is there no one who wants to be Consul?" Varro inquired.

"I second the nomination of Lucius Albinus," another said quickly.

They voted and the absent Proconsul won the election by a wide margin.

"We'll send couriers to recall the Consul," Varro promised.

From his chair, a Senator addressed Varro.

"I have a proposal."

"The Senate recognizes, Senator Alerio Sisera."

"Thank you, Consul," Alerio reacted by standing at his seat. "It appears when I requested a vote to deny the heritage of Lucius Jace Romiliia, I didn't anticipate the loss of so many sons from Roman families."

Lips moved in agreement, but emotions were so high, little sound came out. A few made fists and silently shook them in the air.

"Now, at this moment, we require citizens of noble blood," Alerio continued. "I propose we recognize the Romiliia name and grant Lucius Jace Romiliia the noble title as a Patrician. I submit the proposal for the good of our Republic."

Voting for the name would have been easy. But requesting the acknowledgement of Jace as a nobleman brought pushback from some Plebeians who hated the nobles and several no votes from old Patricians who didn't want anyone new in their ranks. But the proposal carried.

"Where is Lucius Jace Romiliia?" Varro asked while looking around the chamber.

"Consul, he's with Consul Albinus at Rimini," Cornelius answered.

"We'll recall them both. In the meanwhile, you'll take the decree for safe keeping until Romiliia arrives," Varro instructed. After a nod of acceptance from Cornelius, the Consul raised his hands and explained. "You've no doubt noticed the two Senior Tribunes behind me. They organized the retreat of the survivors from Cannae. Without their courage and foresight, we would have lost more of our treasures. I request that you vote for Medals of Bravery for both Appius Pulcher and Cornelius Scipio."

While the Senators discussed compensation and which medal was appropriate, Cornelius leaned over to Appius

"I don't care or want a medal to memorialize a defeat," he complained.

"Just look pleased and act humble," Appius told him. "A commendation for bravery goes a long way in earning public and private backing. You'll be grateful for in when you reach the age of majority."

"Will it help me get appointed as a Battle Commander?" he inquired.

"Yes, and it'll help your political career after your years in the Legion."

Cornelius straightened his posture and thought as he waited for the vote. He had been trying to influence his superiors by his deeds on the battlefield and by sharing his knowledge of Hannibal Barca's tactics. But Appius' guidance pointed Cornelius in a new direction.

Could public support overcome his age limitations? Senior Tribune Scipio would have to explore the prospect.

"The vote carries," Varro announced. "Congratulations to two of our finest Legion officers, Appius Pulcher and Cornelius Scipio."

That afternoon, couriers raced for the port city of Rimini to recall Consul Lucius Albinus and citizen Lucius Jace Kaisa Romiliia. But they arrived three days too late.

Chapter 26 – Spank the Boii

The orders had been issued the night before. As a result, three types of soldiers responded accordingly.

The fearful drank wine and beer until late while bragging about their courage. In the morning, they staggered out of their sleeping blankets. And, while fumbling with packing their gear, they suffered headaches and sour stomachs.

Another type crawled into their beds early but didn't sleep. After a long night of imagined horrors, they crawled out from under their blankets and grimly set about collecting their possessions.

A third type slept because they knew they needed energy for the march. Rising early, they ate to maintain their strength on the trail. After breakfast in the dark, they secured their packs and rested while waiting for orders to step off.

Harsh words from NCOs echoed around the inside of the fort. Outside, where the auxiliary forces had been moved, the Optios for late arriving Legions joined in the process.

"Get up and get dressed," the NCOs sang out, their voices ringing along with the cock-a-doodle-doos of roosters.

"I ain't got all day, honey cakes. You took the Republic's coins, now it's time to earn that pay."

The first and the second types of soldiers scrambled in a mad rush to comply. Meanwhile, the third type waited for the first two to get their merda together.

"File Leader Kasia?" a man called out from the dark.

A few rows of tents over, another echoed the words, "File Leader Kasia?"

From reclining on his long pack, Jace sat up and replied, "Cretan Archers, follow the sound of my voice. Follow my voice."

One of the searchers staggered to Jace while the other limped away, heading for the end of the campsites.

The bowman who appeared in the light of the cookfire looked familiar. But the disheveled man with cuts on his face and one hand tucked into a sling, didn't have the appearance or the bow case of a Cretan Archer.

Jace came to his feet and pointed at the men of his file, "Break out food, needles and thread, ointment, and bandages."

The bowman collapsed but Narkis caught him and eased the man to the ground. His right arm fell from the sling, revealing a burned stump.

"What happened?" Jace ask.

"Cannae and Hannibal Barca," the archer told him. "The Carthaginian pulled the Legion into his belly then chopped off their heads."

Eachann poured wine into two bowls. He handed one to the wounded man and dipped a piece of cloth in the other.

Next, he gently cleaned the stub of the man's amputated right hand.

"Chopped off their heads?" Jace questioned. "How many?"

From the dark outside the firelight, Lieutenant Acis Gergely responded, "All the Legionaries, NCOs, and their officers."

Curses, wailing, and questioning came from the camps around them.

"Three days ago, eight Legions marched into a Punic trap," the Cretan officer announced. From the dark, archers veered around their officer as they staggered into Jace's camp. As the Cretan survivors of Cannae entered the firelight, Jace understood the brutality of the battle. None were untouched by the fighting and several had makeshift bandages wet with fresh blood. As his men drifted by, Gergely continued. "Their center gave, and the Legions pressed forward. But the Carthaginian sides remained stable. As the Legion ranks progressed deeper into the middle, the enemy extended farther along their flanks. We fought with the Thracians. Arrows and spears kept the cavalry off the Legions. Then, the African Corps, infantry we believed fought in the center of Hannibal's army, appeared on the flank. They crushed the light infantrymen and, although we fought with Cretan pride, our archers fell by the File."

Jace couldn't keep track. The wounded flowed by in a never-ending procession of missing arms and hands.

"How many archers escaped?" Jace inquired. "How many survived?"

"None escaped. While survived is a matter of opinion," Lieutenant Gergely answered as he stepped into the light.

Both of his arms ended at his wrists. Bandages, wet from leaks, seeped from the burned stubs at the ends of each limb. The officer fell to his knees, and would have landed on his face, if Jace hadn't dropped down to hold him upright.

"This contract is over," Gergely declared. Jace stretched him out on the ground and propped up his head. Before passing out, the Cretan officer said. "I'm taking the Company home."

Jace peered around. Each of his twelve archers treated at least three wounded bowmen. When they left Crete, the Company numbered five hundred. Only fifty-two would board a transport for the island. And of those, only twelve were fit enough to take another contract.

"How many Legionaries escaped?" he inquired to no one in particular. "Any news of Tribune Scipio?"

"Scipio commanded a Legion in the center," an archer informed him. "I'm sorry to tell you File Leader, no Legionaries or officers escaped once the iron jaws closed."

Jace thought of the first time he saw Cornelius Scipio. Arrogant on his big horse and trying to appear stern, the Tribune had been easily confused by simple word play. Jace would grieve for Scipio later. At the moment, he had a task to perform.

"Marsyas, take Gyes and go to the harbor. Find a transport for the Company," Jace instructed. "Make sure there is plenty of deck space."

"I understand," Marsyas assured him. "But shouldn't you go? With the Lieutenant down, you're the only File Leader left."

"I'm resigning my position," Jace announced. "I will not be returning to Crete. In the instances where Lieutenant Gergely is unavailable, File Leader Narkis is in command."

"Narkis?" Egidio questioned. "He's reckless and self-serving."

"Exactly," Jace confirmed. "He has just the style of leadership a broken Company needs. He'll cheat, steal, fight, and negotiate to get home. But he'll take the Company along with him. Because, for all his flaws, File Leader Narkis won't leave any archers behind."

"What are you going to do?" Eachann asked.

"I'm going north with the Legions," Jace told him. "The auxiliary troops are Samnites, Etruscan and Greeks. I'll join them as a scout."

The sun topped the horizon and NCOs shouted, "Fall into your Centuries. Form up by fours. And stand by."

Jace Kasia shouldered his long pack and bowed to the archers. Then he marched away from the Cretans, moving towards the Samnite camp.

"Standing by, Optio," the rows of Legionaries responded to their NCOs.

***

Legion Velites jogged from the fort, howling like wolves. Wolf pellets pulled over their heads even though it was a warm morning, gave the illusion of half-man-half-beast savages.

"They always put on a show at the start of a march," Paccia, a Samnite soldier, remarked.

"Once out of sight of General Albinus, they'll settle into a stroll," another, named Herennia, stated. "And for the next twenty miles, the skirmishers will swap jokes and tell lies as they hike."

At the mention of Lucius Albinus, Jace Kasia paled. He had attempted to catch a glimpse of one of the men who destroyed his father's reputation. But the Proconsul resided in the city with the wealthy merchants and hadn't come to the fort until that morning. Darkness, in that instant, replaced distance in preventing Jace from getting a look at the General.

"Pick them up," a Samnite Lieutenant called out. In response, the Company of soldiers from the Apennine Mountains slung their packs onto their backs, hung their shields over the packs, and picked up their spears. A moment later, the officer called. "Forward."

Stuck between two Legions, the Samnite auxiliary followed the wagon train of the lead Legion.

A few miles into the march, Jace asked, "Shouldn't we be out there?"

He indicated the sides of the roadway.

"Being off the trail would slow up the march," Herennia told him. "That would delay the General's plan."

"I though we were going to punish the Boii for sending warriors and supplies to Hannibal," Jace commented.

"Punish?" Paccia laughed. "This is the Republic showing shields to impress the tribe. Oh, we may burn a couple of villages to spank the Boii, but the tribe is too smart to take the field against two Legions and the Samnites."

"But I lost archers to a war patrol and the Republic lost Legionaries," Jace insisted. "Surely that rates some kind of restitution."

"That's us, stomping around their territory for a couple of weeks," Herennia described. "It'll be enough to get their leaders to sue for peace. In the treaty tent is where the real punishment will take place."

Jace fell silent as they marched through the countryside.

Two competing thoughts flowed through his mind. On one hand, he pictured putting an arrow into the heart of Lucius Albinus. Hitting the man during a battle wouldn't be a problem. Escaping unnoticed presented the tricky part. Cretan Archers trained to complete a variety of jobs, but no lesson ever covered a suicide mission.

Thus, if they didn't have a battle, he wouldn't have an opportunity to get vengeance for his father. Which led to the other thought. Without a battle, he wouldn't get revenge for Hali Adras and the other archers murdered by the Boii.

"I guess they both depend on the same action," he whispered.

"Did you say something, Kasia?" Paccia inquired.

"No, just thinking out loud," he responded.

As Herennia predicted, at twenty miles, the Legions stopped for the night. Jace and the Samnites relaxed while the Legionaries dug trenches and erected the stockade walls of their marching camp.

"Those Latians sure do work hard," Paccia observed. "It makes me sweaty and hot just watching them."

"Come on," Herennia suggested, "let's go to the river and have a swim."

The three took their gear and hiked the short distance to the river. Due to farming in the area, most of the land was cleared with only groups of trees between farms. Along the riverbank, however, the forest grew thick with unharvested timber.

"These trees are taller than a temple," Jace remarked.

"You think these are tall," Herennia responded, "wait until we reach the Silva Litana. The trees in that forest make these seem like saplings."

"On Crete, we have a lot of trees, but none this tall."

They strolled between the towering trunks to reach the riverbank. And while the Legionaries toiled in the afternoon sun, Jace and the Samnites cooled off in the waters of the Savio River.

***

Another day of marching followed, and at the end of twenty miles, the Legionaries constructed their marching camp. As night fell on the Legions of Lucius Albinus, Jace looked across the cookfire at Herennia.

"A full day of passing through the land of the Boii," he noted. "But I haven't seen a young adult, let alone a warrior of the tribe."

"I told you, they don't want a fight with the Republic," Herennia replied. "Come on, would you?"

"Hannibal's victory down south might give them hope," Jace suggested.

"Hope is a lot like going to a temple and exchanging bushels of grain for prayers to cure your mule," Paccia said in a low voice as if revealing an ancient truth. Jace leaned forward to absorb the message. "What you get is a shortage in your winter stores and, in the spring, a plow strapped to your back. Oh, and a fat priest."

Both Samnite soldiers laughed while Jace sat confused.

"You've been waiting all day to use that one," Herennia accused the storyteller.

"I have," Paccia admitted. He chuckled and repeated. "And a fat priest."

"What does that have to do with the conversation?" Jace demanded.

"It means if the people are working hard and the priests are fat, only the priests have hope," Herennia explained. "All the people have, like the Boii, is a day-to-day struggle to survive."

"They won't attack the Legions," Paccia assured him. "A Legionary assault line is too strong."

The logic sounded convincing and Jace considered resigning as a scout. His archers were gone and in reality, he had no ties to the Legions. But the night had closed in, so he settled back and went to sleep.

Before dawn, the shouts of sentries woke the Legions and auxiliary forces.

"Scouts to the forefront," the call went out. "Enemy patrols sighted."

"How stupid are the Boii," Herennia complained from under his blanket, "to get spotted in the dark? Couldn't they see the campfires?"

Jace secured his long pack and pulled the war bow from its case. He wanted to agree with the Samnite soldier. But he refrained from talking while he packed for fear of hearing another unfunny fable.

***

By mid-morning, Jace, along with a handful of men from different backgrounds, hiked in advance of the Legion skirmishers. They were hunters with nothing else in common. Animal tracked for food, or human footprints for coins, it was all the same to the scouts.

"This is odd," a tracker a few steps away from Jace noted. "The war parties rushed to come together. But now, they're setting their own sweet pace."

Jace drifted over and examined the length of the strides. Mimicking the distance, he matched one set of footprints for several paces.

"They're moving slow," he observed. "Probably, so we don't lose them."

"I'm a hunter," the tracker admitted, "not a military man. Why would they want the Legions to follow them?"

"Typically, the ploy is used to draw an enemy force into an open location where they can be ambushed from a tree line or a hilltop," Jace described. "A place where the Boii can attack the marching Legions from the side. Kill a few Legionaries, then run off, and fade into the landscape before we can react."

"Well, that's not the case here," the tracker assured Jace. He pointed ahead. In the distance, the treetops of giant trees stretched into the sky. "There's no open location for an attack in the Silva Litana forest."

Chapter 27 – A Good War Chief

As the scouts reached the opening to the forest, they closed distance to fit across the dirt roadway. On both sides, trees over a hundred feet tall, supported branches as wide as sixty feet in some places.

"The tracks have changed," Jace pointed out. Two other scouts leaned over to see the footprints. "They sprinted from here."

"Why'd they run?" a tracker inquired.

"Maybe they're afraid our cavalry would catch them," the hunter volunteered.

"With the woods nearby, where the horses can't follow?" Jace offered. "That doesn't make sense. I'm going to report this."

He slowed, turned, and hiked to the Centurion of the lead infantry Century.

"Sir. I'm worried about the war party we're following," Jace said while falling in step with the officer. "They've changed their pattern of..."

"You're with those Cretan rats," the combat officer accused. He pointed to the bow and the long pack. "Why are you talking to me? If I wanted to listen to waste plop into a latrine, I would call you. But not on a beautiful day like this."

286

Jace touched the tip of his bow to his forehead and jogged back to the front.

"What did the Centurion say?" the hunter asked.

"He said it's a beautiful day," Jace answered. "Maybe you should go talk with him."

"Not me," the hunter resisted. "Legion officers don't like me any better than they do you."

"The Boii warriors are peeling off from the patrol and going into the woods," the other scout warned.

"Jace said the forest isn't a choice spot for an ambush," the hunter commented.

Jace studied the woods on both sides of the roadway. He could see where the members of the Boii patrol left the roadway and pushed through the brush between tree trunks. But there were no other signs of human passage.

"Spears, javelins, and arrows from the woods won't disable a Legion of heavy infantrymen," Jace remarked. "This isn't a good place to attack the Republic. And yet, something feels wrong."

The hunter peered back over the skirmishers and the marching Legionaries, to the mounted staff officers. Much beyond them, the view was lost to distance.

"How far back is the end?" Jace asked.

"Got to be seventeen or eighteen miles to the rear guard," the tracker replied.

"And how deep is the forest?" Jace questioned.

"This road runs northwest along the Po River," the hunter told him. "Thirty miles or one hundred miles, it depends on how far upstream General Albinus wants to go. It's forest, all the way."

"And all the way, it's Boii territory," the tracker added.

***

Resembling a giant snake entering a tunnel, the Legions, auxiliary soldiers, horses, mules, and ox drawn wagons marched into the depth of the Silva Litana forest. From Jace and the scouts at the front to the infantrymen at the rear, the ninety-four thousand feet of Republic war machine symbolized strength. Designed purposely to dissuade any aggressive attacks, the message surely wasn't lost on the Boii tribe.

With muscles trained on steel and shields to break waves of assaults, the Legionaries hiked with confidence. At the rear, the infantrymen were grateful when they passed into the shade provided by the giant trees.

Of the marching men, the drunks sipped wine from skins and walked with a slight prance. Meanwhile, the timid Legionaries relaxed in the cool, quiet of the forest. And even the professionals were lulled into a relaxed saunter.

Adding to the tranquility, the Legionaries blinked as they passed through rays of sunlight streaming through the treetops. The bugs and dust suspended in the bands of light seemed magical and even the scouts entered a dreamlike trance.

Crack!

The sound of wood striking wood echoed from the forest.

"A woodworker harvesting lumber," the hunter remarked.

"Or a woodsman collecting firewood," the tracker suggested.

Crack! Crack!

Jace turned his face to the tall tree trunks. Then, he elevated his chin and looked at the branches of the treetops towering overhead.

"If he's not careful," the hunter cautioned, "he'll drop the tree on our heads."

***

A tree did not wait for the ax to chop cleanly through. Rather, the fall started by leaning. Woodsmen used wedges to stress the last connection between the trunk and the stump. And, as the wedges pried them apart, grinding preceded the crack! that announced the separation of the last bit of wood holding the tree upright.

"The woodsman didn't chop first," Jace announced. "The first thing we heard was him tapping in wedges."

"What does that..." the tracker began. He stopped talking and listened.

A falling tree can get trapped in the upper branches of an adjacent tree. Woodsmen were careful to avoid having their wood get hung up in the air. But the sounds of limbs against limbs came cleanly through the forest. Except, the tree did not get suspended against its neighbor.

The tracker rotated his head from side to side, trying to locate the falling tree. He never saw the original. Crack, crack, crack accompanied the cascading of three other trees.

They fell from the forest and crashed into the Legion skirmishers.

Wolf pellets were no defense. The tree trunks crushed rows of Velites. Those not under the bodies of the trees were impaled by branches as if hundreds of spears had fallen from the sky. Farther out from the center of the trees, men got swatted by the limbs. Like bugs smacked by a giant hand, the men screamed from punctured flesh, and cried from broken bones. All the agony came from under treetops that covered the road.

Back in the ranks of the heavy infantry, their armor offered no protection when three more giants toppled onto the Legionaries. In a shield wall fight, they were a powerful force. But under the weight of three cascading trees, the Legionaries became nothing more than broken men, wailing in pain before dying.

Horns sounded, and the voices of Centurions and Optios trying to rally the Legionaries reverberated off the walls of the forest. More trees dropped, separating the Legion columns into small, disorganized units. Unfortunately, those in the small clusters were too busy helping their surviving squad mates. None had the presence of mind to respond to the orders to form their assault lines.

At the rear, the Legion columns and auxiliary Companies fell to the ambush of trees. Ranks of smashed men, animals, and wagons marked the last of the organized resistance. Forest timber had broken the Legions, something tribal tactics could never accomplish. Then, Boii warriors poured from the forest seeking to punish the Legions and end Rome's expedition into their territory.

***

Jace wrapped his hands around his war bow. Using it to point at a small gap under a trunk beside the roadway, he bent his knees and dove for the tiny opening. While digging to enlarge the hole, he heard cries and grunts as Boii warriors swept the roadway clear of scouts and the Velites who survived the trees.

Two warriors reached the far side of the road, stopped, and looked around for their next victim. While there were no more Legionaries or scouts to kill, the pair of Boii tribesmen did find a long pack. Attached to the pack were a wrist shield, two quivers of arrows, a broken war bow, and a case containing a fine hunting bow.

The abandoned items rested beside the trunk of a fallen tree. They began poking at the surrounding bushes with their spears, searching for the owner of the pack.

***

A half mile from the road, Jace pushed through a wall of greenery, and fell. Sliding, he plowed the embankment, catching himself just before splashing into the Po River. In the tall weeds on the edge of the water, Jace Kasia untied the lacing for his sandals and stripped off his clothing. Then he rolled the footwear, his war hatchet, and the tunic inside the water resistant, hooded doublet. Mimicking a snake, he slithered to the side, and nestled down in fresh weeds, under a tree overhanging the river.

Even muffled by the riverbank and the forest, the sounds of fighting and joyous shouts of a victorious tribe were not hard to make out. And they were clear. The Boii had caught the Legions in an ambush of epic proportions.

Master Archer Zarek Mikolas had taught, "When everyone is running around, sit quietly and listen. When the area settles, make your best decision."

Following the lesson, Jace curled up on his side and began picking out sounds. To the east, splashing and Latin cursing alerted him to several Legionaries who had reached the river. Moments after they entered the water, the noise of excited warriors drifted from the riverbank. Screams let him know the Legionaries had been discovered.

Then to the west, a Legion officer ordered, "Advance. Advance."

Shields clashed, and the grunts of men locked in combat washed from upstream. But in moments, Boii warriors gave triumphant yells. Items from a height splash into the water, revealing to Jace the presence of a boat or a bridge.

"Sit quietly and listen…"

Small fights erupted in the forest when Legionaries broke from concealment too soon. Following those hunts proved easy for Jace. The Boii shouted to each other while herding the escaping Romans into dead ends of spear points. But the frequency of skirmishes ebbed until the shouting of warriors moved far away.

"When the area settles, make your best decision."

Jace originally planned to wait for dark, enter the river, and float away from the ambush site. But he was deep in Boii territory and after the ambush, they would be hunting for escapees. Also, he wanted revenge on Lucius Albinus. If the General lived, this was Jace's chance for vengeance. And finally, curiosity captured his imagination. He wanted to know if the Boii tribe actually won the battle against the Republic.

Rolling to his belly, Jace slow crawled westward through the weeds. He'd make his *'best decision'* after seeing if the Boii had a boat anchored upstream or if the unseen warriors guarded a bridge.

***

Piles driven into the riverbed supported an old bridge. The undercarriage consisted of repeating segments of two piles lashed together on the sides with a beam spanning between them to hold up the roadway boards. Additionally, two broadly spaced piles between the end pairs provided stability for the beam. And, to stabilize the bridge, angled boards coming out of the river braced each row of piles from the sides.

Jace waited in the weeds, peering between the branches of a bush. Boii warriors on the bridge talked and scanned the shoreline.

"Floating away in the moonlight is a pretty good idea right now," Jace whispered to himself. Then after long moments, he begged. "Come on, somebody do something."

He desperately needed a distraction. A moment to…The bridge guards shouted, pointed to the forest, and ran to the end of the bridge.

Jace rolled into the river and allowed the momentum to take him in chest deep. Bent forward to submerge his body, he peered around the bundle of clothing and watched the warriors. Underwater, he took big, hurried steps while on the surface, he was no more than a parcel and half a head gliding through the water. If any Boii glanced at the river,

Jace would be dead. Just as he neared the angled support post, the guards started to turn.

Jace reached out, gripped the support, and pulled hard. As quick as a river snake, he slithered under the board. Then, Jace held his breath, waiting for the cry of alarm. When none came, he peered at the underside of the bridge.

The sections of piles were close enough that he could push off and swim to the next section in a few strokes. At the center of the river, however, the Boii had installed split logs from lofty, majestic trees. Cousins, no doubt, to the tall timber that destroyed the Legions.

He waded to a center pile and began swimming to the next. From rows of piles to the next row, he moved away from the riverbank. Near mid-stream, Jace shifted to the pair of piles on the far left. Current pulled at his body, threatening to take him downstream.

Rocking, Jace Kasia prepared to shove off. If his strokes were smooth and strong, he'd reach the row of piles on the other side of the span. If not, the current would carry him out from under the bridge. Then it would only be a matter of which spear took his life.

He released the pile, kicked off, and stroked into the current. Head down, Jace glided into the center of the Po River. With the bundle of clothing in his teeth, he couldn't see anything except the roadway boards overhead. And he appeared to be slipping by them faster and faster. Then daylight touched him, and the edge of the bridge slid…

He bumped into the angled support beam and clamped an arm around it. Safe on the far side of the center channel, he began swimming from row of piles to the next row of piles. Finally, Jace reached the bank on the far side of the river.

***

The bridge guards had the best duty. While their brethren ran around stabbing bushes hoping to flush out a hidden Legionary or two, at the river, the Romans came to them. So, they watched the southern riverbank and the river upstream and down for Latians wanting to try for the other side of the Po.

"Excuse me," a voice called from behind the guards.

Ten strong, they spun. Their spears rotating around, they dropped into an attack formation, intending to defend the bridge.

"Whoa, there," a young man said while holding up his hands to show he wasn't holding a weapon.

"That's a Greek tunic, and a Cretan war hatchet on your hip," a warrior observed. "But you look Latian. You are a Legionary."

"You overlooked these," Jace instructed. He tapped his fingers on the two armlets. "This one recognizes me as a brother of the Carricini tribe. And the other means I'm a son of the Hirpini. Neither makes me a Legionary or a friend of Rome."

"Lāno, take him to Bona," the observant warrior instructed. "Let the War Chief deal with him."

"Maybe Nemeto needs a new sacrificial cup," the Boii named Lāno remarked.

"Don't joke about the priest," the warrior warned. "Get going."

295

Jace strolled across the bridge with a spearpoint at his back. As he walked, he searched the bank for the crushed weeds beside the river. Luckily, the indention made by his body was barely noticeable.

"Tell me, Lāno," Jace inquired as the two left the bridge. "Is War Chief Bona a good commander?"

"Pretty sure of it," the Boii warrior answered. "He just defeated a Roman army and captured their General."

Act 10

Chapter 28 – Hirpini or Dead

The camp of the Boii army might well have been a city festival honoring a tribal deity. Except, there were no sacrifices, vendors, streets, or buildings. Trees and sleeping blankets stood in place of manmade structures, paths between the blankets represented streets, and the warriors strutted around with wineskins found in the baggage trains of the Legions.

"Lāno, where did you catch that one?" a Boii called to Jace's guard.

"He walked in," Lāno replied without breaking stride.

"You're not very chatty, are you?" Jace inquired.

"No reason," Lāno stated.

"Then I better be ready to explain myself."

"Yes," Lāno offered.

The center of attention was a stage of lumber raised a couple of feet above the clearing. A line of men, shoulder to shoulder, acted as a backdrop to the stage. On the platform, two men received visits from warriors.

One locked wrists with the men who defeated a Roman army and said a few words to each. The other man on the platform lifted a finger from a bowl and ran it down each warriors' cheek. The spearmen walked away a red streak down their faces.

Using the shaft of his spear, Lāno reached around Jace and halted his prisoner.

"I guess we'll wait here," Jace commented. Then he asked, although he could clearly see the men performing their duties. "Which one is War Chief Bona? Which one is Priest Nemeto?"

Lāno didn't acknowledge the remark or answer the questions. He and Jace stood as a long procession of Boii warriors marched to their chief and then received a blessing from their priest.

Finally, the War Chief looked up.

"Lāno, what have you there?" he inquired.

With the shaft of his spear, Lāno pushed Jace forward but didn't respond.

"War Chief Bona, I am Jace Otacilia," Jace stated. "A member of the Hirpini tribe."

"I've seen cowards afraid of dying do many things, including dressing as a woman or acting cripple," Bona declared. "In today's battle against the men of the Boii, I've heard many claims by weaklings trying to cheat death."

Jace pointed to his armlets, "This one recognizes me as a brother of the Carricini tribe. While the other means I'm a son of the Hirpini. Neither makes me a Legionary or a friend of Rome."

"Many claims," Bona repeated.

"Lāno, which way was I walking when we met?" Jace asked his escort.

"From the north."

"Was I damp or wet from swimming the river?"

"No."

"There you have it," Jace surmised. "I am a simple traveler, attempting to cross the bridge, when I was detained."

"You look Latian," Bona pointed out. "You're a Legionary."

"I protest," Jace exclaimed. "Allow me to prove it."

"How?" Bona inquired.

"The Hirpini are no friends of Rome," Priest Nemeto intercepted. "There is a test. Jace Otacilia of the Hirpini, pick from the Legionaries."

The line of spearmen behind the platform parted to reveal kneeling prisoners. Some in their armor and others stripped naked. Jace scanned the Romans until his eyes fell on an older man in armor with gold inlays.

"Him," Jace said while pointing at the ornate chest piece.

He hoped it was the man who sent his father into exile.

"General Albinus is not for a test," Nemeto said. "Pick another."

He scrutinized the other prisoners. Then Jace locked eyes with the Centurion he attempted to warn about marching into the forest.

"Him," Jace pronounced.

Nemeto lifted his hand with the red finger while looking at Jace's eyes. When he slashed the air with the side of his hand, a Boii warrior stepped up behind the Centurion. With a quick slash, he cut the Legion officer's neck. Running forward, a young priest shoved a bowl under the cut and collected the blood.

"Any coward can turn on his own," Bona spit out. "That proves nothing."

Jace allowed his face to fall as if defeated. Then he reached to Lāno's shoulder and lifted the rope of a wineskin.

"If you'll allow me," Jace requested.

Walking to the side, he picked up a mug, and blew into it as if that would clean the vessel. Then Jace slowly poured from the wineskin.

"*Castrid and deíkum maimas carneis tanginud ammíd fust tefúrúm or fust fratru'm,*" he recited while filling the mug.

"What does that mean?" Bona demanded. "Am I supposed to understand nonsense?"

Priest Nemeto bent close to the War Chief and whispered something to him.

"My apologies," Bona said.

He stepped back and Nemeto held out an arm. The young priest raced onto the platform with a cup and a wineskin. Nemeto tilted the skin and a stream of wine flowed into the vessel.

"*I pour and speak for the largest part opinions because it's unknown if he will be a victim or a brother,*" Nemeto recited back to Jace. "Come, speaker of the old language, we will take our drinks and see if we will be victims or brothers."

***

Alone with Jace, the Priest stated the reasons for going to war with the Legions.

"Rome is taking our land and our young men," Nemeto complained.

He and Jace sat under a tree with cuts of pork skewed on sticks and mugs full of red wine.

"My mother's estate sits next to taken land," Jace empathized. "I understand, at least partially."

"When Hannibal Barca arrived, we saw a chance to fund a rival to the Latians," the Priest explained. "The warriors who lead the battle today are fresh from Cannae. There, they participated in a great defeat for the Romans. And today is another."

"I have friends who suffered greatly at Cannae," Jace told him.

"From what I hear, the men placed in the center of Hannibal's line took the most casualties," Nemeto said, assuming Jace's friends were part of the Carthaginian army. "I sympathize with you for their pain."

"As do I," Jace agreed.

A warrior walked to Nemeto and informed the Priest, "The water is boiling."

"Very well, I'll be their shortly," Nemeto acknowledged. Looking at Jace, the Priest informed him. "Come and you'll see why Lucius Albinus couldn't be used for a test."

"You're saving him for ransom," Jace ventured.

"Oh no, brother," Nemeto corrected. "I saved him because I need a new sacrificial drinking vessel. I sold my last one to fund this war party."

Jace and Nemeto pushed off the ground. And while the Priest went to the platform, Jace strolled through the Boii camp.

***

At the back of a crowd of dancing spearmen, Jace heard men whining from a distance. But if wasn't in Latin. He circled behind a group of trees, nodded to a couple of Boii guards, and approached a different set of prisoners.

Of the twenty men, only Paccia and Herennia happened to look up. Seeing Jace, they opened their mouths to greet him.

After a chop with his hand at waist level, Jace clamped the hand over his mouth. The Samnite soldiers dropped their eyes to signify they understood the signal to be silent. As he passed by, Jace noted the ropes tying the two friends together.

"How did you manage that?" he said to himself while turning away from the captured soldiers.

A roar came from the direction of the platform and Jace hurried to see what caused the outburst.

Lucius Albinus stood stiffly in his gold and silver armor and white plumed helmet. With his hands tied behind his back, a spearman holding the binding, controlled the Legion General. Beside the Roman, War Chief Bona held a long sharp sword. Behind the stage, Nemeto tended a pair of large deep pots suspended over flames. To maintain the heat, the young priest fed wood into the fires.

"This old man came to our lands to punish us," Bona exclaimed. His warriors booed and hissed the declaration. The spearman rotated Albinus as if the General was acknowledging each sector of the Boii. "And so, he arrived with thousands of armed men to do his bidding."

The audience shouted defiantly at the statement. Again, Lucius Albinus pivoted in small arcs, the spearman making him bow involuntarily to the warriors.

Jace pushed through the crowd to get a better look at one of the men who destroyed his father. At a point, he could look into the General's eyes. And his heart stopped. Lucius Albinus was an old man with tears rolling down his face. Given an opportunity, Jace would gladly put an arrow into his heart. But he would never humiliate and disgrace the old man.

"The grand General, my brothers, did not count on the Boii and our prowess in battle," Bona shouted.

The puppet master yanked back on his hands throwing Lucius Albinus off balance. Once unstable, the spearman shoved his arms upward and the General dropped to his knees. The warriors howled with pleasure.

"Stand that worthless animal up," Bona instructed.

Shoving upward on the old man's arms, caused Albinus to scream in pain as he rose to his feet. Laughter rolled through the thong of warriors.

Bona pointed at the sword, then glanced over his shoulder at Nemeto. The Priest nodded he approval.

"Bend him to the will of the Boii," the War Chief ordered.

By placing one hand on the General's back and pulling up on his arms, the spearmen folded the General into a deep curtsy. The sword flashed over Bona's shoulder before chopping down at the exposed neck.

The helmeted head hung for a moment on a piece of skin and sinew. Then the weight stretched the flesh and tendon until the head dropped away the body. The head of Lucius Albinus hit the platform. Racing for the side, the young priest scooped up the helmet, and carried it to Nemeto.

"You've taken his heart, and his might," the Priest called out. "Now, I will use his head for something other than planning the death of Boii men."

Nemeto grabbed the horsehair comb and shook it until the General's head dropped into the first pot. Drops splashed into the air as Lucius Albinus' face sank into the pot of boiling water.

Wineskins flew into the air in celebration. But none fell to the ground. Each was caught and the warrior drank his reward.

Jace snatched a wineskin in mid-flight and turned to an emptyhanded spearman.

"What happens next?" he asked while handing the wineskin to the man. "Please don't tell me we're going to eat the General's flesh."

"That's barbaric," the Boii said in disgust. He took a long stream of the wine. "What do you think we are, cannibals?"

"I thought nothing of the sort," Jace assured him.

But the Priest planned something because none of the warriors left the area. They talked and drank but no one vacated their place near the platform.

Chapter 29 – Immortality of General Albinus

There was never a sunset in the Silva Litana. Darkness came quickly as the forest filtered out any fading light from the day. In response, the warriors stacked wood and lit three large bonfires. Light flooded the space between the stacks of burning wood, casting the platform in perfect illumination.

Jace had enough of the Boii, the ceremony, and the forest. He edged out of the revelry. Once outside the crowd, he moved to the trees in the back. Away from the light, he blinked a few times to adjust his eyes. Then he pulled his war hatchet and strolled around the trees to where the Samnite prisoners were being held.

With the weapon positioned low and out of sight in the dark, Jace prepared to murder the guards. Killing them would have been quick and easy. But screams from the crowd pulled the two guards away from the prisoners. Rather than adding to the day's death count, he dropped down between Paccia and Herennia.

"You're free," he whispered to the Samnite soldiers. "Help the others or not, it means nothing to me."

With two sure strokes, he sliced the ropes releasing the soldiers. Putting away the hatchet, he dashed four steps towards the forest. Then oohs arose from the warriors.

Jace needed to go. He needed to be out of the forest before first light. But the pleasure in the voices of the warriors pulled him to a stop. Slipping to one side of the audience, he stepped into the light to watch.

On the platform, Nemeto held the General's head in a pair of iron tongs. Turning it, he allowed War Chief Bona to flick bits of boiled flesh from the skull with the big sword. Each small piece flying across the platform brought shouts of joy from the Boii warriors.

Nauseated at the disrespect towards a dead enemy, Jace prepared to go. But a chant started, and curiosity froze his feet to the forest floor.

"Dip him. Dip him," the warriors sang. "Dip him…"

Nemeto held the head up and Bona pointed at it with the sword. Then the Priest walked to the back of the stage and lowered the skull of the Roman General into the second pot. When he pulled it out, the gold coated bones reflected the light from the bonfires.

Jace recalled Lāno's comment on the bridge.

"Maybe Nemeto needs a new sacrificial cup."

It seemed the Priest now have a new gold drinking vessel.

***

The Legions of Co-consul Albinus had stretched over seventeen miles when they marched into the forest. Reversing the trip on a clear roadway would have been an easy run for Jace. But the roadblocks of fallen trees made the route slow and full of trip hazards.

Three miles from the Boii ceremony, Jace squatted in the dark. Considering everything that happened during the day, his soul felt stained, and his spirit crushed. At his lowest point of self-pity, Zarek Mikolas came to him.

"Still your breath so your hands are steady. Calm your heart so your eyes are clear. Focus your mind on the task."

Renewed by the memory, Jace Kaisa took a moment to smile and observe his surroundings. Then he rose, faced southeast, and jogged towards the Apennine Mountains.

Chapter 30 – Dearly Departed

Cornelius Scipio stepped onto the patio of his father's villa. The tray in his hand contained two glasses, a pitcher of wine, and a small scroll. After placing the tray on a table, the young Tribune faced the city.

Rome stretched before him. From the temples of brick to the big commercial structures, the apartment buildings to the slums built of bare timber, he loved the city and the citizens. But his heart ached.

Time and again, Cornelius had stood across the battlefield from Hannibal Barca and each time, the Punic general won. After witnessing the tricks, the brilliant tactics, and experiencing death in far greater numbers than a man of his age should, he wanted control.

Control of the infantry, skirmishers, auxiliary troops, and the cavalry, so that he, Cornelius Scipio, could defeat Hannibal. Given command and the opportunity, he would be victorious where stubborn, narrow-minded generals failed.

Sitting beside the table, Cornelius filled both glasses then placed a hand on the scroll. Another regret settled in his chest. Jace would never know the Senate had acknowledged his citizenship and birthright as a nobleman. Cornelius clinked the glasses together, said a silent prayer for the dead archer, and drank a toast to the memory of Jace Kasia Romiliia.

***

Forty-five miles northeast from the Scipio Villa, on a patio overlooking the Via Salaria, Jace Kasia finished a meal.

"That's a substantial road for being so high in the mountains," he remarked to the owner of the inn.

"For centuries, the old salt route has carried loads of minerals from the seas," the proprietor informed him. "Go left and you'll arrive at the Adriatic. Go right and, on the other side of Rome, your feet will splash into the Tyrrhenian."

"What if I go south?" Jace inquired.

"Then you'll hike through the Apennines until you reach the Messina Strait."

Jace stood, paid for his meal, and glanced in both directions of the salt route. To the east lay Crete, but other than Neysa Kasia, there was nothing for him on the island. To the west sat the city of Rome. But, with Cornelius Scipio dead, he had no reason to journey to the Capital of the Republic.

Shouldering a small pack, Jace Kasia said goodbye, and headed south. Maybe he could find a home among his mother's people, the Hirpini. If not, he would head to Iberia and hire on as a mercenary with the Carthaginians. Would he be happy fighting the Legions? After their arrogance and insults, he had no doubt that he could use his war bow to take Roman lives.

The End

A sample of book #3 in *A Legion Archer* series:

Heritage of Threat

Reject Legion

Benevento 215 B.C.

"Kasia, when the men finish with the defensive fortification," Centurion Thaddeus instructed, "set up a rotation for sentry duty."

"Yes, sir," Jace replied.

In the ditch, Sidia the Hirpinian stopped to wipe sweat from his brow.

"The mountain is just over there," he said softly so his voice didn't carry. "Tonight, we could be out of camp, out of the valley and, halfway up the mountain, out of the Legion."

"Cousin Sidia," Jace stated. He dropped to a knee and leaned forward to keep the conversation confidential. "We can't go home. Bands of angry warriors sworn to the Chief of Chiefs are searching for us. I think the price for us from Carthaginian command is over three gold coins each. And the Centurion of the garrison at Benevento has carved our names on two crosses. He's just waiting for us to call attention to ourselves to put us up on the wood."

"North then, we run north?" Sidia suggested.

"The Boii tribe and I had a falling out over a few Samnite tribesmen," Jace said nixing the direction. "I think here in the middle of the Reject Legion, we're as safe as anywhere. Plus, the Republic feeds us, pays us, and provides the opportunity for lots of exercise."

"Reject Legion," Sidia scoffed. "Is that what you're calling us these days?"

"More correctly, the Gracchus Reject Legion East," Jace corrected his cousin. He stood back from the ditch and sermonized. "You cannot leave out the name of our Proconsul."

The Legion's Senior Tribune strolled along the line of men shoveling dirt from the trench. As always, two Legion bodyguards walked slightly behind him.

"Kasia, is there a problem over there?" Seneca inquired.

Jace saluted the approaching senior staff officer.

"No, sir. We were discussing how to extract a big rock from the defensive ditch," Jace lied.

"Put more men on it," Seneca directed.

The Senior Tribune didn't wait to see if Jace followed his advice. In a few strides, he and his two bodyguards were beyond Jace without even looking into the ditch.

"If he didn't have those thugs with him," a big Gaul boasted from the bottom of the ditch, "I'd take Seneca's head."

"And do what with it?" an Illyrian digger asked. "Dip it in silver and mount him on the mantle of your villa?"

"He doesn't have a villa," a Noricum spit out the insult directing it at the Gaul. He kept digging and added. "The stupid Gaul probably doesn't own a shed in the woods."

The Gaul tossed down his shovel and glared at the Noric.

311

"Anytime you feel the need for light duty," the Noricum told him, "I'll gladly install the damage."

"Gentlemen," Jace pleaded, "can we finish this ditch without bloodshed?"

Sidia tossed a shovel full of dirt at Jace's hobnailed boots, and declared, "Gracchus Reject Legion. Now I get it."

***

High peeks to the west would soon block the light of the setting sun.

"Night's coming," squad leader Anker remarked.

"Is your guard rotation set for this evening?" Jace inquired.

The squad leader held up his hands and counted off on his fingers, "For the number three watch tower, I've got two at dusk. Then, two more during late evening. And another two, after a fight in the middle of the night. Two for the early watch, and the two at dawn will cover my squad's responsibility."

"Can't you separate the Gaul from the Noric?" Jace asked.

"I could, but than my Illyrian troublemaker gets to wake one of them for the next watch," Anker explained. "And instead of a fist fight, it'll turn into a knife fight."

"I noticed he keeps that sica sharp," Jace remarked. "Forget I said anything. Run your squad…"

A guard in watch tower one shouted, "Open the gates for the scouts."

Across the parade ground, Seneca questioned, "Didn't they just leave?"

The Senior Tribune and his bodyguards strutted to the gates. Shortly after the warning call, the gates swung open, and four riders galloped through the portal.

"Senior Tribune, we've located a detachment of the Punic army," one of the cavalrymen reported.

"Are they on the march?" Seneca questioned.

"No, sir. They appear to be setting up camp for the night."

"Then why did you cut your patrol short?"

"Sir, their camp is only two miles from here."

For an older man, Seneca moved fast as he headed for the Battle Commander's tent.

Not much later, a messenger ran from the Colonel's pavilion, jumped on a horse, and kicked it into motion. He raced out of the south gate and galloped a mile to the town of Benevento. Once inside the city walls, he rode to the villa where Proconsul Tiberius Gracchus and his staff were quartered.

As sun set, the courier rode back with orders that surprised a few people. The Legions would form attack lines at first light, per Proconsul Gracchus as delegated by the authority of Consul Quintus Fabius.

**

At dawn, the morning light revealed eleven thousand five hundred heavy infantrymen, thirty-two hundred skirmishers, and nine hundred cavalrymen blocking the Via Appia.

"You can tell Consul Fabius is in Rome," Jace commented. Several heads turned, none understanding the remark. "When he was Dictator, we waited for orders to attack the Carthaginians. He never gave the order."

A portion of the Legion cavalry stood beside their horses near the Calore River. Beside the riders, the Maniples of Gracchus Legion West filled the area just off the riverbank to the edge of the roadside. The paved surface of the Via Appia ran between Fabius Legions North and South. They controlled the center of the Republic attack line. On the right, Gracchus Legion East completed the infantry ranks while the remainder of the Legion cavalry held the right flank.

Seeing the thin ranks of Legion horsemen, Jace recommended to the combat officer, "Centurion Thaddeus, we need to turn our ends and guard the flank."

From the Legions on the far-left side, cheering arose. Moments later, a more robust roar of approval burst from Gracchus Legion West.

"We have cavalry to cover our flank," the Centurion replied when the noise subsided.

Not being in a position to argue his point, Jace Kasia replied, "As you will, sir."

Horns sounded, announcing the arrival of the Proconsul. Battle Commander Ulysses Ovid instructed, "Gracchus Legion East, stand by."

"Standing by, Colonel," the Legion responded.

"Legion, turn about."

The three Maniples and ten Centuries of light infantry about-faced. The Legionaries shuffled their feet, many glancing nervously over their shoulders watching for the Carthaginian army.

Battle Commander Ovid saluted Tiberius Gracchus as the General reined in and halted. After a few words with the Colonel, the Proconsul guided his horse around to face the Legion.

"Men of Gracchus Legion East, hear me and trust my words," Tiberius Gracchus encouraged. "I made this promise to your comrades in Legion West. For everyone who brings me the heads of Punic mercenaries, I will free you. Or, if you're a convict, I will pardon you."

The Legion of slaves and criminals, like the slaves and criminals in the ranks of Legion West, screamed out their excitement. When they settled, Gracchus continued. "Hannibal Barca is near Nola. Up the Via Appia is his Lieutenant General Hanno. And they want to meet and dine together. But to their great disappointment, my Legions stand in their way. My killers, the freemen of Gracchus Legion East. In the name of the Republic and your freedom, you will end Hanno's march right here at Benevento."

Wild cheering broke out when Tiberius Gracchus saluted the Legion.

"Freedom," Anker called over to Jace. "Isn't that good news?"

"Freedom," Jace repeated with a lot less enthusiasm.

"Come on cousin," Sidia teased. "Could you get any less excited about the concept?"

"I might," Jace whispered, "if we'd ever been caught and convicted of a crime. It's unclear if the Proconsul can commute a sentence when there is no sentence."

"What's wrong, Optio Kasia," Thaddeus asked from his position at the center of the Century. "Afraid of being free and having no master?"

"No, sir," Jace replied. "I'm worried about where we're going to put all the heads."

The slaves and criminals of the Twenty-Fifth Century laughed at their NCO's remark.

Before anyone else could comment, Colonel Ovid commanded, "Legion East, turn around. Prepare to earn your freedom. Draw."

"Rah!"

Spread across the Via Appia were ranks of Punic mercenaries. Unsettling to the Legion cavalry, over eleven hundred Numidian horsemen flanked the Carthaginian infantry.

"Freedom," someone shouted.

Only a few repeated the cry as the cost of that freedom plowed into the front ranks of the Legion shields.

***

From his position as Optio for the Twenty-fifth Century, Jace dutifully split his attention. Ahead, he studied the men of the Thirteenth Century to be sure they held the end of the assault line. To the right, he attempted to judge the state of the cavalry battle. But on foot, he couldn't tell if the Legion horsemen were winning, holding the flank, or losing.

Glancing back, he scanned the Thirty-seventh Century to see if they had reacted to anything he'd missed. So far, all three Centuries on the ends were focused on the enemy to the front.

"Our cavalry is holding them," Thaddeus shouted to Jace. "You were worried for nothing, Sergeant."

"Yes, sir, for nothing," Jace repeated.

In combat with tempers running hot, agreeing was preferable to debate. Especially if the statement expressed an outcome while events were still unfolding.

"Stand by to rotate the line," Centurion Hasti of the Thirteenth ordered.

Always being behind the Century in the combat formation, Jace and his men knew Hasti's voice. And the men of the Thirteenth knew Jace's and Centurion Thaddeus' voice. In shield-to-shield fighting, the only orders able to reach the men on the front line were audible instructions, making a familiar voice a requirement for a successful command.

"Standing by, Centurion," the Thirteenth responded.

"Advance, advance, step back, step back," Hasti ordered. "Third line, rotate forward."

The rotation maneuver provided the Republic's army with an advantage. While the front line of the enemy became exhausted, the Legions kept fresh arms and legs on the assault line. For months, the officers drilled them, transforming slaves and criminals into Legionaries. During that period, they practiced the rotation a thousand times.

Twenty-five shields smashed forward, and the Century's attack line stepped into the gap created by the shield thrusts. Then their gladii ripped in to fill the space when the shields withdrew. Before the Punic front rank could recover, the shields lunged again, and the blades stabbed. Anticipating the rotating, the third rank of the Century surged forward to replace those on the front line.

Jace admired the smooth changeover, for a moment.

***

Breaking their training, the exhausted Legionaries on the assault line each grabbed an enemy by his shield and pulled him through the second rank as they retreated. Already tightly spaced, the lanes used by the third line to move up were clogged by the rotating Legionaries and their prisoners.

Plus, the extra bodies created openings and Carthaginian mercenaries flooded through. A heartbeat after the rotate command, some from the assault line attempted to cut the heads off their captures. Others tried to decapitate their prisoners but found they had pulled fighters into the rear of their lines.

"First and second squads," Jace bellowed. "Move up and shut that down."

Twenty Legionaries from Jace's Century raced forward to join the fight and stem the breaches. With the First Maniple battling to its front and rear, Jace glanced over to Centurion Thaddeus for instructions. But the combat officer faced away while directing their third squad forward to patch another hole in the First Maniple line.

Then, a Numidian javelin swept in from the side, taking the Illyrian from first squad off his feet and pinning him to the ground. A second javelin stuck Centurion Hasti, taking him off his feet. An instant later, Jace realized the Legion cavalry had lost the war on the right flank.

"Still your breath so your hands are steady. Calm your heart so your eyes are clear. Focus your mind on the task."

The world slowed as Jace Kasia's archer training took over and his mind sorted through solutions.

***

"Pivot right," he shouted as he calmly walked to the rear of the Thirteenth Century, "Brace for cavalry."

Pulling Legionaries back from fights, Jace shoved them into a line facing to the right. Lance Corporal Anker and the squad leader for the second squad noticed the start of a blocking formation. They began pulling their people out of the melees. Some fought the distraction because the Legionaries were busy chopping at the necks of mercenaries in order to take the head and claim their freedom. But soon, a rough broken defensive wall began to form.

A young staff officer trotted from the center of the Legion and waved for Jace's attention.

"I'm a little busy, sir," Jace told him.

"Optio Kasia, Proconsul Gracchus has a change to make in the freedom agreement," the Junior Tribune reported. "He said to stop taking heads. If you want your freedom, win this fight."

"Timing is everything, sir," Jace told him. Turning from the young nobleman, Optio Kasia inhaled a deep breath, then ordered. "Thirteenth, Twenty-fifth, and Thirty-seventh Centuries, sweep right and form a shield wall, on my line."

Lifting his arms so he was visible, Jace moved deeper into the Legion and planted his feet. Even when a Numidian rider targeted him with a javelin, Jace only moved enough to dodge the sharp point.

Two hundred Legionaries backed up and quickly formed two lines based on the rogue NCO's position.

"Cavalry shield wall," he bellowed.

The order was repeated until stacked shields blocked the javelins thrown by the Punic cavalrymen.

"You've secured the Legion's right flank, Optio," Centurion Thaddeus noted as he marched to Jace. With eyebrows elevated in a questioning manner, the officer asked. "What are you going to do now?"

End of the sample for *Heritage of Threat*, book #3 in *A Legion Archer* series.

A note from J. Clifton Slater

Thank you for reading *Pity the Rebellious*. This is the 21st novel set in the ancient world, and the 30th book I've authored. It's hard to express just how much your support means to me. Because of you, I will continue to explore ancient Rome and write historical adventures. To you I say, *"quantum gratum."* Latin for 'much appreciated.'

Let's examine some of the history in *Pity the Rebellious*.

The art of being a General

About leadership during the Punic Wars, Roman historian *Cassius Dio* wrote.

"...The Romans owed the majority of their reverses to the fact that they kept sending out from year to year different and ever different leaders. And took away their office from them when they were just learning the art of generalship. It looked as if they were choosing them for practice and not for service."

We witnessed this many times in the history of the Roman Republic. Politicians, hungry for glory, campaigned to be Consul/Generals. After a year of hit-or-miss military operations, the Consuls stepped down taking the lessons on leadership they learned with them. Later in history, in the case of the Third Servile War, 73-71 B.C., the Senate sent lesser Generals out to battle Spartacus for fear the victor might become a dominant political force.

Cassius Dio's comment caused me to show how Cornelius Scipio got a variety of combat experiences in his early life. It would make a difference later in his career.

After the Battle of Lake Trasimene

We examined the battle from Cornelius and Jace's perspective in *Journey from Exile.* After the massacre on the banks of Lake Trasimene, Hannibal's forces met and destroyed four thousand cavalrymen from Servilius Geminus' Legions. They were the advanced units sent ahead of the Legions marching from Rimini. Before they received warning about the fate of Gaius Flaminius' Legions, the Legion riders were ambushed and butchered in the mountain valley beside the Tiber River.

With the fourth battle at the start of the 2nd Punic War, Hannibal Barca had cost the Republic dearly in reputation and in the lives of Latins and allies. Losses, Rome could ill afford.

Family Name Romiliia

Lucius Romiliia's story was made up and the Romiliia name in Roman history faded before the end of the Republic. But in 234 B.C., the Ligurians from the area around Genoa, Italy did revolt. Consul Lucius Albinus sailed to the region on the northern coast of Italy and put down the uprising. Although a small piece of history, the revolt helped build the story of Jace's family.

Events in Chapter 5 - Found, but Unwanted

The Greeks' view of Ares, the God of Courage and War, was well documented by ancient writers. In my readings, Ares seemed to be humiliated in almost every myth. In *Pity the Rebellious*, Hektor's speech covered a few of the myths and legends.

The Romans did ask for help building the fleet. Near the end of the 1st Punic War, Rome had run out of money. In the 22 years prior, they had built and lost several fleets. Some sunk in battles while other losses came from poor seamanship and storms. The Senate, in 242 B.C., asked rich citizens to fund the building of warships. As a testament to the wealth of the Roman Republic, the well-to-do constructed a fleet of 200 five-banker, quinqueremes. With that fleet, the Roman Navy defeated the Carthaginians in 241 B.C. which ended the 1st Punic War.

And finally, in 234 B.C., as we discussed earlier, Consul Albinus did march on the Liguria tribe to put down a rebellion, although there was no mention of a land swindle. And as you've read near the end of *Pity the Rebellious*, Proconsul Albinus served again in 216 B.C. as the General for the Battle of Silva Litana. More on the battle and outcome later.

I hope you enjoyed the connections, because weaving story and history together into a book is one of my greatest pleasures.

Oscan language

Oscan is an extinct Indo-European language of southern Italy. I attempted to create an accurate sentence in Oscan for Jace. With it, he proved to the Boii Tribe that he was Hirpini by repeating the challenge greeting he learned from Papia.

Oscan language: *"Castrid and deíkum maimas carneis tanginud ammíd fust tefúrúm or fust fratru'm."*

English: "I pour and speak for the largest part opinions, because he will be a victim, or he will be a brother."

The sentence was pieced together from a list of Oscan words. I love finding creative ways to relate a tale. If there are issues with the translation or ancient syntax, let me remind you, I am a storyteller, not a linguist.

Old Wine Remedy

Greek historian *Polybius* recorded that Hannibal Barca captured wagons and vineyards full of wine. With an abundance of the liquid, he had plenty to use for medicinal purposes. Skin rubbed raw from packs, saddles, and harnesses was treated by bathing the scabby and mangy areas in old wine.

The Greeks, Romans, and Persians also used wine in concoctions to treat various ailments and as a wound cleaner. According to Dr. Norrie, a family physician and wine historian in Sydney, Australia, clinicians used sponges or cloths soaked in wine and applied them to wounds. Norrie stated it wasn't the alcohol in the wine that killed off pathogens, but the grapes' polyphenols.

Consequently, science reinforced *Polybius'* claim about Hannibal's animal handlers using wine as an antiseptic.

No Man of Sound Sense

The bit of philosophy War Chief Papia imparted to Jace at the start of Chapter 18 is quoted from *Polybius* in book #3 of his *The Histories*.

"...since no man of sound sense goes to war with his neighbors simply for the sake of crushing an adversary..."

The Greek historian's words were too poignant to simply note and leave in the pages of my research. Compare the utilitarian ideas to modern times and we can see that the ancients had no leisure time for mindless activities like pleasure sailing or fun arts and crafts.

Mefitis, Samnite Goddess

I mixed the legends of Mefitis the Goddess of Noxious Gases from Swamps and Volcanos, and the founding of the Hirpini, wolf-people. The tribe did claim to have been guided to their homeland by a wolf, but there is little written about it. And Mefitis was one of the Samnite Tribes main Goddesses who eventually had a temple dedicated to her near an ancient volcano vent. War Chiefs needing to gather mud for a fence dedicated to the Goddess is pure fiction.

Hannibal's Escape Route from Ager Falernus

Many maps and resources show Hannibal's escape route running by the town of Teano. I think Hannibal used a different route. Allow me to explain why.

On page 227 of book #3 of *The Histories*, *Polybius* writes:

*"Such being Hannibal's anticipations, he left **Samnium** and traversing the pass near the hill called Eribianus encamped beside the river Athyrnus, which approximately cuts this plain in half..."*

By referencing the Volturno River, which cuts the plain in half and marks the southern boundary of his operations on the plain, *Polybius* brings Hannibal in from the southeast. This works with reports of Hannibal ravishing the area around Benevento, a city on the southern route.

Polybius, page 231: *"They* (the Romans) *were then to occupy the ridge* (Allifae), *so that if the enemy* (Carthaginians) *advanced to any part of it, they might meet and attack him. At the same time, he* (Hannibal Barca) *himself with his heavy-armed troops in front, next them his cavalry, next the captured cattle, and finally the Spaniards and Celts,* **made for the narrow gorge** *of the pass."*

The sources claiming Hannibal passed by Teano would put his army in a wide gap and not 'a narrow pass'. Because he came in from the south, I believe he took a narrow pass over the foothills, avoided Allifae, and headed south to Samnium. Following a familiar route in the dark, Hannibal didn't worry about his vanguard getting confused.

The tactic of driving oxen with burning branches on their horns up the slope to draw the garrison of Allifae out and into a premature battle was clearly genius.

And finally, after escaping the plain, Hannibal sent Iberian heavy infantry back to save his pikemen and the oxen herders. They could only have reached Allifae in daylight and unmolested by the Legions, if the army journeyed on the southeastern route out of Ager Falernus.

Numbered Legions

The question of numbered Legions often comes up. One reviewer of an earlier book was frustrated. He desperately wanted to know what numbered Legion was operating in a battle. Unfortunately, the Legions weren't numbered in the mid Republic era.

Until the late Roman Republic, the Legions took the names of their Generals who were elected Consuls, Proconsuls, or Praetors. As the elected Generals returned to the Senate after their terms of office, their Legions were disbanded to return to the farms for harvest and planting.

The numbering of the Legions came about with the Marian reforms in 107 B.C. With the reforms, Rome created career Legionaries, made their army more professional, and easier to manage in far off regions of the expanding Republic.

No Conspiracy, This Time

Not everything in my historical adventure books are based on actual events. *Pity the Rebellious* had a story thread using Aemilius Paullus, Servillius Geminus, Lucius Albinus, and an unnamed man as conspirators in a land grab. To the best of my knowledge, none of those ancient gentlemen participated in anything nefarious. But the Senate in ancient Rome regularly accused and exiled people. Only later, did the facts show in some cases, the charges were brought under false pretenses for political or business reasons.

The Demise of Lucius Albinus

Lucius Albinus was elected as a replacement Consul in 216 B.C. At the time, he commanded Legions marching north to punish the Boii tribe. The tribe had broken treaties and supplied fighters and supplies to Hannibal Barca. When Proconsul Albinus entered the old forest of Silva Litana, he moved with a strong force. However, once in the forest, the Boii sprang a trap.

They precut tree trunks and left them unsteadily balanced until the Legions marched into the forest. History is weak on how many trees fell, but the results reveal the effectiveness of the tactic. Toppling a few brought down other giant trees and if they fell in regular spaces the tree trunks would have done two things. In what must have been the equivalent of an avalanche, the falling branches crushed Legion equipment and killed Legionaries. And the falling trees would have divided the Legion ranks into smaller, isolated units. Then once the tumbling trees ended, Boii warriors attacked and killed everyone who escaped the timber ambush.

The Golden Skull: Lucius Albinus was beheaded. History tells us, his head was boiled to remove the flesh. Then it was dipped and coated in gold, and the skull used as a drinking vessel by the head priest of the Boii tribe.

Why Author Notes

I started including the notes in my novels because some of the history sounded like fantasy or was hard to believe. The notes are a way for you to separate pure fiction from actual events. Hopefully, you enjoyed *Pity the Rebellious* and found the notes insightful.

I am J. Clifton Slater and I write military adventure both future and ancient.

***

I appreciate your emails and comments. If you enjoyed *Pity the Rebellious*, consider leaving a written review on Amazon or on Goodreads. Every review helps other readers find the stories.

If you have comments e-mail me.

E-mail: GalacticCouncilRealm@gmail.com

To get the latest information about my books, visit my website. There you can sign up for my monthly author report, see all my books, and read blogs about ancient history.

Website: www.JCliftonSlater.com

Facebook: Galactic Council Realm and Clay Warrior Stories

Other books by J. Clifton Slater:

Historical Adventure of the 2nd Punic War

A Legion Archer series

#1 Journey from Exile

#2 Pity the Rebellious

#3 Heritage of Threat

Historical Adventure of the 1st Punic War

Clay Warrior Stories series

#1 Clay Legionary

#2 Spilled Blood

#3 Bloody Water

#4 Reluctant Siege

#5 Brutal Diplomacy

#6 Fortune Reigns

#7 Fatal Obligation

#8 Infinite Courage

#9 Deceptive Valor

#10 Neptune's Fury

#11 Unjust Sacrifice

#12 Muted Implications

#13 Death Caller

#14 Rome's Tribune

#15 Deranged Sovereignty

#16 Uncertain Honor

#17 Tribune's Oath

#18 Savage Birthright

#19 Abject Authority

Fantasy – *Terror & Talons* series

#1 Hawks of the Sorcerer Queen

#2 Magic and the Rage of Intent

Military Science Fiction - *Call Sign Warlock* series

#1 Op File Revenge

#2 Op File Treason

#3 Op File Sanction

Military Science Fiction – *Galactic Council Realm* series

#1 On Station

#2 On Duty

#3 On Guard

#4 On Point

Printed in Great Britain
by Amazon